Judging Laura

Peter Rizzolo

Judging Laura

Create Space, a division of Amazon Publishing
Original art work by Joe Rizzolo
Cover Design by Ruth Eckles
First Edition: March 2016

Peter Rizzolo

Dedication

This novel is dedicated to victims of sexual abuse, who frequently neither obtain nor seek justice. The perpetrators of these crimes are infrequently prosecuted successfully; the victims, when they do come forward are often met with skepticism and blame and are accused of behavior that contributed to the assault. This repudiation by authorities, friends and even family, amounts to what many survivors consider a second victimization.

ACKNOWLEDGEMENTS

I would like to thank the members of my writing workshop, who endured the long journey to the completion of this manuscript. Those offering advice and encouragement were Charlotte Hoffman, Orman Day, Robin Kirk, Frank Stallone, Donald McKinney, Carol Mann, Beverly Lemons, Neal Paris, Lucia Peel Powe and the late Chuck Hauser.

I would also like to thank Mark Finkelstein and Walter Bennett for their help in critiquing the legal and courtroom intricacies of the novel.

Chapter One

South Orange, New Jersey

October 2003

"Hey, sweetheart, let's do it," Bruce said, looking over his shoulder at Laura as he leaned back on the couch. "In a couple of years I'll be in line for regional manager. You can quit your job and enroll in college full-time."

But the thought of going to a gynecologist terrified Laura. She knew her own body; there was something terribly wrong. Until she started birth control pills, her periods had been unbearable. Even her husband didn't know the full extent of the horror she had endured that night six years ago.

Laura tried to match his conversational tone. "Quit? I like my job. Besides, we're not ready for a baby. This small apartment...."

She walked across the room, sat beside him and put her arms around his waist. He pulled her over onto his lap and ran his fingers through her honey-blond hair.

"All the guys at Carmart have kids," he reminded her. "Some already in school. All we have is an arthritic cat, who thinks she owns the place. She won't even let me pick her up."

"She knows I'm jealous. She wouldn't dare."

Jubilee, their obese tabby, was sprawled on a sheepskin rug in front of the fireplace. She stood and snapped her tail defiantly in Bruce's direction, then waddled toward the front door.

Laura opened the door, and Jubilee gazed into the dark. It was mid-October. The evening air was a reminder how soon they would be face-to-face with another New Jersey winter. Having second thoughts, Jubilee backed off and walked to her favorite spot in front of an air vent in the front hall. She pawed an old feather cushion Laura had placed there and settled, tucking her forelegs under her chest. Laura returned to the living room and sat on the sheepskin rug next to Bruce.

Of course he had the right to want a family, Laura thought, but that didn't make her feel better.

Bruce placed his arm around her, drawing her to him.

He's about as complicated as a teddy bear and just as cuddly, Laura thought. After five years, I'm still the center of his universe, if you don't count Monday night football, racquetball at the Y and surfing the net.

They stared in silence at the dancing flames rising from a cluster of ceramic logs. She ran her finger along his square jaw-line.

"Throw away those pills, honey. It's time we moved on."

"You know I love babies," Laura whispered. "I just don't feel ready." *Why couldn't he let it go?*

Laura agonized for weeks, finally agreeing to put away birth control and give motherhood a try. When she didn't become pregnant after a few cycles, she called Dr. Jane Corbett, a fertility specialist who had recently joined the staff of St. Joseph's where Laura worked as supervisor of the medical records department.

Dr. Corbett's office was conveniently located a block from the hospital. The doctor, a pleasant-looking woman with penetrating light blue eyes and a touch of gray in her hair, looked up from the detailed medical history Laura had completed.

"Would you like to tell me about it?"

Laura began to cry. Why had she even gone to the damn party? She knew Michael Greene was bad news, and she had let him hand her a drink. Maybe her mother was right. It was her fault. Stupid, stupid, stupid.

She must have said that out loud because Dr. Corbett was shaking her head. "Laura, so many women feel that way," she said. "It's alright. I understand. I was molested by my baby-sitter's boyfriend when I was twelve."

Laura was shocked that Dr. Corbett confided in her. She was determined to continue, but her mouth was so dry she could hardly speak.

Chapter Two

Allentown, Pennsylvania

November 1994

Laura, a high school senior, had been studying for an English exam when the phone rang. The voice at the other end said, "Hi, Laura, it's Martha."

"Martha?" Laura was surprised to hear from her. They weren't friends, though they had been in a couple of classes in their junior year.

"Luke's parents went to Florida. He's having a fifties party at his house Saturday night. He asked me to get a date for his friend, Michael."

"Michael?"

"Michael Greene. He was in our chemistry class last year. He's gotten early acceptance at Yale. He's brainy, like you."

"No, thanks." Laura knew exactly who Martha was talking about. He had sat next to her in class. He asked her to a basketball game. In the bleachers, they were scrunched close together. He kept reaching over and resting his hand on her thigh, acting as if it were an accident. After she pushed his hand away a few times, he finally quit.

On the drive home he pulled the car over on a dark side street. He grabbed her and started groping and kissing her. He reached under her dress. She pushed him hard and got out of the car. As she walked, he rolled down the passenger side window and followed her.

"Come on. I'm sorry. Okay?" he said. "Get back in the car."

The last block or two, she ran. Michael didn't bother to follow. That had been their first and last date.

At our senior year homecoming dance he kept cutting in on me and Bruce. After that he phoned a few times. He was good-looking enough to have his pick of girls. Why was he hitting on me? I couldn't honestly say I hadn't been attracted to him, but Bruce and I had started going out the previous summer. We hadn't made any promises, but I really wasn't interested in anyone else.

"Is the problem the party or Michael?" Martha asked. "There'll be plenty of other guys there. Luke says half the senior class is gonna show. He throws really cool parties. No uptight chaperones. It'll be a blast."

"His parents let him?

"They'll never know. A bunch of us are going over the next day to clean up."

"I don't know...."

"Jimmy and Ginger are coming," Martha said.

"Oh?" *She knows they're my best friends.*

"Yeah. You can hang out with them. And if you're not having a good time, somebody'll drive you home early. I promise. How's that?"

6

Laura was hesitant---it did sound like fun. "What'll the girls wear?

"Fifties stuff. Check out the movie, *Grease.*"

"I don't have things like that."

"Who does? Some of the girls are going to the Bygone Times Thrift Shop after school tomorrow. Come along. The clothes cost next to nothing."

"Well...okay, but make sure Michael knows this is not a real date."

"I don't get it. He's cute as hell. Most of my friends would kill to go out with him."

"Good; call one of them. Besides I already have a boyfriend. He's away at college."

"You'll have fun, I promise," Martha said. "And bring your bathing suit. Their pool is heated. Forget Bruce for one night."

As Laura approached Luke Marshall's home, its winding tree-lined drive, and two-story white house with massive columns, she imagined Scarlett O'Hara's mammy meeting them at the door. However, a mid-November dusting of snow and below-freezing temperature quickly dispelled that image.

Word of the party had gotten around, and kids kept showing up, until you could hardly move in the two-story living room. Quadraphonic sound blasted Elvis' *All Shook Up* and Buddy Knox's *Party Doll*, and Jerry Lee Lewis' *A Whole Lot of Shaking Going On.* Laura welcomed the more typical fare by Bonjovi, Paula Abdul, and Michael Damian.

Luke and some other boys moved the dining room table to one side and rolled up the Oriental rug.

They had already transformed his parents' incredibly austere dining room into a beer pong lounge

Laura tried to avoid Michael but he was persistent, cutting in on her whenever he spotted her dancing. When he did, he clung to her like a wet shirt. Along one wall was a gigantic mirror. Every time they danced past he'd stare at himself approvingly.

Between dances he asked, "How come you're not drinking?"

"I don't like beer." She grabbed a can of coke from an iced cooler.

"Try some of this." He pulled a small silver flask from his jacket pocket and opened it.

She sniffed it. "What is it?"

"Vodka. It's from my father's stash. It's half water. I didn't want to take so much that he could tell."

"I've never tasted vodka."

"It's good stuff. Smirnoff."

She took a sip. It burned going down her throat but didn't taste bad. "It's better than beer." She added some of her coke to the flask, and as she did, spilled some onto the leather case that enclosed the flask.

"Damn. Why'd you do that?"

Laura took a sip. "Now that's better." She noticed that his initials were embossed on the leather case.

A girl grabbed his arm. "Hey, gorgeous, you wanna dance?" They drifted off. Laura slipped the flask into the pocket of the red cardigan sweater she had picked up at the thrift shop. Whoever had owned the sweater had earned a varsity letter.

A boy wearing a white t-shirt with rolled-up sleeves and tight-fitting black leather pants asked Laura to dance.

"Yo, an athlete," he commented as they jitterbugged.

"Earned my letter in football before they discovered I was a girl and threw me off the team."

"You must of never took showers after practice. huh?"

She was glad when the dance was over. No chemistry there. She wandered off looking for Ginger and Jimmy. She guessed they were already in the pool.

Oversized French doors opened onto a flagstone patio, and beyond that was a lighted swimming pool. She noticed Michael snapping her picture with a stubby little camera that looked like a pair of binoculars. *What was it with that guy? When he goes off to dance, I'm getting the hell out of here!*

She went into a room where coats were piled high, found hers, and slipped outside. Clouds of steam rose from the surface of the heated pool. On the patio, kids were dancing to music blasting from outside speakers. A few brave souls had stripped off their clothes and plunged into the pool. Dancing on the patio would have been fun if Bruce were there. He was probably at some frat party at Penn State, but he'd soon be home for Thanksgiving break. Laura counted the days.

She stretched out on a chaise, pulling her black woolen coat to her chin. She had seen a rerun of *Dr. Zhivago*, and the coat reminded her of one that Julie Christie had worn in the movie. She bought it at the thrift shop, where she also picked up a pair of penny loafers, her sweater and a pleated woolen skirt.

She watched guys doing cannon balls, competing to see who could send up the most spray. Martha, Ginger and Jimmy were already in the pool.

"Hey, Laura. Come on in," Martha shouted. "We're gonna play polo against the guys."

There were nets at both ends of the pool. It looked tempting but Laura hadn't brought her bathing suit.

"Thanks. I'll watch."

"Come on. We need a couple more girls."

"I really can't," Laura whispered.

She wanted to remind Martha that she had promised to get her home early. But soon the girls were starting to win their game, and Martha was a key player. She'd wait until the game was over.

The evening grew colder as it wore on. Laura took a sip from the flask Michael had given her. She drew her knees to her chest so that her coat covered her legs and feet. It was becoming more and more difficult to focus her eyes. She was feeling sick. Was it the vodka? She had only had a few sips. After pouring what was left of the vodka onto the patio deck, she checked her watch. It was already nine-thirty. She slipped the empty flask back into her coat pocket.

"I gotta get going," she called out to Martha. Her lips and tongue weren't working quite right. "Sposed to be home by ten."

Martha, who was at the far end of the pool, apparently hadn't heard her.

When Laura stood, she felt dizzy and nauseous. She held onto the edge of the chaise to steady herself.

Her mouth filled with bile as she walked along the edge of the pool. Her legs seemed to have forgotten how to work. She teetered at the edge, leaning back, wind-milling her arms, trying not to fall in.

"Hey, look at Laura," someone said. "She's totally wasted."

She toppled over, landed on her backside, hitting her head on the metal edge of a chaise lounge. A boy knelt beside her.

"You okay?" He helped her to her feet.

He seemed really nice. "Sure, I'm okay." Her knees gave way.

He laughed as he caught her in his arms.

"I think maybe I'm a little drunk," Laura whispered.

"You hit your head pretty hard. We better ice it." He carried her into the house. She reached back to feel her head. She already had a bump. She thought that was funny and started to giggle. As he carried her upstairs, some kids gave a thumbs up. She smiled and waved back. And there was Michael, the creep, with his funny little camera clicking away.

When she woke up she was naked, her arms stretched above her head and tied to the bed post. Someone on top of her, someone holding her legs. Her eyes and mouth were covered.

She tried to scream but couldn't. There was an eerie quiet as they penetrated her with such force she could feel herself tear. The smell of blood and beer breath made her gag.

She struggled with whatever was binding her hands to the bedpost, swinging her upper body from side to side. The pain was unbearable. She fought desperately to free her legs.

Somehow she managed to free one leg and drew her knee to her chest. She kicked someone hard. He toppled off her and onto the floor.

"Goddamn bitch," he shouted.

Michael had screamed at her! She recognized his voice. Someone else grabbed her free leg and pressed her knee to the bed.

"Hey man, she's bleeding pretty bad," someone whispered.

She could sense them gawking. There were at least three voices, Michael's and two others.

"I'm out of here," someone said.

"Yeah, me too."

In seconds she was alone. She rolled off the bed and onto the floor, stood and removed the blindfold and cloth they had used to cover her mouth. With her teeth she tried to undo the knot that bound her hands, but couldn't. She looked down and saw blood streaming down her legs. She screamed.

Moments later, Martha and Ginger rushed into the room. Martha helped untie Laura's wrists. Ginger ran to grab some towels. Laura couldn't stop shaking. They gathered up her clothes from the floor, helped her dress, then got her into her coat.

"Who the hell did this? Was it that guy who carried you upstairs?" Martha asked.

"I don't think so...I don't know. There were at least three of them. My eyes were covered, but I'm sure Michael was one of them."

"My God. I can't believe this!" Martha cried.

"We'd better take you to the hospital," Ginger said.

"No, no...no! Just take me home. I want to go home."

"Why not see a doctor?" Ginger pleaded. "The way you're bleeding, you may be torn inside."

"She's right," Martha said. She put her arm around Laura's shoulders.

Laura knew they had a point. But at that moment she'd just as soon die as have a doctor or nurse stick his hands or instruments inside her.

Ginger and Martha helped her out of the car and as they walked to the house, blood gushed from between Laura's thighs and down her legs.

Her mother must have heard them pull up. She opened the door as Martha and Ginger half-dragged Laura up the front steps. When her mother saw the blood covering Laura's legs and shoes, the color drained from her face. She clutched her chest. Laura was afraid she might have a heart attack.

"What have you done? What had you done to my girl?" her mother yelled. She didn't wait for them to answer. She grabbed Laura, pulled her into the house and slammed the door behind them.

Neither of them spoke as she led Laura to the bathroom, where she undressed her. She was still bleeding. She put on a sanitary pad. Laura was freezing cold. Her mother got her into a nightgown and led her to her bedroom.

As she propped a second pillow under Laura's head she asked, "Who did this to you?"

"I was at this party..."

"You said you were going to a movie."

"I'm sorry."

"You've been drinking. I smell alcohol."

Laura told her mother what happened. She listened in silence until Laura was finished. Her mother's face was like stone. She had never ever looked at Laura in such a cold, disgusted way.

"You said you were going to a movie. How can I ever trust you? I would never have given you permission to go to that party. You damn well knew that!"

Laura's bedroom had always been a place where she felt safe and comforted. Just a small room, but bright with tiny lights strung along the casement window above her bed. The wallpaper was a cheerful pink and yellow. Now the room seemed strangely menacing, as though she didn't belong here.

"I'm sorry. I got drunk. But that didn't give them the right..."

"Who's going to want you now?" her mother shouted. "Did you think of that? No man wants damaged goods."

"How can you say that?" Laura gasped. "What does that mean? I'm still the same person I was. I'm still your daughter."

Her mother began to pace. She was wearing a gray dress Laura always hated. It seemed to hang on her. Had her mother lost weight? She looked haggard, drawn.

"I tried hard to bring you up the right way. All by myself since you were three. I thought I was doing a good job. You've ruined everything. I'm ashamed of you." Her mother left the room.

A real mother would forgive her daughter, Laura thought. *Forgive what? It wasn't my fault. Mother will feel different tomorrow.*

The next morning, her mother told her that she had soaked everything in strong bleach, but still the blood stains didn't come out. She had thrown the soiled clothes away. By this time Laura was frightened. Why was she still bleeding, and why did she hurt so much inside? It was stupid not to get medical help. She pleaded with her mother to take her to the doctor. But her mother said the doctor would report the rape to the police, and then the whole ugly mess would be in the papers.

"And don't complain to me," her mother snapped. "You behaved like trash, drinking and partying. This is what happens."

Laura ran to her bedroom, slammed and locked the door. She sobbed so hard, she started to gag. After about a half-hour her mother came to the door and asked to be let in.

"I'm damaged goods. Trash," Laura screamed. "Go away. I might as well die."

"I didn't mean it. You know that, Laura. I'm sorry. I'll take you to the doctor."

"I hate you. Just leave me alone."

******

"Weren't you worried about becoming pregnant?" Dr. Corbett asked.

"It was the last day of my period. I didn't think I could have gotten pregnant. But I did get one of those kits from the drugstore. I checked it two or three times."

"You haven't mentioned your father."

"My parents divorced when I was three. I barely remember him, mostly from old photographs. He's living somewhere out west."

"You must have felt terribly alone."

Laura nodded. She bit her lip to keep from crying. "After that God-awful night, the worst was at school. The things kids said as I passed. The looks the boys gave me. Even Ginger and Jimmy avoided me. I wanted to call Bruce, but I was too ashamed. I thought maybe someone might have told him. Who knows what they would have said about me? He'd probably stop talking to me too.

"I decided to drop out of school, to leave home. I took all my money out of the bank. Twelve hundred and fifty-five dollars. Money I earned from babysitting and summer jobs, savings for college. What a joke!"

"Hadn't you already applied for admission to college?"

"No. I needed to work for at least a year. I didn't have nearly enough money."

"You told no one where you were going?"

"I didn't know myself. I got on a Greyhound bus heading south. When the bus stopped in South Orange, New Jersey, I decided to stay."

"Why there?"

"It's a college town. Lots of young people. It looked appealing."

Dr. Corbett nodded. "I don't understand why you didn't call Bruce once you got settled in."

"I was sure he would reject me the same the others had. The night before he went away to college we almost made love. But we'd been going out only since summer. I wasn't ready. He'd go off to college and have other girls. I'd be just another conquest. I told him I was a virgin and wanted to stay that way. After what happened to me, I couldn't face him."

There was a long silence. Laura's heart raced. She realized that her most private secrets were now part of her medical record. She was aware St. Joe's hospital kept psychiatric files separate from the rest of a person's medical record. But she didn't know how sensitive information was handled in Dr. Corbett's private office.

"Doctor, who has access to your medical records?"

"It is my practice to keep sensitive information in a separate, locked file. No one on my staff has access to that, and I would never release it without your written permission."

Judging Laura

Chapter Three

A sense of impending disaster and sleepless nights preceded Laura's second visit with Dr. Corbett. How would Bruce react if she could never bear a child? Would the events of that awful night cast a pall over their entire marriage?

"I'm terribly sorry to tell you this, Laura." Dr. Corbett removed her glasses and slowly polished the lenses with a tissue. "Both your fallopian tubes are badly scarred and cystic. I suspect one of those boys must have given you a sexually transmitted disease."

"Disease? What kind of disease?" Laura asked.

"The changes in your internal organs are consistent with untreated gonorrhea. Women are often asymptomatic or have minimal symptoms."

The word gonorrhea struck Laura like a blow to her chest. She realized how stupid she had been not to see a doctor after the party. She took slow deep breaths to calm herself. "Would the disease have damaged my tubes if I'd gotten treated?"

"Early treatment would almost certainly have prevented the damage. But you mustn't blame yourself. You were seventeen, frightened, confused...."

"Is it too late for treatment?" Laura interrupted.

"There's no active infection at this time, so there's no need for antibiotics. The natural history of untreated gonococcal infection is spontaneous resolution after a few weeks or months. But of course, by then, I'm sorry to say, it had already damaged your reproductive organs."

I dread having to tell Bruce that I had a venereal disease. How can I? Laura began to cry. Dr. Corbett came from behind her desk. She sat beside her, placed her hand on her arm, and handed Laura a tissue.

"What about babies?" Laura asked, after she blew her nose.

"There's nothing wrong with your uterus, but with closed-off fallopian tubes you'll never be able to have babies the way nature meant. Fortunately you have other options. *In vitro* fertilization, for example."

"A test-tube baby?" Laura asked. To conceive a baby in a test-tube? That seemed weird. It was something Laura had never dreamed she'd have to do. She had to talk it over with Bruce, of course.

"Is that something you might choose?"

Laura scanned Dr. Corbett's small office. How many women have been given news this bad, or even worse, in this room? Is that why she had resisted trying to have a baby---did she somehow know that her insides had been irreparably damaged? Tears flooded her eyes. "If it were the only way,"

"I'm afraid so. I'll give you some information about the procedure."

"I was such a damn coward," Laura said. "I should have gone to the police. I wish I had."

Dr. Corbett returned to her desk. "You were very young. You believed you were partly to blame. Many women do exactly what you did."

"I was furious about what those boys did to me, and couldn't understand why my mother treated me as she did."

"Family members often blame the victim."

"She called me damaged goods."

"What an incredibly brutal comment!" Dr. Corbett said.

"That comment was so unlike her. Of course she was hurt, angry...just as devastated as I. It took me a long time to understand that."

Dr. Corbett nodded. "I believe there's a chance you can still make those rapists pay for what they did."

Laura was stunned, confused. How could she do anything now? Those guys had trashed her life. "The assault was so long ago, and I have no witnesses."

"You said Martha and Ginger came and untied you. They may have seen the young men leave the room."

"If they did see them, they never told me. I'm sure they would have."

Bringing the whole dirty episode out in the open might be too difficult for either me or Bruce to deal with. And what if I can't prove them guilty? I'd live under a cloud of malicious rumor and suspicion.

"There's another possibility," Dr. Corbett continued. She stood and walked to the office window. "If we remove your diseased fallopian tubes, there's a chance the tissues might contain the DNA of one or more of those young men who attacked you."

"Remove my tubes? Just on the remote possibility you might find DNA?"

"If you decide to undergo *in vitro* fertilization, removing those tubes will increase your chances of success."

I know rapists can be identified through physical and DNA evidence gathered soon after an assault. But after so many years?

"I didn't think you could find DNA inside a woman's body other than her vagina," Laura said.

"Recovery of DNA from fallopian tubes years after the fact has never been reported," Dr. Corbett answered. "But I've had this theory ever since my residency. I've searched a number of times for DNA in pathology specimens, but as yet I haven't found any. That was before there were new procedures that can detect even the minutest of genetic material. There is some research evidence that suggests that sperm may be able to produce a protective shield... like the U-2 Spy plane... that may allow them to fly below the radar of the woman's immune system."

Laura knitted her brows. "I don't get it."

"I guess that wasn't a very good analogy." She smiled. "Let me try that again... A woman's immune system is generally very efficient at identifying and destroying foreign proteins. A group of British researchers believe that sperm may have figured out a way to fool the immune system's killer cells that ordinarily hunt them down."

"Are you saying it's possible sperm may survive in a woman's body?"

"No. The sperm do not store enough nutrients to survive very long, but their DNA might persist."

"But for how long?"

"No one knows. Maybe indefinitely. But if we are able to identify DNA that is different from yours or your husband's, despite how long it's been, you would be in a position to take legal action."

"Is it a serious operation?"

"It would require general anesthesia, but it's not much different from an appendectomy."

"They transplant all sorts of organs. Is it possible to transplant fallopian tubes?" Laura asked.

"Any transplant requires taking anti-rejection medication for the rest of your life. Tubal transplants are not being done because IVF works better, is safer and much less expensive."

Laura took a deep breath. She was aware of the risks of surgery. She had served on the audit committee reviewing a case at St. Joe's during which a surgeon had damaged a patient's uterine artery in the course of removing a benign tumor. They had to remove the woman's uterus. That was only one of the many bad outcomes she was aware of. She had confidence in Dr. Corbett. But still... She grasped the arms of the chair, her fingers digging deeply into the fabric.

"Yes. I want to have the operation. I want you to look for DNA evidence."

Judging Laura

Chapter Four

Laura and Bruce lived in a two-bedroom apartment complex in suburban South Orange, a fifteen-minute drive from Seton Hall, New Jersey's oldest Catholic University. Two neighbors, Rose Gatti and Lilly Mendez, became Laura's closest friends. She looked forward to their weekly get-together for lunch, often at Little Naples Pizzeria. They talked about books, clothes and men. If you were reckless enough to bring up religion or politics, you got stuck with the tab.

Rose, an in Italian language instructor at Seaton Hall, was working on a doctoral degree in Italian cinema. She was dating Jamie, owner of Little Naples. Nothing serious she insisted...just fun to be around.

Lilly worked as assistant to the assistant editor at Seaton Hall University Press. She sorted the mail and screened the dozens of query letters that arrived weekly, passing on the most promising to her boss.

The trio turned more than a few heads. Rose, slender, bordering on undernourished, had prominent cheek bones, full lips, long dark brown hair, and expressive light brown eyes. Lilly, petite, had a voluptuous figure and jet black hair that surrounded her face in a pillow of tight spirals. She had had surgery for a cleft lip as a child. The barely visible scar drew her mouth slightly to one side as she smiled. A perfect mouth for wisecracking.

"Six years married. Where are the *bambinos*?" Rose teased Laura.

Laura sipped her coke as they waited for their pizza. She was dying to tell them about her visit to Dr. Corbett, but this wasn't the right time or place.

"And where are yours, my hot-blooded Italian friend?" Laura retorted.

"Do you not know of the bees and the birds? First a woman is in need of a man," Rose said.

"But you already have a man, *cuora mia*," Jammie said as he placed a large Margareta pizza on their table.

Rose blushed. "That was not meant for your ears, Jammie. Besides, I am not so special. I see how you flirt with the other women."

Laura loved Rose's Italian accent. *Do Americans sound as charming when we speak a foreign language? She doubted it.*

"With them it is business," Jammie said.

"Monkey business," Lilly remarked.

Jammie sighed and moved on to a nearby table, where a copse of teenage girls beckoned.

"A new crop of interns will soon arrive at Saint Joe's," Laura said. "One is handsome, single <u>and</u> Italian. I can arrange a meeting."

"Interesting!" Rose said. "But your interns are too...too *al dente.*"

"I thought Italians preferred *al dente,*" Laura said.

"For pasta, yes. Not for a man," Rose responded

"Half-baked is a better choice of metaphor," Lilly suggested.

As they munched their pizzas, Rose talked about her many boyfriends when she was a university student in Bologna. Laura was envious. She had missed the college scene entirely. *I had the good fortune of meeting the right guy, but the timing could have been better.*

"If Gino is as good in person as he is on paper..."

Rose stood. "I must run. I will be late for class. He sounds very *interessante. Caio!"*

*****

At Saint Joe's medical records department, Laura had gone from file clerk to departmental supervisor in a few years. Not bad for a high school dropout. She had been a straight A student in high school, hoping for a college scholarship, when her life took that abrupt detour. For years afterwards, she'd awaken in a cold sweat, shaking uncontrollably, sobbing, and thankful that Bruce was there to gather her in his arms.

Laura couldn't afford psychiatric care. Bruce and time, the great healer, were her therapy. She knew the anxiety and panic attacks would never completely set her free, but daily life had been getting easier. Bruce and her friends, Lilly and Rose, were the only people with whom she shared her secret.

Within months after having dropped out of high school, Laura had taken and passed her general equivalency examination. She obviously couldn't rise in the ranks at St. Joe's without at least a high school diploma. And she had grown to love her job. She was responsible for assuring the completeness and confidentiality of the patients' medical records. A misfiled or incomplete record could result in poor care, even a disastrous outcome.

At the time a patient is discharged from the hospital, his or her medical charting had to be complete before the hospital could get reimbursed from the insurance company. Timely completion of the chart was a high priority. Laura at times had to send her staff doctors and interns notices threatening them with suspension unless they completed their charting by noon on such and such a day.

While working full-time at St. Joe's, Laura was studying for a paralegal degree at Pace Junior College. She got to thinking about it ever since she saw a movie about a woman who single-handedly confronted a water-polluting industrial giant. Of course Laura didn't dress as provocatively as Julia Roberts, in the movie *Erin Brockovich*. The nuns at St. Joe's wouldn't tolerate cleavage or mini-skirts. Still, most of the young female employees pushed the dress code restrictions as far as they dared.

Laura didn't have enough fingers to count all the doctors, young and old, single and married, who had hit on her. She'd smile, flash her wedding band, and tell them she was married to a man with a jealous streak, and the strength of a sumo wrestler. That usually capped off the gushers.

Every July St. Joe's received a fresh crop of interns. One of them, Gino Romano, was exceptionally hot-looking. Born and raised in Sicily, he had graduated from medical school in Bologna. At five-feet-ten, he moved with the grace of an athlete. But his English was a bit awkward.

One morning, soon after he started his internship, he came to the record room looking for a patient's chart. He didn't have the correct unit number. Usually Laura would politely ask the doctor to look up the number on one of the terminals scattered throughout the hospital. But the new interns often expected her to drop everything when they needed a chart or wanted something copied or faxed, and in general acted as though she and her staff were their private secretaries. Laura usually straightened them out early on, but she was more than willing to accommodate Gino.

"Come on around here," Laura said to Dr. Romano. "I'll show you how to look that up."

He peered over her shoulder, their faces inches apart. She walked him through a few simple sequences. His patient's record appeared on the computer screen. Laura jotted down the unit number.

"That was easy. Why does it not work for me?"

"Computers are finicky."

He stepped back, apparently realizing that his face was still close to hers. He blushed. "Feenicky? I do not know that word."

"The spelling, the spacing, everything has to be just so."

She noticed him glance at her legs. Bruce had once joked that even if she weren't gorgeous, he'd have married her for her legs alone.

Laura, although boasting only a trace of Italian descent, had gotten her full lips and naturally curly hair from her Roman ancestors. The other seventy-five percent, her Irish/Scottish heritage, no doubt accounted for her blond hair, blue eyes, fair complexion and slim ankles.

Her skirt often hiked up well above her knees, after sitting in the same position a long time. As she swiveled from her computer stand to her desktop, she handed Gino the patient's unit number.

"Thank you." He extended his hand.

"For what?"

"You are kinder than most. Miss...?"

"Laura." They shook hands.

That was her first encounter with Gino, the dreamy-eyed intern from Palermo. Laura had served on the selection committee and was privy to his application. He was unwed; his parents and most of his close relatives lived in Sicily. His medical school credentials were excellent. He had played semiprofessional soccer and had a passion for movies, especially westerns. A perfect match for her friend Rose.

*****

Laura's new intern friend, Gino, would seek out Laura in the hospital cafeteria. In fact, she'd sit alone, hoping he would. Their enjoyment of each other's company raised a few eyebrows, but she didn't care. She was helping him with his English, especially the slang, and he was adding a little spice to her life, even though he never once made a pass.

Whenever she asked about his life in Palermo he quickly changed the subject. Was he connected to the Sicilian Mafia? There were no outward signs, but then again, you never know.

"How did you end up interning in New Jersey?"

"My father's brother lives in South Orange. He owns a small importing business. He wrote to me about this hospital. It is known well for having an utmost training program in cardiology."

He liked the word *utmost*. "You want to be a heart specialist?"

"Yes, but first I must get through my internship. Then a residency in internal medicine. Then two years in a cardiology fellowship."

"I envy you. You know what you want and exactly how you intend to get there."

"But it is not so certain, Laura. Many who start the race do not make the end."

"I'm on the selection committee for the internal medicine residency. How rich is your father?"

Gino frowned. He looked around. "You shouldn't say such things."

She laughed. "Just joking, Gino. I don't really have any influence on their decision. I submit a few chart audits that deal with your record-keeping skills.

Their decision is mostly based on evaluations by your attendings."

"That is what concerns me," he said. "The other interns are much more familiar with hospital procedures. Some are very...determined." He was silent for a moment or two. "Do not take this in the wrong way, but I find that American women are very....I do not know the right word... bold, rude at times."

"Are you saying that in Italy, women know their place?"

"You see, you prove my point. You insinuate I am a chauvinist because I make an honest observation."

"A handful of ambitious lady doctors is hardly a representative sample of American women."

He blushed. Did he realize she was teasing him? He was so incredibly polite and formal. She smiled, hoping to relieve the tension

"Drawing conclusions from a series of observations is the scientific method," Gino said. "It is how I was trained."

Laura couldn't help herself. "Did you include any men in your sample?"

He stood. "You make a good point. Of course you are right. Next time I will observe the men and report to you. I must go. We have rounds in five minutes. *Ciao*."

He hurried off. Had she offended him? *God, it's fun talking with him. I want to know more about his uncle. Exactly where in South Orange does he live? And what does he import?*

She had heard through the grapevine that Gino was a hard worker, well-liked, and knowledgeable, but that his clinical skills were not on a par with most of the other interns. She had been told that doctors graduating from Italian medical schools generally have less hands-on experience than students trained in the United States.

He was on his general surgery rotation. Laura knew the nursing supervisor, Mrs. Timmons, because they had worked closely together on the audit committee. As head nurse she was often first to know when an attending physician ordered a particular procedure. Laura decided to ask Mrs. Timmons to make sure Dr. Romano got his share.

Judging Laura

Chapter Five

On the drive to Dr. Corbett's office for her preoperative workup, Laura had an urge to turn around and head back home. Why not just forget the whole damn business? In a way she was allowing Michael Greene to once again mess with her life. The below-freezing temperature and sunless sky added to her apprehension. She was about to commit to major surgery, that may or may not produce anything worthwhile....*I can do this. I must!* Determined, she pulled into the employee parking lot at St. Joe's Hospital, left her car and headed for Dr. Corbett's.

Her doctor described the operation and post-operative care. If was hard for Laura to imagine it was her body the doctor was talking about dissecting and then putting back together again. Laura was surprised she experienced no visceral reaction to Dr. Corbett's recitation of the gory details. There was plenty of time to panic; after all, she hadn't fully committed to going through with it.

A laboratory technician came in and drew blood. Dr. Corbett handed her a sheet of instructions.

"You and I have already spoken about test-tube babies," Dr. Corbett said.

"Yes, but I'm not sure how it works."

"Let me give you some reading material about that approach. Read through it before your next visit. Discuss it with your husband. You can also search 'test-tube babies' on the internet. Loads of information there."

Laura read what Dr. Corbett had given her and googled the subject. The volume of information was overwhelming. There were thousands of websites. She learned that the first successful case was in 1978. *In vitro* fertilization was considered almost science fiction back then, but by now, the year 2000, the procedure was being done routinely by fertility specialists like Dr. Corbett.

IVF involved giving the woman a hormone such as Clomiphene to induce ovulation. To harvest the eggs, Dr. Corbett would place an instrument in the vagina and aim a needle, guided by ultrasonic imaging, at Laura's ovary. Several eggs are aspirated, and then incubated for a few hours. They are then separated and placed on individual glass dishes. Bruce's sperm would be added to each Petri dish. After fertilization, they again incubate the fertilized eggs until they begin to divide, and at a certain point, usually three doublings, the doctor inseminates the woman's womb with the fertilized eggs.

The doctors use more than one egg because there is no way of knowing which egg, if any, will actually implant. Often none of them do, and the procedure has to be repeated. But sometimes two or more eggs take hold. When that happens, the couple might be blessed with twins or triplets.

Bruce accompanied Laura on her follow-up visit. They had talked it over prior to their appointment. He had a pretty good idea what IVF involved. His main concern was whether the baby might be at risk of having birth defects.

"No abnormalities associated with the procedure have been reported, and there's no reason to anticipate any," Dr. Corbett assured them. "It's your sperm and her eggs. There's nothing unnatural about it."

Bruce and Laura exchanged glances. "Yes," Laura said, "but how they get together isn't exactly what Mama Nature had in mind."

"And what about that hormone you use to make her ovulate....how safe is it?" Bruce asked.

"I understand your concern," Dr. Corbett said. "But no problems have been reported with its use." She leaned forward. "The process has become routine for me. That is exactly why I have asked for this meeting."

Laura looked about Dr. Corbett's consultation room. It resembled a cozy den: Oriental rug, shelves stacked with books, journals and framed photographs, a blinking computer screen sat off in one corner, a couch, coffee table and two comfortable side chairs. No one spoke for a few moments.

"I have pretty good health insurance through work," Laura said. "Will that cover most of the cost?"

"IVF is considered an elective procedure. Most carriers don't cover it. But all the preliminary testing and the operation to remove your fallopian tubes would be covered."

"Can you give us a ballpark figure?" Bruce asked.

"It's difficult to say for sure what it might cost. On average it takes three cycles for a successful outcome. In my clinic that would come to around $60,000. The total bill could be close to $90,000. That does not include pregnancy care and delivery. But that part would be covered by your insurance."

Bruce and Laura were stunned. There was no way they could afford that.

Later that evening as Bruce and Laura prepared dinner they discussed the meeting with Dr. Corbett.

"Let's not do anything just yet," Laura said. "Maybe we should think about adoption?"

Bruce was mincing onions as she stir-fried some frozen vegetables. He tossed the onions into the wok. "Hell, that could take years," he said, "and it's not the same."

Laura added some soy and hoisin sauce. She was tired of thinking about eggs and sperm and babies. She had also been given information about surrogate pregnancy. But even with that, you still have to go through the IVF procedure to obtain and fertilize your eggs. And neither she nor Bruce was interested in using donor eggs.

Laura dumped the contents of the wok into a large serving dish. As the pungent steam rose from the bowl, she was carried back to the heated swimming pool at Luke's house. The kids shouting, the loud music and everything spinning out of control. She turned to Bruce, her eyes brimming with tears. "Won't it ever stop? Won't I ever stop paying for that night?" Bruce put his arms around her. She pressed her wet cheek to his.

"I'm sorry about pushing you on this baby business," he said. "Let's let it rest...."

She pulled back enough to look into his eyes. He was good at saying the right thing, but his eyes couldn't lie. They were not happy eyes. He was worried about her, about their future. She couldn't give him the children he had always dreamed of. Would he grow weary of a barren marriage?

"No, Bruce, I'm not going to let this rest. With Dr. Corbett's help we *are* going to have a baby. And one way or another, Michael Greene will pay."

Judging Laura

Chapter Six

1995

A year after Laura had left home, she was no longer furious at her mother for treating her like a tramp, for not standing by her when she needed her. Now that Laura was on her own, struggling to pay her bills, she had came to realize how her mother, on a high school librarian's salary, must have had to scrimp to support them both and to put aside enough to buy a home. Why had her parents divorced? Her mother never complained or talked about her father in a negative way.

Laura came to realize that it was wrong not to let her mother know she was alive and well. Her anger had dissolved, replaced by a sense of guilt and longing.

A phone conversation would be awkward. She decided instead to write. She composed a long, rambling letter about her new life, the hospital where she worked, her friends. She wrote that she was sorry for having said she never wanted to see her mother again.

She waited a couple of weeks, looking every day for a response. None came. Finally she telephoned and learned that the number was no longer in service. That was strange. Had her mother moved? Laura wrote to her mother's sister, her Aunt Lena, and explained that she had been trying to get in touch with her mother. Could she send her an address or phone number?

A week later Laura received a letter from her aunt. Her hands shook as she opened the envelope.

Dear Laura,

It makes me sad to tell you this, but your mother died of breast cancer six months after you left home. She knew she had a lump in her breast but did nothing until the cancer was too far gone. She said she really didn't care. With you gone she felt useless, unnecessary. She was always making novenas for you and cried every time your name was mentioned. I'm sorry, Laura, but we had no idea how to get in touch with you.

Your father came to the funeral. Someone must have called him. I can't imagine who. He didn't talk with anyone. Just stayed off by himself. He left right after the church service. You got a little money coming, Laura. She asked me to put it aside for you. I had to sell the house to pay property taxes and other expenses. I sold the furniture. Some of your personal things like school papers, diplomas, albums, yearbooks, clothes, I stored away.

Doctor bills, funeral expenses and paying off what was left on the mortgage ate up most of what we got for the house. I set up a trust account in your name at the BB&G Bank. She wanted you to have the money

42

when you turned twenty-one. Call Mr. Rudolph at the bank. He's in charge of your trust fund. The number is 610-123-2265.

Walter and I are doing okay. He's got almost twenty-five years in at the post office. He wants to retire in five years and sell our house. He wants to buy one of those fancy motor homes. Travel through the US and Canada. We'll see.

Love,

Aunt Lena

The letter slipped from Laura's hand as she dropped to her knees. "Oh, mother, oh, mother, I'm so sorry."

How could a cancer take her so quickiy? She had seemed perfectly well when Laura left home. But then Laura recalled how thin and pale her mother had looked that awful night. Had her mother already known about the cancer? If she did, why would she keep such a thing from her? She had not been there for her mother's final days. Had she suffered? Her remorse was unbearable.

One evening, several weeks after having received Aunt Lena's letter, she returned from work and was stunned to find her old boyfriend sitting on the front stoop.

"My God! Bruce!" She flew into his outstretched arms... "How did you know where to find me?"

"Your Aunt Lena called. I couldn't believe you were just a few towns away."

Laura grabbed his hand, pulling him into her apartment. "It's so amazing you're here. Have a seat. You must be hungry. I'll microwave some dinner."

"You look great, Laura. You haven't changed at all."

"It's only been a year. What did you expect, an old lady?"

She opened the freezer compartment and pulled out a couple of Lean Cuisines. "Chicken Alfredo or macaroni and cheese?"

"Macaroni and cheese sounds good."

"I'll duke you for it," Laura said.

He laughed. "God, I missed you." He looked about the tiny apartment. "Nice place."

She pried up a corner of each of the cartons. "You're looking at the entire apartment, except for the bathroom."

"It's cozy."

It looked even smaller than usual with Bruce there. "You've grown taller since I saw you last."

"Yeah. And wider."

He looked great. She learned that he had dropped out of college in the spring of his first year. He had gone mainly to please his parents and to try out for the baseball team. Most of the other kids going out for the team were on scholarship.

"I wasn't in the same league as them. I worked out in the weight room. Tried as hard as I could, but got dropped from the roster. I quit school and got a job at a body shop."

"Your uncle's?" Laura asked as she removed the dinners from the microwave.

"Yeah. I had worked with him summers. He's a great guy. The pay's good. No term papers. How about you?"

"First I waited tables. Then I saw an ad in the papers. Saint Joseph's Hospital was looking for a file clerk to work in their medical records department. When I interviewed I didn't think I had a chance."

"How come?" Bruce asked.

"They said you had to be a high school graduate. But when I told them about my GPA and SAT scores, they hired me and suggested I take the GED examination."

"How'd that go?"

"The reading comprehension and social studies questions were a breeze. Good thing, because I needed the extra time to work on the math and science questions."

"Would have been just the opposite for me. I bet you aced it."

"I did okay. The job at St. Joe's pays less than waiting tables but it's a lot more interesting."

"Filing? Interesting?"

"I hand-deliver charts to the emergency room, clinics and the hospital wards. They have conferences for the doctors and nurses practically every day at noon. I eat my lunch and listen. At first a lot of it went over my head, but after awhile I began to get used to the medical jargon."

Bruce seemed lost in thought. "Hey, you okay?" Laura asked.

"No. I'm not okay. I went half crazy this past year. Not knowing what happened to you and why you never called me." He went to her and gathered her into his arms.

"I was ashamed. I was afraid you wouldn't want me anymore..."

Bruce drove down from Allentown every Friday after work. The first few Fridays he didn't stay overnight. He had to be at the body shop by seven the next morning. Then one night they discovered a place called *Mamma's and Tapas*. They served appetizers and beer by the pitcher. They ate and danced and drank until the restaurant closed.

"You can't drive back tonight." She gently took his car keys from him. He didn't resist. She slipped behind the wheel of his Miata.

He leaned back in his seat. "Guess I had one pitcher too many. I'll get up at six. It'll only take me an hour that early."

Laura spread a blanket on the floor next to her pull-out bed. Bruce was asleep before she finished brushing her teeth. She walked over to where he lay, slipped a cushion under his head, and whispered "I love you, Bruce Hamby."

She kissed his cheek, then crawled into her own bed. After that night, Bruce brought a sleeping bag and stayed over every Friday. She had fitful nights with him sleeping on the floor beside her. Was he holding back because of what she had gone through? Or was the thought of having sex with her somehow repulsive to him? Each time he left, she was afraid he might not return.

Yet Laura was grateful that he had given her all the time she needed. It was exactly eight weeks after he had appeared on her front stoop that they made love. He was gentle and considerate of her feelings. She was into her tenth Hail Mary before she realized it wasn't going to hurt. Fear receded at the same rate that passion accelerated. It was a joyous release of inhibitions. Afterwards she silently said another decade of the rosary in thanksgiving.

After a few months, Bruce began looking at local classified ads. An auto parts franchise was advertising for a clerk. They were looking for someone familiar with cars and willing to learn the business. He got the job. That night he came by with a bottle of champagne and a corsage of gardenias. They sat on folding chairs at a card table covered with a doubled-over bed sheet.

"Here's to the new job," she said as she raised her glass.

"Here's to my future wife," he said.

Laura was shocked. Well, not entirely shocked. "You have anyone particular in mind?"

He looked confused. "Yeah."

"Was that a proposal of marriage?" She had to resist the urge to rush to the door and bolt it for fear he might change his mind.

"I guess it didn't come out like I meant."

"Do you love this future wife of yours?"

"Oh, God yes!"

"In that case, she accepts."

Six months later they were married by a justice of the peace. She was nineteen, Bruce was twenty. It had been almost two years since she left Allentown. She didn't want ever to go back.

"I'm still a little pissed at you for not letting me know where you were going," Bruce commented one evening at dinner. They were having spaghetti and meatballs, his favorite. Her smidgeon of Italian ancestry spiced up her cooking.

"I felt it was partly my fault. I was ashamed to talk about what they did to me. Especially with you."

"It must have been hard for you to trust anyone."

"I couldn't bear the thought that you would look at me like I was dirty. Like I was damaged goods."

"God almighty. I would never think that." Bruce bit into his third meatball. "After you left town, Michael Greene figured he didn't have anything to worry about, so he began hinting that he was one of the guys. You know how kids talk. A friend of mine told me about it when I was home on Christmas break."

Laura didn't want to dredge up the past, but she had to know where this was leading.

"I didn't know for sure who the other guys were," Bruce said, "but my friend said everyone was saying that Michael Greene was one of them. One day before going back to school, I went to Central High and waited by the school entrance. When Michael went up the steps I grabbed him from behind, dragged him by the collar and threw him onto the lawn. Neither of us said a word. Kids gathered around us. Others leaned out of classroom windows. We fought for maybe ten minutes with practically half the school watching.

"We were both bloodied, but he had the worst of it. When the cops arrived there was Michael groaning on the ground. They took him to the hospital emergency room. I learned later that he had a broken nose and two fractured ribs. Me, they took to the police station. My parents came down. I didn't tell them why I had started the fight. I said it was something that had been building up between us for a long time.

"I learned later that Michael's father went to the hospital emergency room. He's some kind of big-shot corporate lawyer. My guess is that he knew already what his son had done, and that's probably why they didn't press charges."

Laura listened in silence, imagining she was Bruce, pounding Michael with every ounce of her strength, enjoying the crunch of his nose under her fists, the snap of his ribs.

"Weren't you afraid his friends would come after you?" she asked.

"I hoped they would. But I was pretty sure they wouldn't."

"I wish I would have known what you did. God, I'd loved to have been there."

On her twenty-first birthday, Bruce brought home Chinese takeout and a bottle of Chianti. After dinner they snuggled on the living room couch, watching an old black-and-white movie featuring Spencer Tracey and Katherine Hepburn. She knew Bruce would have preferred a Clint Eastwood western, but it was her birthday after all. He reached for the bottle of wine. As he poured the last into their glasses she asked, "So how does it feel to be married to a wealthy, not-unattractive woman?"

He knew about the inheritance she was due to collect when she turned twenty-one.

They banged glasses.

"So how wealthy is my not-unattractive wife?"

"There's a little over ten thousand dollars in the trust fund."

"Maybe you should trade your Beetle in for something safer, like a Lincoln Continental."

"My bug's as safe as your Miata. Besides, it only has 150K. I'm shooting for 200."

"Volkswagen Beetles are like little old ladies."

"How so?" she asked.

"Their bottoms rust out long before their engines call it quits."

"I'll forgive you for that, Mr. Hamby, assuming you've had a bit too much to drink."

He lifted the empty bottle and sighed.

"The bank trustee advised that I roll the trust fund over into an IRA Account. That way interest and capital gains can accumulate tax free."

"Sounds like a good idea to me."

"But before retirement, you can't pull your money out of an IRA without a big penalty," Laura said. "What if we need it for an emergency?"

"Yeah. Maybe tax free municipal bonds might be a better way to go."

"I like that idea, mister financial advisor."

Chapter Seven

South Orange, NJ

September 2002

"Sweetheart," Bruce said, "it's your decision whether we to go after Dr. Greene and those guys, but we'll both have to live with the fallout."

She walked to where he was sitting at his computer desk. "That sounds a bit less than lukewarm." She pulled up a chair and sat next to him.

He swiveled toward her, taking both her hands in his. "At first I would have said no way. Let it rest. There's no way we can win this. You know his lawyers will come after you...say all sorts of hurtful things. You don't deserve that."

Laura laid her head on his lap. "What about justice? Shouldn't that figure in there somewhere?"

"It's a crapshoot. Good guys get convicted. Bad guys get off," Bruce said.

"I know our chances of winning this aren't great, but how else can we afford to have a baby?

He leaned over and kissed her. "You know I'll support whatever you decide."

He knows I want to make those guys pay. Our first step is track down Michael. Laura decided to search the internet. There were several Michael Greenes listed, but only one in Allentown, Pennsylvania.

Michael D. Greene DOB 7/14/1976
Central High Allentown, PA (1991-1995)
Yale Univ. New Haven, CT (1995-1999)
Jefferson Medical School, PA (1999-2002)

With his family connections, he could have gone into business or politics. Why medicine? It just didn't seem a likely fit. She stared at the screen in disbelief. If she had gone to the police that night, and he ended up with a rape conviction, his life would have been different. What medical school would have admitted a convicted felon? And a political career would have been out of the question. It was her uncertainty that enabled him to move ahead with his life. She wished it were possible to go back and redo her actions.

"Bruce," Laura shouted, "get your head out of the fridge. Come here and look at this."

"How did you know where I was looking?" he asked as he came into the spare room they used as a home office.

"A not-so-wild guess."

He leaned over her shoulder. "Michael Greene? That can't be him. Medical school?"

"Of course it's him. Look at when and where he graduated high school. He probably started his residency this past July."

"I suppose you're right. Damn."

"I would never have guessed medicine."

"You know, it drives me nuts to think this guy's DNA may be inside you." Bruce said. "If Dr. Corbett finds out there is, you should definitely press charges...."

"We've talked about that...it would mean dragging out all that dirty laundry. And what if he claims we had consensual sex. How do we disprove that?"

"I don't get it...you agreed to have an operation to prove his DNA was still in your body, and now you say there's no way to make him pay for what he did."

When she turned to face him there were tears in her eyes. She embraced Bruce. *My mother died believing I hated her. That more than anything else makes me want to prove what Michael Greene had done. He had wanted to humiliate her.*

"How many men like him have gotten away with rape because the victim dreaded public scrutiny?" Laura asked.

"Sweetheart, this guy put you through enough crap. We'll figure out a way to have a family. We don't need his money."

She turned to face the computer monitor. "Part of me wanted to forget the whole business, to go on with our lives. It's not just about the money. We need to expose him for who he is, for what he did. He ruined my reputation, my health and my ability to have a baby."

"If he's only earning a surgery resident's salary, he might claim bankruptcy," Bruce said.

"Did you know the Pennsylvania State Senator, Joe Greene, is Michael's uncle? And that his father's the head corporate lawyer for Pennsylvania Mining?"

"I knew his family wasn't exactly poor," Bruce said. "Not many guys at Central High drove around in a BMW convertible in their junior year."

"The 120 grand it might cost for our test-tube-baby would be nothing to that family."

Bruce nodded. "You make a good point. But it may not be his DNA. There were two other guys."

"God. I wish we knew which ones they were."

"After you left town, there were rumors about them," Bruce said. "They could be tested."

"I'm not sure you can force someone to get tested based on nine-year-old rumors. Besides, I don't have to go to the police."

He spun her chair around. He was kneeling on one knee. "You're not thinking about blackmailing the guy, are you?"

"No. The whole purpose would be to expose what he did, not cover it up. An attorney could advise whether to pursue criminal prosecution or civil action."

Bruce laughed. "You sound like a lawyer..."

She brushed the tears away with tissue. "Someday...maybe."

"But if we take him to court and lose, we're the ones with pie in our face," Bruce said. "And what if he had used a condom? He would know it wasn't his DNA. They'd have him tested. Without a match he'd be off the hook."

"I hadn't thought of that. Damn. Only thing left to do would be to get a sample of his DNA," Laura said.

"It's all speculation. What if Dr. Corbett doesn't find anything unusual?" Bruce asked. "Let's not drive ourselves crazy." He stood and walked toward the kitchen.

"Come back here. We need to think this thing through."

He returned to the den and sat beside her.

"What if we go to the police with a report from Dr. Corbett saying she found DNA evidence? I tell them my story. Couldn't they issue a court order to test him and a few of the guys who were at the party?"

Two weeks later, Dr. Corbett removed Laura's fallopian tubes. Laura's ovaries were normal, but both tubes were scarred and cystic. Laura was surprised how little pain she felt after surgery. She was home in a couple of days, back to work the following week. She called Dr. Corbett's office several times to see if the tests were back. She said some unkind things to Dr. Corbett's office nurse, for which she later apologized. Finally, after two agonizing weeks, Dr.

Corbett called and asked that she and Bruce come in to discuss the results.

"There was no chance of you ever becoming pregnant," Dr. Corbett told Laura. "Both tubes were obstructed. There wasn't enough normal tube left to even consider reconstructive surgery."

"What about the DNA test?"

She nodded. "Yes, of course. The pathologist at St. Joe's made dozens of paraffin sections of your fallopian tubes. The specimens were tested using a recently developed technique that detects minute fragments of DNA."

Laura nodded. "PCR analysis?"

Dr. Corbett raised her eyebrows. "You've done your homework."

"And what did they find?" Bruce asked impatiently.

"They found three distinct DNA genotypes. One was consistent with bacteria, probably gonorrhea; the other two were human."

Laura was stunned. There was a chance they wouldn't find anything and she would have to let the whole ugly business go away. "You're sure of the results?"

"Yes. A second lab confirmed the findings."

"I'm concerned curious staff in the hospital lab may have seen the test results."

"No. The analysis was done by an outside laboratory that specializes in DNA analysis. The report came directly to me."

Laura was relieved but not surprised. Many of their staff doctors used outside labs. Contract labs were staffed twenty-four hours a day. They pick up specimens from the doctor's office, fax results the same day, and usually charge less than hospital-based labs.

"Laura, I believe the infection may also have contributed to the preservation of the DNA."

"I don't understand. . . ."

"As I explained before, foreign DNA would be attacked and destroyed by the immune system under ordinary circumstances. But beside the sperm's innate ability to ward off the immune system, the inflammation and scarring that resulted from the gonorrhea may have also helped shield some of the sperm DNA from the body's armies of attack and destroy cells." Dr. Corbett looked intently at Laura. "These findings could have broad implications."

She wanted to jump up and hug Dr. Corbett, but she wasn't sure what she meant by broad implications. "Are you saying that other women who have been raped may be carrying the evidence around with them for years, maybe their entire lives?"

"Most rape goes unreported," Dr. Corbett said. "Fear, guilt, and shame are some of the emotions that hold women back. DNA evidence, when gathered from examination of the woman, is usually done immediately afterwards or certainly within a few days. My review of the medical literature failed to reveal even a single instance where DNA evidence was still present in the victim many years later."

"Why is that?" Laura asked.

"Mainly because doctors haven't thought to look. Finding foreign DNA in a pathology specimen is like searching for a needle in a haystack. It's tedious, time consuming and very expensive."

Laura hadn't as yet gotten the bill. She didn't want to know how expensive. She looked at Bruce. He shrugged.

"Laura," Dr. Corbett continued, "I must share this knowledge with the medical community. Hundreds, maybe thousands of women might benefit."

"But what if my case is just a fluke of nature?"

"My medical intuition tells me not. A month from now I'm scheduled to present at the annual meeting of the Society of Fertility Specialists. I would like to discuss your case, if you don't mind."

Laura blanched. Dr. Corbett quickly added, "Your identity will be scrupulously guarded. Your medical records will be kept in my locked file. The laboratory records will be purged from the computer and filed as *Jane Doe.* No one will be able to connect this report to you."

Laura looked at Bruce. He nodded.

"Yes. Go ahead, Dr. Corbett," Laura said. "Maybe some good might come of this."

"Are you considering taking legal action?"

"I'm not sure. I've waited this long. I want to keep that option open."

"While you decide, your records will be safe with me," Dr. Corbett said. "But remember, once you bring the case to court the most private parts of your life will be made public."

Chapter Eight

Laura had to know whose DNA she had been carrying around in her tubes for so many years. Just thinking about that made her sick. Dr. Corbett had said Bruce wasn't likely responsible for one of the DNA samples, because her tubes were probably already scarred long before they were married. But just to be sure, Dr. Corbett arranged for him to have blood drawn. A week later Bruce and Laura visited Dr. Corbett to discuss the results.

"Neither of the DNA specimens matched yours, Mr. Hamby. Frankly, I never expected a match."

"So it's an open-and-shut case if we do decide to press charges?" Laura asked.

"No. Especially not an eight-year-old case. The DNA evidence only proves they had intercourse with you. We can't establish when that DNA found its way into your body."

Bruce leaned forward. "Are you suggesting we shouldn't go after those guys?" he asked.

"No. I'm saying it's not a slam dunk. And the emotional and financial cost to you and Laura will be immense, no matter what the outcome."

"If we decide to go ahead, what do we do?" he asked.

"You'd have to file a complaint. Then the police would get a court order to do DNA testing on the suspects. They would talk to people who were at the party. Try to determine who the other two young men were."

"I know the guys Michael hung out with," Bruce said.

"And there are the girls who came into the room when I started to scream," Laura said. "Remember? You suggested they might have seen someone leave."

"Yes, that would certainly help. But it's been years since the incident, and you told me everyone was drinking. They might not be very credible witnesses," Dr. Corbett said. "Of course they saw you injured and bleeding."

"What other options do we have?" Bruce asked.

"A civil suit might be the way to go."

The thought that they would press charges and not be able to convince a jury was worse to Laura than doing nothing. "Dr. Corbett, Bruce and I have a lot to talk about. Thanks for everything. We'll let you know when we want to go ahead with the business of getting me pregnant."

The following day Laura called the Dean's office at the Jefferson School of Medicine. She learned that Michael Greene had been accepted in the surgical training program at the University of Pennsylvania. That afternoon she paged Dr. Gino Romano and asked if he would meet her in the hospital snack bar for a few minutes.

Laura was sipping a coke at a booth at the far end of the room when Gino walked over. They shook hands as they always did on meeting. It was an Italian thing. She didn't know how to start. They talked about his surgical rotation. He was pleased that he was getting plenty of procedures. Almost too many. "Chest tubes, spinal taps and cut-downs are coming my way every day. Ms. Timmons, for some reason, has befriended me. I cannot think who might have spoken for me." He smiled.

"Beats me."

"How are you feeling since your operation?"

"A little sore, but not bad really. Thanks for stopping by to see me. I almost freaked out thinking about having some of my organs removed. You were very kind and reassuring."

"It was my pleasure."

"How much time do you have, Dr. Romano?"

"I start evening rounds in one hour."

Laura had no choice but to swallow her pride and jump into her story. "When I was a senior in high school I went to a party at a boy's home. His parents were away. Half the senior class was there. I was drinking...just sips of watered down vodka. I became sick...I passed out..."

"You do not have to do this'" Gino said.

"When I woke up, three boys...three boys were attacking me."

"My God."

"My arms were tied the bedpost. My mouth and eyes were covered."

Gino squeezed her hand. His eyes glistened. "In my country those boys would be long dead. You are brave to tell me this. Is there something I can do? You need only ask."

She wondered again if his family had Mafia connections. She dallied with the thought. A couple of *soldati* breaking a leg, or grabbing Dr. Greene's balls in a vise-like grip. She was tempted, but decided not to go there. But what did Gino mean when he said she need only ask?

"I know you're in the process of interviewing for an internal medicine position," Laura said. The record room had sent off copies of service evaluations to the programs to which he had applied. One had gone to the University of Pennsylvania. "When is your interview at U. Penn?"

"In two weeks I'm taking a one-week holiday. I hope to do all my interviews then."

"My gynecologist identified two different DNA thingies when she examined my fallopian tubes."

Gino leaned forward. "DNA thingies? Is that what she tells you?"

Laura smiled. "I think maybe she said, 'fragments'...is that right?"

"Yes, that makes sense. It is truly amazing. But whose DNA?"

"One of the guys who raped me is a first-year surgery resident at U. Penn."

"But you cannot be certain. You said your eyes were covered."

"I'm absolutely certain. I need a sample of his DNA."

"That is a matter for the police. You must not do this."

So much for her Mafia theory. "No, not yet," she said.

He looked so distressed, she was almost sorry she had taken him into her confidence.

"You are asking me to somehow get you a sample of this person's DNA?" he said, barely above a whisper.

"No, of course not. But I wonder what their policy is on testing house staff for HIV."

Gino took a deep breath. He was obviously relieved. "When I joined the program here, it was required."

"That's because St. Joe's is self-insured. We don't want someone who is already HIV positive to claim they got the infection while employed here."

"You want me to ask them what if any laboratory tests I have to take to join their program?"

Laura nodded.

"And what if he has had a blood test?"

"Then I must get hold of a few drops of that blood. Can you find out what they do with the specimens here at St. Joe's? Where they're stored and who has access to them?"

"I am in the hematology lab almost every day, looking up test results. I have become friends with one of the technicians."

"Close?"

He smiled. "I have little time for close."

Had she waited too long to introduce him to her friend Rose? "What is her name?"

"Sylvia Conte. You know her?"

"No. Is she *bella*?" Laura had picked up a paperback Italian phrase book. She liked to throw in an Italian word here and there. He did the same.

"*Ma certamente! È bellissimo*. Like you, she has Italian ancestry. Both her parents are from Italy. It's good to have someone to speak to in Italian."

"I would like to meet her sometime." Laura stood. "*Ciao*."

They shook hands. "*Arrivederci*."

A couple of long days later, Laura received a call from Gino.

"Laura, I have been so busy there is no time even to eat lunch. But I do have the information. The blood is kept in a freezer in the lab."

"How does it get there?"

"Sylvia said the person who draws the blood gives it to one of the laboratory technicians. They draw off enough blood to do the test, and the rest is stored in the freezer."

"How long is the specimen kept?"

"Hematology specimens are discarded after one week."

"Damn. So much for that idea."

"But HIV testing is done in the immunology lab," Gino said. "Those are kept for three months."

"That's better. Michael started his hospital rotations in July. That's probably when they did his blood tests," Laura speculated. "But that was five months ago."

"That's true," Gino said. "The original specimen was probably discarded. But the surgery residents are getting tested all the time. Their gloves tear, they prick themselves while suturing. They are like fish in a sea of blood."

"So he may have had a more recent test?"

"It is an utmost possibility."

"*Grazia*, Gino; you've been of utmost help."

If Michael had pricked his finger within the past three months, Laura thought, there would be a record of the incident. If she could somehow get her hands on that report she'd know for sure. She knew that, at St. Joe's, copies of incident reports went to the risk management department, one to the department head, and one to the nursing supervisor. A copy was also placed in the employee's personal file.

As a member of the St. Joe's audit committee, Laura was only privy to incident reports discussed by the members from risk management. A few months back they had looked at which departments had the highest incidence of exposure to HIV. It wasn't surprising that the Emergency Department topped the list. General surgery was a close second, OB/GYN third. The committee recommended that the department heads routinely discuss incidents at their monthly staff meetings as a way to keep the issue alive. The committee promised to revisit the matter in one year.

Laura figured it was a safe bet that the hospital of the University of Pennsylvania wasn't much different from St. Joe's when it came to staff, residents and medical students not complying with safety standards. If she could figure out a way to get her hands on a recent incident report at St. Joe's, the same technique might work at U. Penn. After thinking about it for a day or two, she decided on a plan.

Laura was beginning to enjoy this.

Jeff Coleman was an attorney in the risk management department. Laura dialed his secretary's number at 12:30 PM on a Friday afternoon. His regular secretary would be out to lunch. Someone else would be covering the phone.

"Hi, Janet. This is Laura Hamby."

"Janet's out to lunch. This is Suzie Weston. How may I help you?"

"I'm medical records supervisor. I'm preparing a presentation for the next meeting of the audit committee. I need a copy of the incident reports from surgery for the month of November."

"I'll check with Mr. Coleman. I have no idea where she keeps them. Could you hold on a minute?"

"Of course." So far so good, Laura thought.

"He said he'd bring copies to the committee meeting next week."

"That won't work. I need to audit the charts ahead of time. Can I stop by say in a half hour?"

"Hold on, please." There was a long pause. "Okay. I'll make the copies. I'll leave them in a folder on my desk."

When Laura stepped into Jeff Coleman's outer office, she found the folder sitting on his secretary's desk. She had never met Suzie Weston, so for all the secretary knew, it could have been anyone on the phone. Laura was feeling very clever. As she picked up the folder, Jeff came from his office. He was a young attorney the hospital employed full-time to advise them on malpractice claims, and to develop and monitor policies to reduce the number of screw-ups by hospital personnel.

"Would you step into my office, Laura?"

Chapter Nine

A trickle of perspiration ran from Laura's upper back to her lower spine as she walked into Jeff's office. "Of course. How are you, Jeff?" She sat beside his desk in his cramped windowless office. Her voice remained calm. Her stomach didn't.

Jeff was a short, plump, pleasant-looking man in his mid-thirties, his hair already thinning. He had the habit of winking when he believed he had made an effective argument. He picked up a pencil and chewed for a moment on the eraser. She had seen him do that many times at committee meetings. It wasn't a good sign.

"What the hell's going on, Laura?"

She wasn't about to tell him any more than she had to. "What do you mean?" she asked innocently.

"I got the agenda for the audit committee meeting just yesterday. I phoned the audit committee chairman, Dr. Silver. He said the agenda was set. He had no idea what you were talking about. He was pretty upset."

"This is great," Laura said, trying hard to sound pleased.

"A potential breach of security? I fail to see what's great about that."

"Do you recall about six months ago we had a lengthy discussion about the security of documents?" she asked. "We discussed how lawyers use a variety of tricks to get their hands on sensitive material?"

He raised one eyebrow, then winked. "Yes. And we talked about how they might use a hospital employee to do their dirty work."

"Right. And we made some changes in our protocols. So I wanted to see just how secure incident reports are. I knew another secretary would be covering for Janet over the lunch hour. I figured she might not be familiar with our protocols."

"All our secretaries go through a thorough orientation."

"True. But we throw an awful lot at them. I was going to present the results of my little experiment at the next meeting. Your secretary did exactly the right thing. Risk management passed the test!"

"I would suggest, Laura, that the next time you plan an experiment such as this, you first consult the committee chairperson. You know how doctors are. They don't like anything that undercuts their authority." He winked.

"You're absolutely right, Jeff, I should have." Laura winked back. She handed him the envelope. "I won't need this."

Her plan had back-fired. It would be too risky to use a similar approach at U. Penn. She would have to figure out some other way to gain access to Michael Greene's incident report, assuming one existed.

The day Gino returned from his interviews, he and Laura met in the hospital snack bar. She asked him how it went.

"Most well. I was impressed with the program at U. Penn."

"It is of utmost quality?"

He nodded. "Yes. Compared to the others. The interns and residents I met were *simpatico*."

"Mostly women, I bet."

He smiled. "I told them I was interested in cardiology and immunology. I got to visit both labs."

"Ah! You are clever. Tell me about the immunology lab." She added an extra envelope of sugar to her coffee.

"It is a large room with many work stations separated by . . ." He used his hands as he searched for the word.

"Partitions?"

"Yes. Partitions. The freezer is like a small room in the back. It was very orderly. They store many specimens other than HIV. They are kept in trays. The drawers are numbered."

"Is it kept locked?" she asked.

"Not when I was there. The technicians were in and out most frequently."

Gino told Laura that all incoming house staff get a battery of blood tests, including HIV. And that they kept the initial specimen for four months.

"Would you do me one more favor?" she asked.

"Ma certamente."

"I need a small disposable syringe and needle."

He nodded. "Yes. You will have it tomorrow. I will also bring you a pair of surgical gloves. Be sure to wear them when you use the syringe. And remember, you will have to warm the blood before you can draw off the serum."

"I know just where to put it."

That afternoon Laura called the U. Penn operator. The woman connected her with a public relations type.

"I'm moving to the area, and I'm thinking of getting my care at your institution. Could you send me a listing of the internists on your staff and information about the kinds of quality control methods you employ?"

"Of course. We'll get that right out to you."

A week later she received the list of specialists in internal medicine. They also provided the names of several committees and their chairpersons. The topics included quality assurance, peer review, credentials, morbidity and mortality, and risk management.

Quality assurance sounded like their equivalent of St. Joe's audit committee. She chose a name of one of the listed internists. On her computer she went to the Yahoo website and set up a free email account in the name of Martin Dunlop MD. There were already several Martin Dunlops. She chose Martin Dunlop 007. She then called the Medical Director's office at U. Penn. She told the secretary that she was calling for Dr. Martin Dunlop. "He lost his list of the hospital committee members. Could you send us another?"

"Just ask him to stop by the office. We can give him a copy."

"He's always so busy on rounds. Would it be possible to email it to us?"

"Okay. Would you like me to send it to his university mailbox?"

"No. He uses a different email address for his office mail." Laura gave her his Yahoo address.

An hour later the list of U. Penn hospital committees, chairpersons and committee members were in Laura's new mailbox at Yahoo. On the list of Quality Assurance Committee members was someone named Cathy Atwood. Each member's departmental affiliation was included. She was supervisor of medical records. Cathy Atwood! She would be Laura's key to getting into U. Penn Hospital.

Laura had read on their website that they had gone from the usual ponderous paper-based medical records to a totally computerized system. St. Joe's had once considered such a conversion but determined that it would take a gaggle of full-time IT types to set up and maintain it.

Laura dialed U. Penn and asked to speak to Cathy Atwood. "Hello, my name is Laura Hamby. I'm supervisor of the medical records department at St. Joseph's Hospital in South Orange, New Jersey."

"What can I do for you?"

"We're considering converting to a computer-based medical record. I understand you've done that."

"Yes. It hasn't been easy. But we're just about there."

"Could I spend a couple of days to get a first-hand look at what you've done?"

"Mrs. Hamby, we've had so many people come through here that we have had to hire extra personnel. It's developed into a three-day workshop. For each session we can accommodate up to five people. We do charge a fee. The tuition is two hundred dollars a day."

"I understand. Do you have a brochure describing your workshop? I'll need something to show my medical director."

"We do. I'll send you a copy."

"Could you fax it?"

"Of course. Our next workshop is in two weeks. We only have three signed up. You can attend if you like."

The next day, with the brochure in hand, Laura headed for the medical director's office. She knew Dr. Cummings was a strong advocate for conversion to a computer-based medical record. Although there wasn't money in Laura's budget for travel, Laura knew the director had a slush fund for pet projects. He studied the brochure for a few minutes, then agreed to pick up the tab with the stipulation that Laura report on the workshop at the medical board's February meeting.

"It had better be a dynamite presentation, Laura. That's what it'll take to move those old farts."

Laura called Bruce at work and informed him that she was taking him to dinner.

"What's the occasion, sweetheart? They put you in charge of the hospital?"

She had to struggle not to tell him what she was up to. "Not yet. But I do have something to celebrate."

That evening they went to their favorite Mexican restaurant. Bruce ordered a pitcher of Corona beer. They studied the menu.

"You're looking gorgeous-er than usual tonight. You've done something with your hair."

"Thought you'd never notice. It's been a week since I had it styled."

"So what's the big news?" Bruce asked. He poured them both a glass of beer.

"St. Joe's wants me to visit U. Penn Hospital. They're hosting a three-day workshop on converting to a computer-based record. St. Joe's picking up the tab for a hotel room, meals and tuition. They're cutting me a check for one thousand bucks."

He looked incredulous. "What's the catch? They expect you to baptize a few babies while you're there?"

"Maybe I should bring a bottle of holy water." They banged mugs. "Take off a couple of days. The workshop runs from nine to three. We'll have a couple of free evenings in Philly."

"That would be great. We could maybe take in an Eagles game. But there's no way. We just lost a couple of guys at work."

"Any idea where?"

He laughed. "I fired them. They've been stealing auto parts for months. A regular tag-team. We had assumed it was shop-lifters."

Laura was sure Bruce was relieved that she hadn't brought up DNA or *in vitro* fertilization. But a sample of Greene's blood might be sitting in a freezer at U. Penn, and she wasn't going to take a chance that Bruce would talk her out of her plan. Even if they had discarded the initial HIV specimen, as Gino had told her, there was a good chance Greene may have had reason to get another specimen drawn.

"Hey, you're awfully quiet," Bruce said. "What's up?"

"I decided not to register for any courses at Pace Junior College for the spring semester."

"How come?" he asked "I thought you were looking forward to graduating next year."

"I need a break." She didn't tell him she needed time to concentrate on her plan. She was more determined than ever to make Michael Greene pay dearly for what he had done. She wasn't sure whether it was revenge or justice she was seeking. She would be satisfied with either, or better both.

Their steaming plates of chicken and beef fajitas arrived. "It is very hot. Very hot," the waiter said. He placed the metal platters on the table.

As Laura breathed in the steam from the platter, she experienced the sickening smell of bad breath, sweat, semen and the terror of being unable to scream or resist---images and memories flooded back. She relived the fear that her body would explode from pain as the rapists thrust violently into what felt like an open wound.

She pushed her plate toward Bruce. Her heart raced. She grabbed her chest. It seemed someone with a bellows was forcing air deep into her body. She grasped the edge of the table to steady herself.

"God! What's going on?" Bruce asked.

"I don't know. . . ."She began to fall to the side. Bruce jumped to his feet and caught her. He lowered her to the floor. He held her head up with one hand. She opened her eyes.

"What happened?" she asked.

"You fainted. Just lie here a minute, sweetheart."

A man came over and knelt beside Bruce. "I'm a physician." He felt her pulse. "Try to slow down your breathing." He turned to one of the waiters who had rushed up to where she lay. "Get me a paper bag. Hurry."

The man returned with an oven mitten and handed it to the doctor. The doctor told Laura to breathe into the glove. He cupped it over her nose and mouth. As she breathed the glove inflated and deflated, causing the thumb of the mitten to flick up and down. She heard people at nearby tables laughing. Slowly her head began to clear. Bruce and the doctor helped her into her chair.

"You were hyperventilating," the doctor said. "It's usually caused by anxiety. But you'd better see your doctor to make sure it's nothing more serious."

Bruce thanked him. "God almighty," Bruce said. "I thought you were having a heart attack. You've got to see somebody."

Laura glanced about the restaurant. People were staring like a bunch of idiots. She felt so damn foolish. "What do you mean...see someone? You're talking about a psychiatrist?"

"I was reading about post-traumatic stress...."

"Since when did you get your medical degree? Damnit. I'm not going to let some shrink turn me into a zombie."

"Hey, I'm sorry, okay?"

They ate the rest of the meal in silence. Laura was sorry too, but she was too pissed off to apologize for that crack about his aborted education. She had suppressed her anger for so many years, but since finding out that she could never have a child normally, she could no longer hold back her rage. She knew now that there was only one way to deal effectively with anger. Someone, she didn't remember who, once said, "Don't get mad, get even!" And that's exactly what she intended to do.

Chapter Ten

There was an outside chance Laura might run into Michael Greene at U. Penn. How would she react? Would he recognize her? Of course he would. She hadn't changed that much. The afternoon of the day she was to leave for Philadelphia, she went to Helen's Salon.

"I want you to take out all the curls and pull my hair into a bun."

"Why? You have such beautiful curls," Helen said.

"I'm going undercover. They will come back, won't they?" she asked.

"Of course. Your hair is naturally curly."

"Do it, Helen, quickly before I change my mind."

After leaving Helen's, she stopped at a toy store and bought a pair of Harry Potter glasses with plain lenses. The next stop was a sporting goods store. There she picked out a sports bra two sizes smaller than she would ordinarily have worn.

In the dressing room, she could barely squeeze her breasts into the bra. Breathing might prove to be a problem, but she was going for the teenage-Russian-gymnast-look. She convinced herself that the bra would probably stretch out enough to keep her lips from turning blue.

Late that afternoon the temperature dropped sharply, and gathering grey clouds obscured the sun. Laura drew her heavy calf-length woolen overcoat about her as she headed for Walmart. She bought a pair of gum-soled, flat heeled orthopedic-style shoes. Her final stop was the PTA thrift shop for something she wouldn't ordinarily be caught dead in. She found a loose fitting, dark brown tweed jacket with leather elbow pads, and a dowdy brown skirt. A white cotton shirt with a button-down collar completed her outfit. She checked herself front and back in the dressing room mirror. Decked out as she was, she could sit down to lunch with Dr. Michael Greene and he wouldn't recognize her.

The short drive from South Orange to Philadelphia took forever. She was glad she had worn a heavy coat. The heater in her beetle put out a steady stream of not-so-hot air, the car radio wasn't working and shifting in bumper-to-bumper traffic was causing her left calf to cramp. Maybe Bruce was right about trading in her bug. Laura exited the highway at the next rest stop. She phoned Bruce. He was probably at home planted comfortably in his favorite chair watching Monday night football.

"Hey, sweetheart, I'm halfway there."

"Figured you'd be there by now. The traffic must be something."

"Yeah. I had to pull off the road. My clutch leg was cramping."

"I wish I were there to massage it."

She could hear him chewing. "What are you eating?"

"I stir-fried some of that veggie mix you had in the freezer. Love that stuff."

"Sure. Let me guess. A double cheeseburger, large fries, and a side of chicken fingers."

"Lady, you belong in the circus. We could make a fortune."

"Don't forget to feed Jubilee."

"She's nibbling my fries as we speak."

Laura didn't want to tell Bruce exactly what she was planning to do, but it wasn't fair not to. "There are so many things I'd like to tell you, but..."

"You've been a little weird lately. Those panic attacks and all of a sudden this trip. It's some coincidence that St. Joe's decides to send you to the same hospital where Dr. Greene happens to be a surgery resident. When will you tell me what the hell's going on?"

Laura sensed he was trying hard to control his frustration. His voice betrayed his anxiety. He had every right to be angry with her.

"You're right. I probably wouldn't have signed up for the workshop if he weren't there." Laura took a deep breath before going on. "I want to get a sample of his blood."

"I knew you wouldn't let it rest! How do you plan on doing that? You gonna slash his wrists?"

"I hadn't thought of that."

"That's not funny," Bruce said.

"I have no intention of seeing him, and my chances of running into him are pretty remote."

"So how are you going to get a sample?"

She went on to explain to Bruce about HIV testing performed whenever a doctor, who is exposed to an infected patient, doesn't use proper precautions, like not wearing protective goggles or pricking his finger with a needle.

"How will you know that's happened?"

"The workshop's in the hospital record room. I'll figure out a way to get a peek at his medical record."

"And what if he's careful as hell and hasn't been tested?" Bruce asked.

"Then I'll have to slash his wrists."

"Seriously."

"I made a list from the internet of the ways to get a DNA specimen besides blood. Let me get it."

She searched through her purse. "Here it is: Sweaty t-shirts, underwear, a pillow, a paper or plastic cup, a water glass, ear wax, fingernail clippings, socks, urine, licked stamps, hair, hair brush, comb, chewed gum, dental floss, cigarette butts, used tissue, and a used razor."

"You should've applied for a job in housekeeping."

"First I have to figure out if he's had an HIV test recently, and if he has, then figure out how to swipe it."

"Shit."

"What?"

"I'm worried about you, Laura. The dreams are coming back, those panic attacks . . . "

"Don't worry. I'll be careful. I'll go crazy if I don't do anything."

The workshop was conducted in a small conference room in the medical records department; each of the four workshop attendees had the use of a laptop computer. Cathy Atwood, the record room supervisor, a handsome, imposing middle-aged black woman close to six feet tall, welcomed the group and handed out their study materials. Her posture was that of a military officer.

They were given a loose-leaf syllabus divided into several sections, each of which covered a particular aspect of the medical record: patient demographics, diagnostics, and ultrasonography. Each section in turn was divided into specific departments.

For demonstration purposes, they were given a password to enable them to access the various parts of the medical record. They were provided with a stack of CDs that contained the records they would be working with. Patient identification had been deleted.

Just as all hospital personnel are not privy to the complete paper-based medical record, U. Penn had limited access to the computer record. Employees, for instance, in the business end had access to patient demographics. Laboratory technicians could access information pertinent to their areas of responsibility. It became more complicated when nurses and doctors had to access a medical record. A physician can access his patient's chart or the chart of a physician with whom he works, but he can't snoop into other doctors' charts. On the other hand, interns have access to all the charts because they are called on to assist with the care of a large number of patients. Likewise in a teaching hospital, supervising faculty have access to patient records in their particular departments. They had to develop a complicated system of access codes to insure patient confidentiality. A nurse's access is limited to the hospital section to which she is assigned. There is also provision for emergency access.

"What if a doctor is asked to consult on a patient? How does he access the record?" Laura asked the instructor mid-morning of the first day.

"When the attending physician asks for a consultation, he or she enters the name of the consultant," Ms. Atwood responded. "The consultant is then able to use his or her access code for that particular hospital admission."

"Who can look up a patient's unit number?" she asked.

"It varies by department. In medical records, anyone with access to a computer can."

That's how I'll get into Michael Greene's medical record, Laura thought. All she would need was a few minutes at one of the record-room computers.

Later that morning Laura asked, "When a patient is discharged, who checks the computerized record to make sure it meets hospital and Medicare standards?"

"We're working on automating that process by building it into the computer software. But for now that's done by medical records personnel."

"So their access code must enable them to get into any medical record, not just hospital discharges?" she asked.

"That's right. In any given week we get dozens of requests from physicians, pharmacies, insurance companies and attorneys asking for information contained in the patient's record. Of course those requests must be accompanied by a release form signed by the patient."

"Speaking of attorneys," Laura said, "they love to get their hands on incident reports." Everyone in the class nodded. "How do you restrict access to sensitive material like that?"

"If an incident directly involves a patient, we have no other option than to make it part of their electronic medical record."

"At our hospital," she said, "incident reports also go to our audit committee and risk management committee. I imagine you have similar watchdog committees."

"Yes, of course. As members of the American Hospital Association, we're required to do so."

It had been a very productive morning. Laura now knew that she could easily get Dr. Greene's unit number. That if he had had an accident involving exposure to potentially infected material, the report would be on his record. And she also knew that many of the computers in the medical record room would have access to individual records. Five minutes at one of those computers would be all the time Laura needed. That afternoon, while on break, she sat at a small table in a corner of the record room sipping a cup of coffee. She made small talk with a computer type from Milwaukee, who was also taking the workshop. He looked to be barely out of his teens, but despite his youth he had an air of confidence that Laura noticed in so many of those IT experts.

"So, Mark, how secure do you think their data base is?" she asked. The workshop attendees wore name tags and temporary ID badges.

"It wouldn't take much to crack into their system. Give me a half-hour, tops. But think about it, Laura, how secure is the paper record at your hospital?"

"You're right," she said. "Once a chart leaves my record room it passes through dozens of hands."

As they talked, Laura watched as a record-room employee stepped from her work-station and headed toward them. At St. Joe's her outfit would have caught the attention of Mother Superior. She was wearing a silky mini skirt and form fitting low-cut jersey. She poured a cup of coffee and sat at the table with Laura and the man from Milwaukee.

After introductions and some small talk, Laura asked if she could spend five minutes checking her email on her computer. The young woman shrugged.

"Can I do that without an access code?" Laura asked.

"I'm already signed on. Just hit the mail icon."

Laura stood. "Thanks."

"Sure, no problem." She turned to Mark. "So, tell me about yourself."

Laura slipped into the clerk's work space and in a few seconds brought up her email. She then hit the minimize button to get back to the screen the clerk had been working on. It would take a quick click to restore the email window in case someone approached.

Laura typed in Michael Greene's name. His demographic data, including his unit number, popped up. There was no mention of a wife or children. She entered his unit number to access his medical record. It wasn't much-- a complete history and physical, blood and urine tests, immunizations, a tuberculin test and one incident report. Hmm. This is interesting! He was treated with cryotherapy for venereal warts. *Too bad they didn't freeze his entire dick.*

As she continued to read the report, she saw the supervisor, Cathy Atwood, heading her way. Damn it. Laura restored the email screen just as Cathy Atwood stepped into the work area. She was obviously startled to see Laura sitting at a computer.

"What are you doing here?" she snapped.

Laura gulped, momentarily unable to speak. She pointed to the screen. "Checking my email. Margarette said it would be okay."

"These computers are off-limits for the workshop participants. Come to me the next time you want to get onto the internet."

"I'm sorry. I'll sign right off."

"It's not your fault. Margarette should have known better. Finish checking your mail, then sign off."

As Cathy headed to where Margarette and Mark were sitting, Laura quickly restored the incident report window. An RN had signed the report. Dr. Michael Greene pricked his surgical glove while assisting at an appendectomy on an HIV positive patient. Blood was drawn and sent to the immunology lab. It was dated mid-December, less than a month ago!

She exited his record as Margarette approached.

"I'm sorry," she said. "I hope I didn't get you into any trouble."

"Screw her. The old battleaxe thinks she's still in the Army," Margarite whispered. "And thanks for the intro to Mark. He's taking me to dinner."

"Whoa. Fast worker. You'd better be careful. Those computer geeks can get into some pretty secure places."

Laura could hardly sit still through the afternoon workshop. A vial of Greene's blood was sitting in the freezer in the immunology lab, just waiting for her.

Chapter Eleven

Participants at the workshop were from a variety of professions. There were two medical records personnel, one IT-tech, a physician and someone from hospital business administration. Because of their varied interests and responsibilities, U. Penn allowed time during the course for individual work. Laura asked if she could spend an hour or two the following day in the immunology laboratory to see how they were incorporating sensitive information into the computerized record.

The part of Laura that did not want to see Michael Greene lost out to the part that was curious to see if he had changed, and if he would recognize her. How would she react? Would she pretend not to recognize him? Or would she stomp over to his table and smash his mashed potatoes into that arrogant face of his? Then as he wiped away the potatoes, she'd say, "Hi, Michael, remember me? I'm the girl you raped." Three other doctors seated at his table would be too startled to move. As she turned to exit with her head held high, the people at nearby tables, who heard what she said, would give her a standing ovation.

She was halfway through her meal of meatloaf, mashed potatoes and asparagus when a young man in scrubs approached her table.

"You mind if I join you?"

"No. Sit down." He had a stethoscope draped around his neck.

He glanced at her guest identification badge. "I'm Nate Jefferson." He placed his meal tray on the table and reached out his hand.

"Hamby. Laura Hamby. Nice to meet you, Dr. Jefferson." They shook hands. He looked too old to be a medical student or resident. "Are you an attending?"

"I'm a nurse practitioner. I work on the pediatric ward."

She wasn't really in the mood for small talk. On the other hand, maybe he could be of help. If for some reason she were unable to obtain a blood specimen, she would need a backup plan. They chatted about his training and what Laura was doing there. She asked him where the doctors stayed when they were on call. He said that the major departments had their own on-call rooms.

"There's a pecking order." He smiled. "Nurses, medical students and interns sleep four to the room. More senior residents usually double up. The chief residents and attendings have private rooms."

She told him that an old high school acquaintance of hers was a first-year surgical resident. That he didn't know she was visiting the hospital and that she wondered if he might be on call that night. Nate pulled a Palm Pilot from his pocket.

"What's your friend's name?"

"He's not exactly a friend." She said "friend" with emphasis. "His name is Michael Greene."

"Hey, I've met him. He came to pediatrics with his attending physician to consult on a boy I thought had appendicitis."

"Oh?"

"Don't take offense." He glanced at her name-tag. "He was sharper than most interns, but more than a little on the arrogant side. He did his best to humiliate me in front of the kid's mother."

Laura nodded. "That sounds like him."

He read from his Palm Pilot. "Here we go. He's not on call tonight," he said as he looked at the tiny screen. "He is on call tomorrow."

"I assume you're on call tonight?"

"Yeah. I'm glad he won't be around if I need a surgery consult."

They had both finished eating. Her coffee was cold. She pushed it aside. Should she confide in this stranger? She would need help to get a DNA specimen from Michael's shaving pouch. This person clearly didn't like Michael. Even if he refused to help, he'd not likely expose her. But would he risk getting into trouble on her behalf? She decided to take the chance.

She told him that she had been raped when she was a senior in high school. How she had been tied down, blindfolded and gagged. Laura was unable to see her attackers, but she was certain Dr. Greene was one of them. She could see that Nate was shocked and moved. His eyes brimmed with tears.

"My baby sister, Ayana, was raped and murdered when she was seven years old. They never found the monster who did it."

"Oh, my God. I'm so sorry . . . "

"It's been over twenty years. But at times I feel as if it's just happened."

"I know," Laura said.

"Is there anything I can do to help?" he asked quietly.

She told him about the surgery she had had. And about the DNA Dr. Corbett had found. When she told him how Dr. Corbett had discovered someone's DNA in her fallopian tubes, he gasped.

"My God. That's amazing. After all those years!"

"My gynecologist was very excited about the finding."

"I can understand why. It's probably never been done."

"I want to prove it's his DNA before I go to the police. Can you help me?"

"You need a specimen of his DNA?"

"Yes." She asked if the residents brought their shaving kits with them each time they were on call.

He nodded. "Should be lots of DNA in one of those. As a surgical resident he'd have a private locker in the surgery dressing area."

"Would his name be on the locker?"

"Yes. Most of the residents leave their toilet stuff there. Maybe an old pair of shoes."

"Are they locked?"

"Rarely."

Nate agreed to help. He gave her his cell phone number. She gave him hers.

The following morning the workshop leader presented an overview of how U. Penn dealt with conversion of voluminous paper records into digital information. First they used a high-speed scanner to copy the records. A trained team then went through the digitized record and used very specific criteria, which had been developed by a committee of doctors, nurses and other staff, to decide which information to include in the computer-based record. The materials not selected for inclusion were not destroyed, but copied onto compact disks and stored. The original paper records were housed at a remote site.

Early that afternoon, Laura reported to the immunology laboratory. It was pretty much as Gino had described. There was a small area where several patients waited to have blood drawn. Double doors led into the main laboratory, where gloved lab technicians in long white coats scurried about. Others were seated at cluttered desks, or on the phone, some at computer workstations. Along one wall were shelves of chemicals and exotic-looking glassware. The secretary of the laboratory supervisor gave Laura a quick tour. Laura noticed staff going in and out of the walk-in freezer.

"Dr. Carmine is away at a meeting," his secretary said. "He won't be back until tomorrow. I understand you want to meet with our IT person."

"Yes, please."

She led Laura to a small, cluttered office. An austere middle-aged man sat at his desk, typing at a computer keyboard.

"Excuse me, Jimmy, the visitor I told you about is here."

He glanced in her direction, then abruptly returned to his computer monitor. He motioned for her to sit. After sitting a few minutes, Laura removed her Harry Potter glasses and hiked up her skirt a bit before crossing her legs. She cleared her throat.

When he looked up she smiled and introduced herself. He went from grumpy to charming in an instant.

"Excuse me, please. That was rude of me. How can I help you?"

She explained that her home institution was considering going to a computer-based medical "I'm interested in how U. Penn treats sensitive data related to HIV and other sexually transmitted diseases."

"Think of the record as a large house with many rooms, some of which are easy to open, while others are accessed only by a very limited number of people."

"Can you tell me what happens when a specimen is brought to your laboratory?"

"The lab tech enters the patient's name and unit number on a form. She then removes the original label from the specimen and replaces it with one that displays only the patient's unit number." He opened his desk drawer and removed a sheet of paper. He swung his swivel chair from behind his desk and rolled to where Laura was sitting. He handed her the paper. "The original label is attached to this form." He leaned toward her as he spoke. "The technician keeps the form in a file until the results of the test are known, then enters the data on the form and brings it to me. I enter the data in the record in one of those locked rooms I told you about."

He kept glancing at her ID badge. Or was it her flattened breasts? "What do you do with the paper record?" Laura asked as she drew back in her chair.

"I keep them in a locked file." He pointed to a file cabinet across the room.

"Patient unit numbers at our institution are not that hard to get hold of," Laura admitted.

"Not so here. Everyone who uses the computer data system has a very specific access code. For example, in our lab only the laboratory supervisor can access patient unit numbers."

"It must be a nightmare keeping track of all those codes."

"Not really," he said. He rolled back to his desk. "We have a computer program that automatically reassigns them monthly." He looked at his watch and stood. "I'm sorry, Laura, but I'm already late for a meeting. It is okay if I call you Laura? We're not very formal around here."

"Yes, of course. I'd like to chat with the laboratory supervisor and maybe one of the technicians."

He shrugged. "Why not?" He gave her a crooked smile. "I'll be back in an hour. Maybe we can continue our conversation over a cup of coffee."

Laura next spoke with the laboratory secretary, who introduced her to the lab supervisor, Dr. Lin Chen. She looked much too young to be a doctor, much less head of the laboratory.

"I'm especially interested in what you do with the HIV specimens after testing," Laura told her.

"We keep them for four months. Come, I'll show you where we store them."

She walked Laura to the freezer. A white-coated technician exited as they entered. The room was eight-by-ten with slide-out drawers on three sides, pretty much as Gino had described it.

"How do you know when a specimen is to be discarded?"

"Jimmy makes a simple computer program. A kind of tickler file. It produces a list of specimens to be discarded each week. Otherwise we run out of space."

"And what do you do with them?" Laura had memorized Dr. Michael Greene's unit number. She glanced about to pick out the drawer that contained his specimen.

"I remove the labels and place the specimens in a hazardous material disposal container."

Laura slid open the drawer that held Michael's blood. Her heart thumped against her ribs. "There are so many. These can't all be HIV specimens." Her eyes came to rest on the vial sporting his unit number. Laura prayed that Lin's beeper would go off or someone would come into the room. Anything to distract her.

"Most are for diagnostic tests the physicians order. Others are specimens drawn for research studies. We keep research specimens many months, sometimes years."

Laura shivered and hugged her chest. She looked toward the door "It isn't possible to be locked in here, is it?"

As Lin turned and walked toward the door, Laura quickly slipped out Greene's specimen and placed it in her bra.

"This lever on the wall can open the door even when it's locked from the outside."

"Ah! That's reassuring." she said, as she quietly slid the drawer shut.

After Lin and Laura left the freezer, they made small talk as Michael Greene's specimen thawed between Laura's breasts. Lin had earned a PHD at Stanford when she was twenty-four. She was born in Taiwan and came to the States as a teenager. She still lived with her immigrant parents. She had eyes and cheek-bones Laura would die for.

They were about the same age. Laura was a high school dropout, Lin had a PHD. Laura felt more than a little envious.

"Could you tell me where the nearest ladies' room is?"

Laura hurried off. She sat in one of the stalls and removed the vial from her bra. The blood was clotted. There was a serum layer at the top. Gino had told her that red blood cells didn't contain DNA, that all she needed to draw up was some of the serum. She removed the syringe from her purse, attached the needle, filled the syringe with a little air, stuck the needle in the rubber stopper, injected the air and then sucked up about half of the serum. Her hands were shaking so badly she scratched her left index finger with the needle as she withdrew it from the vial. "Damn it!" She had forgotten to put on the surgical gloves. She replaced the plastic cap over the needle, and placed the syringe with the attached needle into a sandwich bag. She slipped the bag into her purse. She hurried to the sink and scrubbed her hands with soap from a wall disperser. She could express a drop or two of blood by pressing her finger. *Was that a good thing to do?*

According to the incident report, Dr. Greene's initial HIV test had been negative. So she probably had nothing to worry about. Or did she? Laura wrapped a piece of toilet tissue around her finger. She headed back to the immunology lab.

Should she bother replacing Dr. Greene's blood specimen? Gino thought it would be "of utmost importance" to do so. He had said, "When it is time to discard the specimen, and they find it is not there, someone may recall that you had been in the freezer and perhaps had been left unobserved for a few moments."

She agreed. She didn't want to get the reprehensible Dr. Greene alerted any sooner than she had to.

It had been relatively easy removing the specimen from the freezer, but how the hell was she going to get it back? She looked at her finger wrapped in toilet tissue. Maybe that scratch wasn't such bad luck after all.

She asked the secretary in the immunology lab if she could again talk with Dr. Chen.

"Of course. She's on the phone. She'll be free soon."

Laura sat at Dr. Chen's desk and removed the tissue from her finger as she waited. She noticed that tiny droplets of blood had clotted along the path of the scratch.

Lin Chen's eyes widened when she saw Laura's finger. "You did this in my lab?"

"I didn't notice it until I went to the ladies' room. I don't know exactly where I scratched it."

She led Laura to a sink and pointed to a soap dispenser. "You scrub it for five minutes. And think where maybe this happened."

When she returned, Laura told her that when she had opened one of the drawers in the freezer she now recalled bumping her hand, but had thought nothing of it at the time. Dr. Chen said she did not recall which drawer Laura had opened. As they spoke, she dried Laura's finger with a paper towel and applied a Band-Aid.

"Let me show you where I think it happened," Laura said. "Maybe there's a sharp edge that needs to be taken care of."

Laura had removed the vial of blood from her purse and was cupping it in her hand. They walked to the freezer. She knew exactly which drawer she had opened, but pretended to be confused. She opened a drawer on the opposite side.

"No, I believe it was on the other side," Lin said.

"Yes, I think you're right. But which one?"

"Somewhere in the middle, I believe."

Laura opened one or two others before she placed her hand on the drawer from which she had taken Dr. Greene's specimen. She opened it only a few inches. "I think maybe this was the one."

Dr. Chen checked the corner and edge of the drawer. "It is quite smooth. I will check the others." She went about checking the corners and edges of the other drawers Laura had pulled partially open. As she did, Laura replaced the vial.

After leaving the freezer, Laura and Lin walked to the doctor's desk. "Although I can't explain how you scratched yourself, you obviously were not in contact with needles or contaminated material. Still, we should report the incident."

The way she fidgeted with some papers on her desk, it was obvious she was not anxious to raise the issue. "It's nothing really," Laura said. "I'm sure you have better things to do."

"Are you certain?" Lin asked.

"Yes, and thanks for all your help." Laura could tell the doctor was relieved. It wouldn't look good to have visitors scratch themselves in a laboratory filled with deadly viruses.

Deadly viruses! The thought of millions of those invisible demons pouring into her bloodstream was terrifying. According to Michael Greene's incident report, his blood had tested negative. But why do they repeat the test after a few weeks if they're so sure?

Chapter Twelve

After workshop that afternoon, Laura called Nate on his cell phone. "Mission accomplished," she announced.

"Hey, good going," he said. "So what about the other item we talked about?"

"It doesn't seem necessary now, does it?"

"It wouldn't hurt to have a backup. Labs are known to lose specimens," he said, "Hey, I'm on rounds. Can I call you back in about an hour?"

Laura sat at a table at the hospital snack bar drinking her second cup of coffee as she awaited Nate's call. Three men in scrub suits and surgical caps entered, picked up some coffee and sweet rolls and headed in her direction. Although it had been years since she had seen him, she immediately recognized Michael Greene. Her heart raced. Her mind flashed back to those days and weeks after the rape. She had been terrified of running into him at school. Every time she rounded a corner her pulse quickened, her hands grew clammy. He was no longer human. He was a predator. She had been his prey.

They glanced about for a table and finally settled no more than a few feet from where Laura was sitting. She opened her course workbook and pretended to be studying. When she glanced up, Michael was staring at her. Oh God, how she remembered that stare. Those light blue eyes set a bit too close. Even in a scrub suit it was obvious that he had gone from a wiry teenage boy to an athletic-looking man. Had he recognized her? She certainly recognized him the instant she saw him. Then again he had no reason to be thinking about her. When she looked up, his head was turned toward one of the other doctors. She was pleased to see that his almost perfect profile had been permanently altered by Bruce. There was a slight bump on the middle of his nose. Thank you, darling, she thought.

She returned to studying her wordbook, concentrating on taking slow, shallow breaths. After a few minutes Nate called.

"Hi," she whispered. "I'm sitting just a few feet from you-know-who. This would be a good time to check out his you-know-what."

"Roger. Call me when he leaves."

She glanced toward their table as she slipped her phone into her purse. They stood, preparing to leave. She could call Nate and warn him. But this was a perfect opportunity. She couldn't let it pass. She had to prevent him from leaving.

He had his back to her. "Dr. Greene, can I have a word with you?" Laura called out.

He turned. There was no sign of recognition in his expression. He waved off the other two doctors and approached her table.

Laura removed her glasses and reached back undoing the bun. Her blond hair fell to her shoulders. He stared, unable to speak for a moment.

"Laura?"

"Hello, Michael. Have a seat."

He sat. He glanced at her guest ID badge. "I can't believe this. Are you visiting someone here?"

"I'm taking a workshop in medical records."

He took in the gold wedding band on the fourth finger of her left hand. "You're married?"

"Yes. I think you know the guy. His name is Bruce Hamby."

The color drained from his face. He nodded. "Laura, I had nothing to do with what happened to you. Because you were my date..."

"Your date! I wasn't your date."

"Kids got that impression. Rumors started up."

"I know how nasty rumors can be," she said.

"I didn't press charges when Bruce attacked. I knew it would have gotten in the papers. I wanted to protect you and your family."

"Here you were, trying to protect me." She raised her voice. "And all these years I believed you were one of the three guys who raped me."

"My God!" He looked about the snack bar. "How could you even think I'd do a thing like that?"

"You know how we bitches are."

He looked like a trapped animal. "Laura, please..."

"Would you say, 'Goddamn bitch' for me?"

"What?"

"One of the boys who raped me called me a 'Goddamn bitch.' It was you, wasn't it?"

The muscles in his jaw twitched. "I don't blame you for feeling bitter. You have no idea how bad I felt about what happened to you." He looked at his watch. "I have to get to the OR. How long are you going to be here?"

"The workshop ends tomorrow afternoon."

"How about dinner this evening?"

Is he totally insane? "I have other plans."

"How about tomorrow?"

"I'm leaving right after workshop ends. You ever find yourself in New Jersey, look us up. I'm sure Bruce would love to see you."

He looked as though he was about to extend his hand, but the intense stare she gave him caused him to reconsider.

He turned and left without saying another word. Did he think she had believed him? Even for one millisecond?

That awful night he had been careful not to speak, or if he had, he must have disguised his voice. But those memorable words had burst forth from his mouth in response to sudden and unexpected pain.

Laura's cell phone rang. It was Nate. "You still at the snack bar?" he asked.

"I was just getting ready to leave."

"Don't. I'm on my way."

When Nate arrived, he scanned the room. He didn't immediately recognize Laura. She waved.

He sat at her table. "Man, I haven't had this much fun in a long time."

"Mission accomplished?"

He nodded.

"Tell me about it and don't leave out a thing."

"When I got to the locker room in the general surgery suite, there were a couple of medical students changing into fresh scrubs. I went to a cabinet and pulled out scrubs, a surgical cap and shoe covers. I sat on a bench close to Dr. Greene's locker. Like most of the others, it wasn't locked. After the students left, I opened the locker. On the top shelf was a battered-looking leather shaving pouch. As I reached for it, one of the surgical attending physicians came into the room in street clothes."

"Hey, Nate. What are you doing in these here parts?" the guy said.

"Every now and then I like to see exactly how you guys are treating my patients."

"You're welcome to look over my shoulder anytime you like."

"Thank you, Dr. Ewing. I appreciate that."

He had swung the locker door open all the way when he entered so he wouldn't see Greene's name on the door.

"Fortunately Dr. Ewing's locker was on the opposite side of the room. As he sat with his back to me, he began to tell me about the patient he was about to operate on. I pretended to listen as I opened the pouch, slipped on an oversized surgical glove, removed a plastic comb and turned the glove inside-out over the comb."

"And Dr. Ewing didn't see you do all this?" Laura asked.

"He was busy picking his toes and telling all about some woman's gallbladder. So I closed the locker door, said goodbye, and got the hell out."

Nate looked about to make sure no one was nearby. He reached into his pocket and placed the glove on the table. He had tied a knot at the open end. The palm and fingers bulged with air.

"Thank you, thank you, thank you." She placed the glove in her purse. "You are one cool dude, Nate."

"Hey, what's with the Band-Aid?" he asked. He pointed to the index finger of her left hand.

"I meant to ask you about that. I scratched myself with the needle as I was drawing up the serum. I washed it really good with soap and water."

"Did it bleed?"

"I could squeeze out a few drops. Not exactly a gusher."

"Didn't your doctor friend tell you to wear gloves?"

"I had them in my purse. I was so excited I forgot to put them on."

"You should have told me about this."

"I wasn't worried because I saw in the incident report his specimen had tested negative."

"The test they do doesn't check for the presence of virus particles. They check for antibodies and that takes time to develop."

"So why do they do the test?" she asked in disbelief.

"In order to get a baseline reading. And if it's a high-risk exposure, they start drug therapy as soon as possible."

She told Nate she recalled from the incident report that the patient to whom Dr. Greene had been exposed had AIDS.

He shook his head. "You can't find a higher exposure risk than that. But there's no need to panic. The statistical risk is only three in a thousand for a superficial wound. And taking a couple of drugs for a month will reduce that risk by seventy to eighty percent."

"When I get back I'll call Dr. Corbett."

"The sooner you take the medicine the better." He removed a prescription pad from his breast pocket. He wrote her two prescriptions. "One of the medicines is AZT and the other is Lamivudine. You take one of each twice a day."

She had the urge to check Nate for wings. A black guardian angel. Maybe God *is* black. Nate gave her directions to the pharmacy.

"Take the first dose immediately and the second dose tonight. After today, take one dose in the morning and one at bedtime."

"I wish you hadn't noticed the Band-Aid."

"When you get back home, tell Dr. Corbett what happened. You're going to need urine and blood tests and a follow-up HIV test."

"You sound like an expert."

"I've had to become one. AIDS is a common problem on the pediatric ward."

"I don't think I would have the courage to work with dying children."

"Early on, it was tough. Children were dying. We were helpless. But the newer drugs have made a tremendous difference."

"There's no way I can thank you enough. You and your family must come visit us sometime. Bruce would love to meet you." This time she meant it.

They exchanged home phone numbers and email addresses.

As Laura had promised, she called Bruce that evening. She didn't leave out a thing. Every startled expression, every cocked eyebrow, Jimmy's lewd glances, Michael's shocked expression when he first recognized her, and how it looked as though someone had sucked every bit of air from his lungs when she had asked him to say goddamn bitch. The only thing she left out was her scratched finger. Why throw a wet blanket over all the good news?

"You lucked out, okay. You took too big a chance. What if you had gotten caught?"

"I had to. Can't you understand that?"

"No, I can't. This business is making you nuts."

If Bruce had done anything that risky she'd be just as upset. "I should have told you, but I knew you'd sit on me until I agreed not to do it."

There was a long silence.

"I miss you, babe. You got everything you set out for. Why not head home tonight?"

"I can't, sweetheart. St. Joe's paid big bucks to send me here. The workshop ends at three tomorrow. Should be home around six."

Laura couldn't wait to hand over the specimens to Dr. Corbett. She was reminded of a line in her favorite book, *The Things They Carried,* by Tim O'Brian. A soldier in Vietnam ran his jeep off the road. He was able to jump out before it rolled over several times, then caught fire. He said, as he shook his head, looking forlornly at his demolished jeep, "The f---ing f---er's f---ed!"

Yes, if the DNA sample she had in her purse matches what Dr. Corbett retrieved from her body, then the soldier's jeep and Dr. Michael Greene were in exactly the same predicament.

Chapter Thirteen

Michael Greene spent a sleepless on-call night. Aside from having assisted at two emergency surgeries, he lay awake thinking about the night of the party. Why had he gone to such lengths to humiliate her? He had had a monster crush on her. He respected her. And after screwing up their first date, he became obsessed with having her. She was different than any girl he had ever known. He had had his pick of girls at Central High, but no matter who he dated, he wished it was Laura. His obsession in time turned to anger, then aggression.

When he saw her that afternoon at the hospital, he felt overwhelmed by conflicting emotions. He should have told her he was sorry; told her that the guilt he felt that night was with him constantly. He should have begged her to forgive him. He had admitted to his father that he had had sex with Laura, but lied and said that she had wanted to be tied up. And while they were going at it, Luke and

Arnold came into the bedroom. Luke locked the door and soon after that things got pretty wild.

Instead of telling Laura what he really felt, his father's admonitions filled his head: "Deny everything, son. It's her word against yours. What's the big deal? Just some teenagers sowing a few wild oats."

In those frightening days following the rape, his father had insisted Michael not have any contact with Laura. He was only eighteen, frightened, confused, terrified of going to prison. And when Laura ran away from home, he was desperate to find her. There was no way to make up for what he had done. He wanted to be punished. It was no accident that he told one of Bruce's friends that Laura was kinky and had wanted him to do it with her hands tied. He knew Bruce would come after him. He endured the merciless beating he had taken, but it did little to ease the pain he carried with him whenever he thought of Laura.

Was it a coincidence that she had suddenly reappeared in his life? If it wasn't just an accidental meeting, why had she come? The intensity of her anger had startled him. Could she still go to the police after more than six years? He would have to check with his dad about statutes of limitation.

Arnold, Luke's friend, could testify to the fact that Laura was falling-down drunk when he carried her upstairs. Besides, Michael had taken some pretty incriminating photographs.

Michael looked at his watch. It was five-thirty in the morning. Rounds would start in a half-hour. Just enough time for a shower and coffee.

Michael looked through his shaving pouch for his comb. It wasn't there. But he remembered distinctly putting it there the previous day. Probably some penniless medical student stole it. He checked to see if anything else was missing. No, everything was there: his electric shaver, nail clippers, after-shave, Swiss Army knife, toothbrush, dental floss, and tooth paste. Someone obviously just needed a comb.

In an operating room at U. Penn Hospital, Michael Greene, two medical students and a senior resident assisted an elderly surgeon doing a partial gastric resection. Michael's role was not challenging. He held retractors. His mind drifted back to the days following the party at Luke's. He was terrified that Laura would go to the police, and he would end up in jail for twenty or thirty years.

"Dr. Greene," the surgeon snapped. "Hold those damn retractors wide."

"Sorry, Dr. Cornblatt. I didn't get a wink of sleep last night." The old prick, Michael thought. He had seen second-year residents get in and out of a patient's belly in the time it was taking Cornblatt to expose the patient's stomach.

"Interns today are a pampered lot," Dr. Cornblatt said. "On call every fourth night and still bellyaching. When I trained, we had call every other night and were happy to do it."

"The nurses were more help back then, Doctor," Michael said. "They could apply the suction cups and leeches while you went about your business."

The residents and surgical nurse didn't dare laugh, although a snicker could be heard from behind the screen that separated the anesthesiologist from the surgeon.

"I like a young man with a sense of humor, Greene," Dr. Cornblatt said. "But as usual you are misinformed. I personally applied the leeches and suction cups."

Michael's morning of surgical scrubs lasted until three in the afternoon. He was starved. The cup of black coffee he had had that morning was working its way through the wall of his stomach. He hurried to the hospital cafeteria, where he sat by himself as he continued to dwell on the past. His father had been concerned that soiled items of clothing might be a source of evidence tying his son to the scene. But as the days passed it was obvious that Laura had no intention of going to the police. And after she ran away from home, both he and his father felt relieved the incident had blown over.

But what if Laura had saved her semen-stained underpants? My God! She may be here to gather evidence. He thought of the missing comb. But that wouldn't help her. He was in the habit of washing out his comb after he used it. And how would she have known where his locker was located? Was someone within the hospital helping her? A medical student or another resident?

If he were in her place he'd be trying to figure out how to get his hands on a blood specimen. But how? Then he recalled the HIV specimen he had drawn after a recent needle stick. But that was safely stored away in the immunology lab. Or was it?

He took his mostly untouched tray of food to the conveyer belt and left the cafeteria. He headed for the immunology lab. Laura had said she worked in a hospital. She probably knew something about hospital routines. It wouldn't hurt to check.

Michael was acquainted with the laboratory supervisor. Lin often came to surgical conferences. She seemed surprised and a little flustered to see him.

"Did you come to visit me, or is this business?" she asked.

He gave her what he considered his knock-them-down-dead smile. "A little bit of both, Lin," he said. "All I do is work and sleep. Mostly a lot of work and very little sleep. It's nice to talk with a beautiful woman now and then."

She blushed and looked about the lab. "It is better now than then. Let us go to my office."

She hoisted herself onto the edge of her desk and motioned for him to have a seat. "All work and no play is not a good thing, Dr. Greene."

"No need to be so formal. My friends call me Michael. Do you ski, Lin?"

"I love to ski, but I am not very good."

"Big Boulder is less than an hour's drive from here. Would you like to go skiing with me if I ever manage to get a day off?"

"I would love that. It is best to go during the week. I have gone on the weekend. The lift lines are unbearable."

He had almost forgotten why he was there. She had a great body and was obviously attracted to him. "Lin, I was wondering if you may have run into a friend of mine in the last day or two? Her name's Laura Hamby."

"Yes. She is taking the workshop given by the medical records department. She spoke with our IT person. I showed her around the lab. She is very nice."

"Yes, she is. Do you recall anything unusual happening?"

"Not really. Oh, she did scratch her finger. It was very superficial. I suggested she file an incident report, but she did not want to."

"How did that happen?"

"She thought maybe when she pulled out one of the drawers in the freezer" Lin's eyes opened wide. "Did she come to you? Should I have insisted she file an incident report?"

"No, no. I'm just concerned that she might need drug prophylaxis." The muscles in Michael's back constricted. "Could you show me where it happened?" he asked.

They walked to the freezer. Lin looked about, then slid open a drawer. He noticed the range of numbers on the outside of the drawer. He removed his wallet and checked the plastic ID card that was imprinted with his hospital unit number. As he expected, it was included in the range of numbers listed on the front panel of the drawer. He tried to appear calm but his insides were in turmoil. *God almighty.*

"As you can see, the drawers are very clean. There was no risk of contamination," Lin said.

Michael located the tube of blood marked with his unit number. He looked closely at the stopper. "Could you get me a pair of gloves, Lin?"

When she returned with the gloves, he slipped them on and removed the specimen. "Look here, Lin. There's some dried serum on the stopper." He examined the vial. "And there's hardly any serum in this specimen."

"Yes, I see. I do not understand. A new stopper is inserted when the vial is stored. Someone has drawn blood from this specimen. Why would anyone do that?"

"I don't know," he lied.

"I will check to see who this specimen belongs to."

"That's not necessary. It's my unit number."

"Yours?" She gasped in disbelief. "You believe she has done this?"

"It's possible."

"But I was with her. I did not see her remove anything."

"You're probably right. The specimen has been sitting here over a month. Any number of people might have drawn off some serum."

"I am sorry, Michael. Nothing like this has happened before. I will call a staff meeting. Technicians often go back to do additional tests on stored specimens. If yours was pulled by mistake, that is a serious error and cannot be tolerated."

He stood. "Thank you, Lin. Call me after you've had a chance to check this out." She walked out with him. He winked at her. "I'll call you soon about the ski trip."

"Not too soon. I must first take a few lessons. I am sure you are a very good skier."

Michael was convinced that Laura had taken his missing blood serum and maybe had something to do with the disappearance of his comb. And there was absolutely no reason she would do that if she didn't have some sort of DNA evidence. Most likely an item of clothing. But why now, if she's had that evidence all these years?

Maybe all the news reports about clergy being convicted of sex crimes that happened ten or even twenty years in the past had gotten her believing she could do the same. Things were getting out-of-hand. He decided to confide in his father. He dialed his work number.

"Hi, Dad."

"Michael! Can I call you back later, son? I'm in the middle of a staff meeting."

"It's important, Dad. Don't forget."

His dad had used his knowledge as an attorney, and his political connections, to get Michael out of a number of predicaments, including a couple of DUIs. Michael was sure his father would come through for him. What his dad didn't know, and Michael wasn't about to tell him, was that Michael had spiked the vodka. He had gotten a pill from Luke, who had gotten it after one of his college interviews. At the party he had pretended to take an occasional sip from the flask.

Luke had told him, "You slip this in a girl's drink, and you got yourself a sex slave. Put it in a little booze...she'll never be able to tell. The best part is she won't remember a thing."

He had planned on taking her to an upstairs bedroom himself, but before he could reach her,

118

Arnold picked her up and carried her upstairs. A little later Michael slipped into the room. Laura was asleep. He had only meant to undress her and take a few photographs of her with his new digital camera.

As he removed her clothes she seemed on the verge of waking up. His heart raced as he moved her about like a rag doll. He imagined showing those pictures around school. The stuck-up bitch wouldn't be able to show her face when he was through with her.

He sat on the edge of the bed and fondled her breasts. Then he removed his clothes and lay beside her. In the rush of passion, he forgot about the packet of condoms in his wallet. He was astride her when Luke and his friend came into the room. At first they just watched, not certain how to react. But then Luke began to take off his clothes. Soon they were both naked and clamoring to take a turn. When she began to awaken, they helped him tie her hands, gag and blindfold her with panty-hose Luke swiped from his mother's dresser.

As far as Michael knew, Arnold was not aware of the drug he had given Laura. Both Luke and Arnold were so drunk, Michael wasn't sure how much either of them would remember. He never talked with them about the incident afterwards. After high school, Luke had gone on to Stanford, but dropped out after a couple of years and went to work for his dad's construction company in Allentown. Arnold had gone to West Point and now was making a career in the Army. Neither of them knew about the nude pictures Michael had taken.

After Laura dropped out of school and left home, Michael stopped worrying about the police showing up at his door to cart him off to jail. But as fear receded, the realization of what he had done to Laura gripped him with astonishing force. The world about him darkened and constricted. Like an insect caught in a web, he was immobilized by invisible filaments of guilt, drained of energy and filled with a sense of hopelessness. After he was attacked by Bruce Hamby, he refused to return to school. His parents hired tutors to enable him to graduate. His mother urged him to see a psychiatrist. But his dad insisted that Michael would snap out of the depression without some pill-pushing psychiatrist messing up his head. And his dad as usual was right. By mid-summer, a month at Cape Cod restored Michael's interest in sailing and beach parties. He seldom thought of Laura. That door, he had imagined, had closed forever.

When his dad did forget to call back, Michael wasn't surprised. His dad had always managed to forget school plays, little league games and track meets. It was his mother who bought the birthday and Christmas presents. His dad wasn't stingy with his money, just his time. Michael only merited his father's full attention when he got into trouble.

That evening, after finishing for the day, Michael drove to Allentown to talk with his father. He was uncertain exactly what to tell him, or what his dad might be able to do to help. Should he tell his dad about the photos?

It was ten by the time Michael arrived at his parents' home. His mother would be upstairs getting ready for bed. He quietly let himself in and headed for his dad's study. The room looked like a typical attorney's office. A massive mahogany desk and bookcases crammed with boxed journals. His dad rarely went to bed before midnight. He'd sit at his computer monitor, dashing off emails and sipping a glass of single malt scotch. For Michael, entering his dad's study was like going into the principal's office. His dad always assumed it would cost him money whenever his son set foot in there.

"Sorry I didn't call you back, son," he said, without conviction.

"It's okay. I know how busy you are." Michael flopped onto a side chair. A leather couch had been replaced by a state-of-the-art treadmill. A large TV monitor was mounted on the wall opposite the treadmill. "That's new," Michael said. At fifty-eight his dad looked to be in robust health, although a little overweight.

"My blood pressure is climbing and my cholesterol is out-of-sight. I'm on three different medications. My internist is a man of few words. He said, 'Stop smoking, exercise and take these pills. If you don't you will die.' I jog as I watch the evening news."

His dad came from around the desk. He was wearing gym shorts and t-shirt. He pushed a few buttons and the console on the treadmill lit up. He stepped aboard and started walking slowly at first, then picked up the pace. "What is it you want to talk about, son? Not another gambling debt?"

"You remember Laura Carnahan?"

"Sure. We sweated that one out, didn't we? It was no big deal. A bunch of young bucks having a little fun."

"She showed up at the hospital yesterday."

"So?"

Michael went on to tell him about how he had met her in the hospital snack bar and how angry she sounded. And what he had discovered in the immunology lab. That he was certain she had drawn off a sample of his blood. He also told him about the missing comb.

His dad turned off the treadmill and came over and sat next to Michael. "So she's looking for a sample of your DNA. Why? She must have a piece of evidence tying you to that night. You think she intends to go to the police?"

"That's what I'm worried about. Her underclothes might have been . . . you know."

"But why all the cloak and dagger business? Why didn't she just go directly to the police? They could have gotten a court order to get a DNA specimen based on her complaint."

"Right, Dad. I figure she has DNA evidence, but has no way of knowing who it belongs to. If she files a complaint and it turns out not to be mine, she exposes herself to, you know, all the notoriety for nothing."

"But if it's not your DNA it has to belong to one of the other boys."

"It's me she's after, dad, not them."

"Son-of-a-bitch. What if you knocked her up? If she didn't have an abortion, the kid would be about seven by now. She may want to prove you're the father."

Michael was stunned. Why hadn't that possibility occurred to him? At about the time she left town would have been when she missed a period if she were pregnant. *This changes everything.* "We must find out if she has a nine-year-old child. We need to know when she got married and exactly how old the child is."

"And if it turns out to be yours, she can file a complaint or be even more creative. She might blackmail us," his dad said.

"That investigator Lester uses...can he help?"

"Yeah. I'll get him on it immediately. He can look up births, wedding licenses...shouldn't be hard to trace."

Michael was on the verge of telling his dad about the pictures he had taken of Laura in the bedroom as she was passed out. In the days following the rape, he downloaded the photos. Using a software program, he had manipulated the images to make it appear she was conscious and smiling while she was in fact unconscious. He downloaded the images onto a compact disk. He put a Beetles label on the disk and stored it away with dozens of other CDs in his collection. He deleted the images from his camera and computer.

He decided not to tell his dad about the digitized photos he had taken in the bedroom. For one thing, he'd be furious Michael hadn't told him sooner. And his threat to use them was only a bluff. They would place him in the bedroom at the scene of the alleged rape.

His dad began to pace. He stopped and went behind his desk. "We'd better check when they started forensic DNA testing?"

"I already did. It was in the early 1990s."

"So she could have known about DNA evidence the year you graduated from high school."

"I'm not sure she would have thought of that," Michael said.

"You know where she lives?"

"Her name tag said: 'St. Joseph's Hospital, South Orange, New Jersey.' She was at U. Penn. taking a workshop in the medical records department. They must have a roster of people who attended."

"Good. And don't mention anything to a soul, especially not your mother. I'm going to talk this over with a criminal attorney."

"Some people think they're all criminals."

His father forced a laugh. "Very funny. You know, son, if she's looking for DNA evidence to prove you raped her, we can beat that in court. She has no witnesses other than the other guys. And they're not about to incriminate themselves. No, it's your word against hers. Did you know that your uncle Joe is thinking of making a run for Governor next year?"

"He's been in the state senate as long as I can remember. It's been talked about."

"Yeah. He's got a lot of supporters. He asked me to be his campaign manager. We have to clean this mess up before it picks up too much speed. We don't want something like this coming out in the middle of a political race."

"I'll get her address to you sometime tomorrow morning." Michael stood. "I'm heading back tonight, Dad. Rounds start at six sharp."

"How are you set for cash?"

"Thanks, Dad. I have a job, remember? The hospital actually pays me for what I do."

Before leaving, Michael went to his room and retrieved the CD with the phony Beatles label.

The following morning he stopped by the hospital medical records department.

"Miss Atwood, I'd heard that an old high school classmate of mine attended your workshop. Her name is Laura Hamby."

"Yes, she did. Quite an impressive young woman," Miss Atwood said.

"I had lost track of her. I'd love to have her phone number or address."

"I'm sorry, Dr. Greene, but without her permission I can't do that."

"I know she works at St. Joe's Hospital in West Orange, New Jersey..."

"Good. Call them." and swiveled toward her computer screen.

I'm just a lowly intern in her eyes. She has already given me enough of her time. Arrogant bitch...does everything by the book. He was tempted to say something nasty but still needed her help. He wondered how Laura had known there would be an HIV specimen in the immunology lab. She must have seen his medical record. How else? But how was that possible?

"Miss Atwood, if I wanted to pull up one of my patient's charts to write an order, would it be possible to use one of your computers?"

"No. Not unless an authorized record room employee has already signed into the patient record area."

He looked about the room. There were at least a dozen work stations. "Do all these computers have that capability?"

"Dr. Greene," she said impatiently. "I covered all of this in your orientation. You obviously weren't paying attention." She spoke loud enough to be heard by several of the record room clerks. She had meant to embarrass him.

He leaned over and whispered just inches from her face, "Goddamnit. I need to see you in private, immediately!"

She recoiled as though he had struck her. She led him to a small room where doctors worked on their charting.

They stood facing each other, eye-to-eye. She was a tall woman. She glared, unblinking, her arms crossed in defiance. "I could report you for talking to me like that."

"And I could inform your supervisor that you or one of your clerks caused a serious breach of confidentiality."

"Listen, junior, don't think that MD after your name gives you the right to go around intimidating people. Besides, what in hell are you talking about? What confidentiality breach?"

"I have reason to believe that you allowed a woman in your workshop, Laura Hamby, to get into my personal medical record."

Her expression changed from anger to disbelief. "I did catch her using one of the clerk's computers to check her email...."

"Didn't that place her just a few clicks from my medical record?"

"Yes, but I had no reason to suspect...."

"Your primary responsibility is to protect the confidentiality of the medical record. You didn't do that."

She stood even taller than before. She wasn't one easily intimidated. He could see why she had risen in the ranks. It wasn't the first run-in he'd with her. She had threatened him with suspension for not completing his discharge summaries on time. He would love to see her called on the carpet. But for now he wanted to find out who had been working with Laura.

"Who was the clerk?" he asked.

"A young woman who hasn't been with us very long."

"Does this woman have a name?" Michael glanced about the room. There were several women in the area. Most at work stations, others filing or walking about. He must find out which one had allowed Laura access to his record.

"I'll not have you browbeating one of my girls."

"What is her damn name?"

"How dare you speak to me like that? Believe it or not, I outrank you. Interns come and go. They've got me forever."

"One way or another I'm getting to the bottom of this. If it turns out you're responsible, forever may not be as long as you think."

"If it's a fight you want, you picked the wrong lady." She leaned close to him, saying softly, "Kiss my ass!" She turned and left the room.

The lady has balls, he thought. He regretted having gotten her back up. He wondered if anyone had heard him swear at her. Maybe a call from the hospital attorney might loosen her tongue.

If Laura had an accomplice in the hospital records department, he was determined to find out who that was. He was hoping it was the supervisor herself. She had said Laura was checking her email when she caught her using a computer. There was a chance Laura's email messages hadn't as yet been purged from the computer she had used. He would have to move fast if he hoped to retrieve that information. He headed for the office of the hospital attorney.

Chris Martino sat trimming his nails as Michael explained the reason for his visit.

"And how can you be so sure this visitor, Laura Handbag..."

"Hamby. Laura Hamby."

"Whatever. How can you be so sure she got into your record?"

He wasn't about to tell the lawyer about Laura stealing the HIV specimen. At least not yet. "She referred to a medical treatment I had received. She had no way of knowing that unless she had seen my record."

"And this was rather sensitive information?" Martino asked.

"Yes."

"I see. And you want me to authorize sending a computer nerd to the record room to check twenty record department computers on the chance this person's emails might still be in one of the computer trash bins?"

"The sooner the better," Michael said. "The computers are always up and running. It'll take a couple of hours at the most. Cathy Atwood is not to be told what he's looking for. In fact he should start with her computer."

"Okay, let's assume we do find out who helped this person gain access to your record. What then?"

"I would think that's grounds for dismissal," Michael said.

"It's not that easy, firing an employee these days, but I must admit, a confidentiality breach is pretty damn serious.

"Certainly grounds for dismissal," Michael said.

"Okay, I'll have an IT person try to ascertain if someone logged into your medical record on one of the record room computers."

When Malcolm Greene received his son's email informing him of Laura Hamby's address, he immediately called Lester Knowles and arranged to meet with him. What he wanted to discuss with him was highly confidential, not to be trusted to the phone.

Lester Knowles, a successful criminal lawyer, had been a classmate of Malcolm's in law school. "We know where she lives," Malcolm said. He sat alongside Lester's huge custom-built desk. He gave Lester Laura's address. "I was thinking maybe we should sit tight and wait to see what happens. The DNA samples might not match or she might change her mind."

One entire wall of Lester's office was covered with original paintings by nineteenth and twentieth century masters. Degas, Gauguin, Seurat and others. Malcolm's favorite was one by Degas, titled *Racehorses Before the Stands*. Mal and Lester had little in common except they both loved horse racing. For a time Mal owned several thoroughbreds, but none had ever made him any money. Just tax losses.

Mal had thought Lester a fool, spending virtually every penny he made on art. But time had proven him to be a shrewd investor. His collection was now worth ten times what he had originally paid.

"The more information we can gather ahead of time, the better off we'll be, Mal. I'll get one of my private investigators on this immediately," Lester said. "We need to see what she does with those specimens. That will give us some idea what we're up against."

"You aware that my brother Joe is thinking of making a run for governor?" Mal asked.

"Well, I'll be damned. Can't imagine why anyone would want that kind of life. All that hand-shaking and back-slapping."

"We can't afford a family scandal, Les. We need to find out if she has a seven-year-old kid."

"I doubt it. Why would she wait until now to prove who the daddy is? That shouldn't be too difficult to find out.

"I'll do my best to settle this. But Joe had better begin planning a strategy if we can't contain it. Have you discussed this with him?"

"Not yet," Mal said. "Maybe it's better if I leave him in the dark, for awhile."

"That would be a big mistake. Who would believe his campaign manager knew about this, and the candidate didn't?"

"I'll have to think on that," Mal said.

"Not for too long, my friend. This whole thing could break open at anytime. Believe me, Joe will be pissed if he's blindsided."

Judging Laura

Chapter Fourteen

The afternoon the workshop ended, Laura stuffed her syllabus and notes into her briefcase, exchanged email addresses with the other participants, and prepared to walk to her motel. A winter storm the evening before had blanketed the streets and sidewalks in several inches of snow.

She had never gotten rid of the excitement she felt as a child after the first snowfall. It meant no school and sled riding with her friends on Cemetery Hill, cold feet, hot chocolate, and the smell of cinnamon buns baking in the oven. But on this occasion Mother Nature held no such charm for her. An icy drizzle and frigid wind would make the trek to the motel a bit daunting. She went back into the hospital lobby and asked the receptionist if she would please call her a cab.

"Good luck getting one on a day like this. It could take hours. I'll ask the cabbie to call me when he gets here. That way you won't have to wait outside. You have a cell phone?"

She gave the receptionist her number, thanked her and crossed the lobby to a small shop where they sold coffee, flowers, magazines and newspapers. She bought a cup of coffee and a copy of the Philadelphia *Inquirer.* She sat at a table, sipping her coffee as she scanned the headlines. An article discussing President Bush's State of the Union address caught her eye.

"Mind if I join you?"

It was his voice. God almighty. Go away, go away, she thought. She couldn't bring herself to look up. He pulled up a chair and sat beside her. She finally turned to face him. He was sporting that repulsive grin of his.

"Sorry. I didn't mean to startle you."

She was in no mood to make small talk with someone who had caused her so much pain and destroyed her ability to conceive a child. She gave him her please-drop-dead look.

"The operator told me you're waiting for a cab. I'd be happy to give you a ride to your motel."

"No, thanks," she said, without looking up from her paper.

"It may be hours before a cab gets here. If that happens, you'll be headed for South Orange in the middle of rush hour traffic."

How did he know where she lived? After that exchange in the hospital snack bar, did he think she would ever set foot in a car with him? "I appreciate your concern," she said.

"I use valet parking. An attendant delivers my car to the front door. He can drive you to your motel."

She wondered how many interns could afford valet parking. Maybe she should take him up on the offer. The irony of it somehow appealed to her. She agreed.

They stood inside the hospital vestibule until his car pulled to the curb. Michael gave the driver ten dollars and asked him to deliver her to the Ramada Inn. The attendant said he really wasn't supposed to do that. Michael handed him another ten.

"What the hell, it's not that far," the man said.

Michael opened the curbside rear door. As Laura slipped into the back seat of the Mercedes sedan, Michael tossed a large envelope onto her lap. "What's this?" Laura asked.

"Some pictures I took a long time ago. Never had a chance to give them to you." Then he spoke in a whisper, "I have others, but I'd just as soon hold onto them for now." He stood watching as his Mercedes, driven by the parking attendant, drove off. Laura Carnahan... *I never dreamed I'd ever see her again.* The snow had turned to a freezing rain that crusted his hair and quickly soaked his surgical scrubs. *I'd love to see her expression as she looks at those photos.*

Laura kept glancing at the envelope, almost afraid to open it. Finally, she could no longer resist. She flipped through the 8X10 photographs. She recalled him snapping her picture at the party. Why would he have kept them all those years and why give them to her now?

There were a couple of pictures of her taking a drink from the flask. One of her teetering at the edge of the pool, one of the boy helping her stand, and one of him carrying her upstairs.

"We're here, lady," the attendant said.

Laura was relieved when her Bug jumped to life on the third try to start it. She had plenty of time to think on the drive home. The stop-and-go traffic inched along like a parade of elephants, trunk to tail. Why had Michael gone to the trouble to dig out those old pictures? He certainly didn't carry them around with him. He must have driven back to Allentown to get them. In the picture showing the boy carrying her upstairs, she was awake and appeared to be laughing. Did he think that the photo suggested she was somehow complicit in what followed in the bedroom? And that if anyone had raped her, it wasn't Michael, but the boy in the photograph?

Did Michael suspect that she might have DNA evidence proving that he had intercourse with her? But in that case it wouldn't matter who carried her upstairs. Then she recalled the words he had said to her...*I have others.*

Had he taken pictures of her in the bedroom? The thought of that possibility sent ice water coursing through her veins. My God, he was threatening her! Of course, that's what he's doing. He was saying that if I come after him, he'd make those naked photos public. It didn't matter if he hadn't really taken pictures in the bedroom. He figured the mere possibility they existed would make her back off.

But there was a good chance that his little scheme might backfire. Releasing those pictures, if they could be traced to him, would place him in the bedroom.

Had he figured out that the best way for her to obtain his DNA was to get her hands on a specimen of

136

his blood in the immunology lab? She was glad she had replaced the specimen. *Thank you, Gino.*

On the drive back to South Orange, the heavy snow had stopped, replaced by a freezing rain that was making the roads even more treacherous. She checked the clock display. She had been on the road over two hours and was nowhere near home. She called Bruce. He suggested she turn off at the next exit and find a motel.

"My little bug handles the snow and ice better than most. I'll just plug along. Don't wait up for me."

"How did things go?"

"I can't wait to tell you all about it. I'm reconsidering my career options. Thinking maybe FBI or CIA."

"By the way," Bruce said, "I called Dr. Corbett like you asked. She said you should come by her office tomorrow at nine."

"I hope I'm home by then. The roads are getting slicker by the minute."

Laura arrived at her apartment at two in the morning. Bruce was asleep. Jubilee was curled up at the foot of the bed. Exhausted, she flopped onto the bed fully dressed. But, to her surprise, she was unable to fall asleep. After about an hour of staring at the ceiling, she sat on the side of the bed, clicked on her reading lamp and reached for the envelope of photos. They were printed on ordinary copy-weight paper, suggesting they had not been commercially produced. She assumed he had printed the photos because he suspected she might go to the police.

She had thought that Michael had lost track of her at the party at Luke's. But the photos proved that he had been stalking her the entire time. She'd seen him snap a few pictures inside, but could not understand why she hadn't noticed him take those pictures by the pool.

"Hey! When did you pull in?" Bruce had propped himself on one elbow.

She fumbled as she tried to slip the photos back into the envelope. "Sorry. I just got in a little while ago. Go back to sleep."

"What have you got there?"

"I was going to wait till morning to show you." She handed him the envelope.

Bruce looked through the pictures in stunned silence. "Where in hell did you get these?"

She told him how Michael Greene had shown up at the hospital coffee shop while she was waiting for a cab. "He offered to have the valet parking attendant drive me to the motel. Just before the car pulled away, he handed me the envelope. Then he told me he had more pictures, but that he was going to hold onto those."

"You look like you're having a pretty good time." He handed her the snapshot of the boy carrying her up the stairs. "You're wide awake and laughing."

"I was drunk. Everything struck me funny." Tears filled her eyes. "My God. Are you saying because I'm smiling I was inviting them to rape me?"

"Come on, Laura. You know that's not what I meant."

He came around to her side of the bed and sat beside her, still staring at the photo. "In my head I pictured it a certain way, and seeing these pictures is a little shocking."

Her lower lip trembled. She fought unsuccessfully to keep from crying. "How do you think I felt when I saw them? It made me realize he had planned the whole damn thing. He was stalking me, just waiting for me to pass out."

Bruce put his arms around her, pressing her tear-stained cheek against his chest. "I'm sorry. I didn't mean that you were to blame for what happened."

She sniffed and grabbed a facial tissue from the bedside table. "It was a mistake to let Greene know I was at the hospital."

"But then we wouldn't have known about these." He pointed to the photos.

"I-I guess you're right," she said. "You think he really has others?"

'What the hell does it matter? Either way, he figures to scare us off."

"He's a clever bastard," she said. "But think of this. If he released even one photograph taken of me in the bedroom, it incriminates him, doesn't it?"

"He could say someone mailed them to him," Bruce said.

"Is there a way to trace a photograph to a particular camera?" she asked.

"I don't see how. In a regular camera all it does is focus the image on the film. I don't know about digital cameras. I'm not sure they even had them back then."

"Lots of kids saw him taking pictures," Laura said. "Martha had joked that I had my own private paparazzi."

Laura glanced at the bedside clock. "Damn, look at the time." She stood, kicked off her shoes and began undressing. "You'd better get some sleep. The alarm will be going off in a couple of hours."

After showering and getting into a nightgown, Laura went online to check her email and to do a Google search of digital images and forensics. She looked up the history of the digital camera. She found that Apple came out with a commercial digital camera that they promoted at the Tokyo World's Fair in 1993. There was a picture of the camera. It was called the Apple Quicktake 100. It looked exactly like the camera Michael had used.

Laura continued to search to see if a digital photo could be traced to a particular camera. After going through a few dozen websites, she found this entry:

Just as the rifling in a gun barrel leaves a distinctive pattern on the bullets it fires, a digital camera has a signature of sorts. Today's digital cameras have sensors with millions of pixels. In each camera, a small handful of these are either too bright or are burnt out entirely. When a camera takes a picture, the imperfections leave a unique pattern.

Did Michael know that? Probably not. Because if he had, he wouldn't have given her those photos. Her guess was either no other photographs existed, and it was all a bluff, or they did exist, but he didn't intend to use them unless he had to defend himself in court.

She thought of the blood specimen and comb in her purse. What if the DNA Dr. Corbett had discovered in her fallopian tubes didn't match

Michael Greene's? In that case her only option would be to go to the police or forget about the whole deal. She decided to bide her time. Wait for him to do something stupid, like release photos he had taken in the bedroom.

Jubilee brushed against Laura's leg. She lifted her cat onto her lap. Jubilee rolled over and extended her head, looking directly into Laura's face. She stroked the soft white fur under her cat's chin. Jubilee purred in earnest, and continued to stare, unblinking, into Laura's eyes. "Sorry I woke you, baby." Laura carried the cat to the bedroom and put her at the foot of the bed. Laura crawled under the covers and snuggled up to Bruce. She fell asleep almost immediately.

*****

In a black Toyota sedan with tinted windows and Pennsylvania plates, Rana Akthar, a dark-complexioned, middle-aged man, struggled to stay awake. He looked at his watch. He was parked on the side of the street opposite, and a door or two down, from the Hamby apartment. When the apartment lights finally went out, he ratcheted back his seat, set his wrist alarm and closed his eyes. It hadn't been easy trailing her Volkswagen Beetle with all the super-sized SUVs and trucks on the road. If he hadn't planted a tracking device under her rear fender it would have been impossible.

He'd love to go to a motel and stretch out in a real bed, but he couldn't afford to leave his post. Besides, one hundred bucks an hour plus expenses wasn't bad pay for sitting and waiting to see where she delivered those specimens.

Chapter Fifteen

Chris Martino stepped into Miss Atwood's office in Medical Records. She couldn't recall him ever showing up unannounced. He informed her of his concern that there had been a security breach in her department.

She set her jaw. Dr. Greene, she thought, had no doubt been the source of that information. But she was prepared for that contingency. She was army, born and bred, an expert at the CYA game.

"That will not be necessary, Mr. Marino." She leaned over and pulled an incident report from a side drawer and handed it to Chris. "I completed it yesterday but hadn't had a chance to deliver it to you. I assume this is the incident you were concerned about."

Chris studied the document. "I see. Fine. Well, how do you intend to deal with the employee involved?"

"I'll be meeting with her this afternoon. Since she's been an employee less than six months, she's subject to dismissal without due process."

"You intend to fire her?"

"Yes. Although she hadn't deliberately compromised the confidentiality of the patient's medical record, she displayed a level of carelessness that I cannot tolerate."

Chris Martino called Michael Greene and told him that the issue had been resolved. "The hospital employee responsible is being dismissed," he said.

Michael asked if the IT person had identified the employee involved.

"That wasn't necessary. Miss Atwood reported the incident. She searched the browser history feature on the employee's computer. She discovered that Mrs. Laura Hamby did access your medical record. It appears to have been a screw-up, not a conspiracy on the part of the employee."

"I'm still not convinced this was an unintended breach," Michael said. "And I think the woman's supervisor should be canned, too."

"I sent a copy of the incident report to Dr. Pollack. He'll deal with it as he sees fit."

Michael, dressed in a fresh pair of scrubs, waited patiently for the medical director to get off the phone.

"Excuse the interruption," Dr. Pollack said. "You were saying?"

"A person attending a workshop in the medical records department gained access to my medical record."

He did not mention that she had stolen a serum specimen from the immunology lab. The

Medical Director would certainly be curious as to why.

"Yes, I saw the incident report. Do you have any idea why she would do that?" Dr. Pollack asked.

"We were high school classmates," Michael said. "Probably just curiosity. Her motive is irrelevant."

"How did you discover that she had checked your record?"

"I hadn't seen her in several years. I ran into her in the hospital. She mentioned something she could only have learned by having looked at my medical record."

Dr. Pollack raised one eyebrow. "Something of a sensitive nature?" Dr. Pollack asked.

"Yes."

"I'm sorry that happened. We've gone to great lengths in our new system to enhance security and confidentiality, but no system is foolproof."

"I believe Mrs. Hamby should somehow pay for what she did," Michael said.

"Hopefully legal action won't be necessary. I understand Mrs. Hamby is supervisor of the medical records department at Saint Joseph's Hospital in South Orange."

"That is my understanding." Michael assumed that the Pollack wouldn't want to pursue a lawsuit that would reveal the vulnerability of their new computerized record system.

"I'll give St. Joe's a call. Dr. Paul Davies, their Medical Director, is a good friend. He plays by the book. My guess is that she'll be searching for a new job soon."

Dr. Pollack immediately called the Medical Director at St. Joe's Hospital?

"Got a minute, Paul?" He went on to describe what had happened. "I understand this woman is medical records supervisor."

"I'm shocked," Paul said. "She's been a dynamite employee. Runs a tight ship, never a blip of anything negative. You're absolutely certain of this?"

"Our system has safeguards in place to track this kind of behavior. There's absolutely no doubt as to what happened."

After his conversation with Dr. Pollack, Paul sat at his desk undecided as to how to proceed. This was the part of the job he hated. A bright young woman with an unblemished record---if he put this in her personnel file, she'd have no future at Saint Joe's, or at any hospital for that matter. And if he had an off-the-record fatherly conversation with her, he'd be compromising his own position in the event the incident came to light.

At times like this, Paul regretted his decision to give up general surgery for the prestigious position of Medical Director. He listed his options on a legal pad. He circled one. For now he was preparing a presentation at the AHA meeting in Denver, to be followed by a week of skiing at Snowmass. He'd deal with Laura Hamby after his return.

Chapter Sixteen

Dr. Corbett smiled and shook her head as Laura handed her the sandwich bag containing the syringe of serum and the surgical glove, in which Nate had put the comb. "I don't want to hear how you got your hands on these things."

Laura was dying to recount blow-by-blow how she had cleverly used her knowledge of hospital routines to pull off exactly what she had set out to do. Instead she told her of her finger stick and the medication the nurse practitioner had given her.

"He did the right thing. Although your risk is very small, we had better get some baseline labs today."

Laura nodded. "How long will it take to get the DNA information back?"

"A couple of weeks at least. I'll call you as soon as I get the results."

"When is your medical meeting?" Laura asked. She wondered if she should tell Dr. Corbett that Dr.

Greene and she had met, and that he was obviously suspicious of her intentions.

"Exactly three weeks from today in Orlando."

"I...I'm concerned about the confidentiality issue...""

"Don't worry, Laura. There's no way they can trace this to you."

"What about my office visits, these blood tests?"

"As of today I'll purge your name from my office records. It's not unusual for me to submit specimens under the name of Ms. Jane Doe."

"But the surgery is part of my hospital record."

"You're in charge of the records department..."

"We do have a confidential locked file," Laura said, "but if someone was determined to find out who was the previous owner of those fallopian tubes, they could check the surgical records. You couldn't have taken out that many fallopian tubes in the past few months."

"A half-dozen. You're right. I can't guarantee this couldn't be traced to you. But this finding is too important not to share with the medical community."

"You already have my written permission to go ahead, but..."

"Is there something you're not telling me, Laura?"

Laura had been enthusiastic about Dr. Corbett's presentation at the conference in Orlando, but now she was hesitant. She decided to tell her about the photographs Dr. Greene had given her, and his not-so-veiled threat that he had others that were even more compromising.

"I'm sorry to hear that," the doctor said. "As of now he's probably thinking you saved an item of clothing. But if my report gets into the press, or if he reads it in a medical journal, he'd be stupid not to figure out the rest." She stood and began to pace. "Okay, let's say he puts the pieces together. He had probably assumed you stole his comb to get DNA evidence. He does a little checking and learns you work at the same hospital where I am on the staff. So now he has reason to believe it may not be an item of clothing but a pathology specimen." She sat down next to Laura. "We lose the element of surprise. But that doesn't make a bit of difference if we end up with a DNA match."

The office intercom clicked on. "The OR called, Dr. Corbett. You have surgery at 10:00."

"I have to run, Laura." She sat at her desk and checked off a few boxes on a laboratory requisition form. She handed it to Laura. "Give this to my lab tech."

After leaving Dr. Corbett's office, Laura climbed into her car and adjusted the rear view mirror. She noticed a black Toyota sedan a couple of parking spaces from her. It looked familiar, for some reason. Then she recalled seeing a black sedan as she left her apartment that morning. It's probably just a coincidence, she thought. As she drove past the car, she noticed it had Pennsylvania plates. That wasn't too unusual. She turned her car around and made a second pass. This time she jotted down the license plate number. She could tell from car's exhaust that its engine was running. She made a circuitous trip to the hospital, checking frequently in her rearview mirror. The car was nowhere in sight.

Rana Akthar had gotten careless, believing Laura had no reason to suspect she was being tailed. Now that she had obviously taken notice of him, he would have to rent a different car each day and have it delivered to the motel. He'd keep a healthy distance from her, relying on the tracking device to prevent losing her in traffic.

He snapped open his cell phone and called his boss, Lester Knowles. "First thing this morning she went to a doctor's office. Her name's Dr. Jane Corbett. She's a fertility specialist."

"Good work, Rana," Lester said. "Find out what you can about the doctor; what hospital she's affiliated with; what laboratories she uses; and if she's one of those docs who makes a living as an expert witness. And call the state medical society to see if she's ever been suspended or sued."

"Okay. Want me to continue to tail Hamby?"

"It shouldn't take long to get the scoop on the doctor. After that, get back on her trail. Dig up what you can. See if she's got a boyfriend on the side. You know the kind of stuff we're interested in. Especially see if there's a kid, like a second-grader, hanging around."

"How much you budget for this? It could take a while."

"Our client wants results. He doesn't care about the cost."

"She is a very attractive woman. In my country men would be going after her."

Les laughed. "There's not that much difference between Indian men and American men when it comes to beautiful women. Don't get any ideas, Rana."

Peter Rizzolo

Chapter Seventeen

From the time Laura dropped off the specimens at Dr. Corbett's office until she finally heard about the test results two weeks later, she was busy preparing a power-point presentation of U. Penn's experience in converting to an electronic record. It was a bit daunting to think of standing before the assembled department heads and other hospital executive types, most of whom were not computer literate. And what she was pitching could take years to complete, involving a great deal of disruption and lots of money. The safe approach would be to present the pros and cons and maintain a neutral position, to wait and see how many were ready to commit. But she didn't want to go for safe. If she could successfully spearhead such an innovation, she would be in a strong position to move up the ranks. Administrative assistant to the hospital chief executive officer was one that might open up.

But that was not meant to be. The day Dr. Daves returned from his meeting in Denver, he called Laura to his office. She assumed it was concerning her upcoming presentation.

"I'm looking forward to your presentation, Laura, but that's not why I wanted to talk with you."

Laura searched his face for a clue. Although only in his mid-fifties, his hair was totally white, in striking contrast to his deeply tanned skin. He was normally relaxed and jovial when they met. He'd invariably begin with a humorous story, and then seemingly as an after-thought, he'd approach the business at hand. But this morning he was somber.

"How was the skiing?" Laura asked.

"Fantastic. Fresh powder every morning."

"Sounds like fun. So why the long face?"

"I got a call from Dr. Allan Pollack. He's medical director at U. Penn." He paused. "Do you want to tell me what went on there...besides attending the workshop?"

Damnit. He must have figured out what she'd done. She wasn't going to admit to any more than she had to. "I don't understand."

"He said you accessed, without authorization, the medical record of one of their staff physicians."

Laura bit her lip. Should she deny having done anything wrong? Did they have hard evidence? If not, it would be her word against Michael's. She had no regrets for what she had done. Which was the principle of greater importance, the invasion of someone's privacy or the prohibition against brutal assault on a person's body, a premeditated act that bore lifelong consequences? She recalled a quotation of Goethe that said, "Truth calls for higher powers than the defense of error." What she had done was unethical, regardless of her motive. Was she prepared to deal with the consequences?

"Laura?"

"What he told you is true. I used a secure computer in their medical records department. I read Dr. Michael Greene's medical record."

"Why? You of all people." He stood and walked to where Laura was sitting. He pulled up a chair.

He looked at her so pleadingly she was tempted to take him into her confidence. But that was impossible. If he were to decide to cover up the incident, and it somehow came to light...."I'm truly sorry to put you in this position, Dr. Davies."

"You didn't answer my question. Why did you do it?"

"It concerns a personal matter that I can't share with you right now," Laura said softly.

Dr. Davies took a deep breath. "If I go before the board and they formally reprimand you, it becomes part of your personnel record. You know what that implies."

"They'll recommend you fire me."

"Most likely. But there's another option."

Short of being fired, there were several options, Laura thought. Reprimand—probation—demotion—none of them good.

"If you were to resign, I needn't go to the board. Your personnel record will remain pristine."

Laura hadn't considered that option. She closed her eyes. She had given St. Joe's years of devoted service. Now, a single stroke of a computer key had destroyed all she had worked so hard to achieve. Michael Greene had struck once again. But this time she had brought it on herself. Dr. Daves was right. He had been her friend and mentor, especially in her earlier, more vulnerable years at St. Joe's. Resignation was her only option.

"My husband and I do want to start a family."

"No one could argue with that."

"How soon---like immediately?" Laura asked.

"Of course not. I'd want you to stay on long enough to help us to conclude a search. Yours will be a hard act to follow."

Laura knew that recruiting at the managerial level often took several months, even when qualified persons within the system scrambled to move up the ladder. This was no time to be pounding the pavement looking for a job.

"You'll have my resignation on your desk by tomorrow morning."

****

A week before Dr. Corbett was to leave for her conference in Orlando, she called and asked Bruce and Laura to come in to see her.

"The serum specimen was of course rich in genetic material," Doctor Corbett said. "White cells, as you might know, are a storehouse of DNA."

"And?" Laura asked, irritated that Dr. Corbett hadn't just blurted out what they wanted to know.

Dr. Corbett smiled. "And when we compared his DNA with the two samples obtained from your fallopian tubes, we found that it matched perfectly with one of the specimens. The comb, it turns out, was totally devoid of genetic material."

Bruce and Laura looked at each other. Laura was too stunned to speak. This was the result she wanted, but had never permitted herself to believe it would happen.

"It looks like I beat up the right guy," Bruce said.

Laura hugged Bruce. "I knew it was him. Oh God, I was sure it was him." She turned toward Dr. Corbett. "Now we have to decide what to do."

"Remember what I told you before, Laura. This only proves he had intercourse with you. It doesn't tell us when."

"What are you saying?" Bruce asked. "She never had sex with him before or after that night."

"We know that, but she did go out with him once." Dr. Corbett said.

Bruce turned to Laura. "You never told me you went out with him. What the hell else haven't you told me?"

"We went to a damn basketball game. I went straight home afterwards. That was the first and only time we dated. What was there to tell?"

"You're saying nothing happened..."

"He didn't score, if that's what you're asking."

Bruce took a deep breath. "God. I'm sick of this whole damn business."

"It was months before I dated you. I never thought to tell you."

"Just thinking about that guy alone with you makes me crazy." He put his arm around her shoulder. She covered his hand with hers.

"Maybe we should continue this conversation some other time," Dr. Corbett suggested.

"No, it's okay," Laura said. Bruce nodded. "You were saying it doesn't prove when?"

"Yes. He could claim he had sex with you earlier that evening or even at some other time."

"What if I can get my hands on one of the photographs he took in the bedroom?" Laura asked.

"You would have to be able to prove he personally took them."

Laura reminded her about the photos Dr. Greene had given her. "If I can prove that the photos taken in the bedroom came from the same camera...."

"Is that possible?" Dr. Corbett asked.

Laura told Dr. Corbett what she had learned on the internet about digital photos.

"How do you know it was a digital camera?" Dr. Corbett asked.

"It didn't look like a regular camera. He told me it was digital. Said it cost almost a thousand dollars."

"That guy had no idea what he was getting into when he messed with my girl," Bruce said.

"My advice," Dr. Corbett said, "is to go to the police, or if you choose to go ahead with a civil action, get yourself a damn good lawyer. But no more cowboy stuff. There's no telling what he or his family might do if they think you're intending to blackmail them."

"Amen," Bruce said.

"Laura, you already know that I'm reporting on finding DNA in Jane Doe's fallopian tubes many years after she had been raped. But I want to also report that the DNA we found matches the DNA of the man suspected to be the rapist."

"Sounds like the kind of report that might make the evening news," Laura said. "It's okay with me." She turned to Bruce. "How about you?"

"Yeah. Make the bastard sweat. Why not?"

"What I wouldn't give to see his face when he hears that from his favorite TV anchor," Laura said.

On the day Laura knew Dr. Corbett was to make her presentation, she couldn't wait to get home from work to check the evening news. Dr. Corbett had predicted her presentation would spark a great deal of interest. She was right. There was her doctor on national television!

CNN anchor: "Today at the National Convention of Fertility Specialists our CNN reporter interviewed a key presenter, Dr. Jane Corbett, an attending physician at St. Josephs Hospital, in South Orange, New Jersey. Her report caused quite a stir at the meeting."

"Dr. Corbett," the reporter asked, "had you anticipated finding the alleged rapist's DNA in the woman's body after almost nine years?"

"Yes. I meticulously dissected the surgical specimens in the hope of finding his DNA."

"What made you suspect that was possible?"

"There are biologic parallels. Many infectious diseases such as tuberculosis, trichinosis, malaria, toxoplasmosis, chicken pox and herpes, to name just a few, are caused by organisms that can survive in the body's organs, tissues, and musculature for many years."

"So a person can have some really bad organisms just sitting there waiting for a chance to break loose?"

"Exactly. They appear to have developed mechanisms that shield them from the immune system. But in debilitated persons or persons given medicines that inhibit the immune system, the foreign organisms can raise havoc with the host, causing illness and even death."

"Why didn't the woman's immune system destroy the sperm?" the reporter asked.

"We can only speculate on how the sperm DNA managed to survive. There is some early research that suggests sperm may be able to shield themselves from the host immune system, similar to the way bacteria and viruses are able to do. This finding may support that hypothesis."

"Thanks to you, Dr. Corbett. Perhaps now more rapists will be brought to justice."

Laura flipped around to the other news channels. As she suspected, the report was picked up by Fox, CNBC, NBC and CBS. There was no way Michael Greene could have missed it. For now, she could sit tight. The next move was his.

Chapter Eighteen

Mal Green increased the incline and revved up the RPMs on his treadmill, going from a power walk to a brisk jog. As usual he watched the CBS evening news.

"At a meeting today of fertility specialists in Orlando, a physician reported that nine years after a sexual assault, DNA evidence has been recovered from the victim's internal organs. Stay tuned for an interview with the doctor who presented this startling discovery."

If a land mine had gone off under the treadmill, Mal Greene would not have been more shocked. He momentarily stopped jogging, causing his feet to fly out from under him. He lunged forward in a desperate, unsuccessful attempt to grab the handrails, falling face-down onto the rear surface of the treadmill. The safety mechanism kicked-in, bringing the treadmill to an abrupt stop.

He was stunned, but conscious. His nose bled profusely. He grabbed a towel. His wife rushed into the room, startled to see him sitting on the floor, holding a bloody towel to his face.

"My God, what happened?"

"I just broke my nose, that's what the hell happened."

"I'll get some ice. And it's better to lean forward when you have a nose bleed." She ran from the room.

He got to his feet, keeping one eye on the television, waiting for the interview the news anchor had promised. He had never dreamed that incident almost seven years ago would come back to haunt him. His wife returned with a plastic bag filled with ice. She pressed it to the back of his neck.

"Why the hell you putting it back there?"

"My little brother had nose bleeds all the time. That's where our family doctor told us to put the ice."

"That doesn't make a bit of sense."

"Should I call the doctor, Mal?"

"No." He dabbed his nose. "The bleeding's just about stopped."

"You'd better see him tomorrow. Your nose looks a little bent out of shape."

"My nose *is* bent out of shape, *I'm* bent out of shape, the whole goddamn world is bent out of shape. Pour me a glass of scotch."

"Alcohol will make the bleeding worse."

"God almighty! Just leave me alone. I'll get it myself."

He went to a sideboard and poured himself several fingers of scotch, then sat at his desk, sipping his drink as he held the bag of ice over the bridge of his nose. As Mal watched the news, the anchor droned on and on about President Bush's call for medical liability reform. Mal impatiently switched around to other news channels, then back to CBS. Finally at the very end of the show the interview of the doctor came on. It was even worse than Mal had anticipated. It wasn't just any doctor, it was *her* doctor. He immediately dialed Lester Knowles.

"Les, turn on the television."

"I'm already watching it, Mal."

"What in hell are we going to do?"

"One thing we're not going to do, Mal, is panic. Think for a minute. That pathology specimen probably passed through many hands. They certainly didn't follow strict forensic techniques. It could have been contaminated at many points along the way."

"But the report said they found DNA of the suspected rapist in the pathology specimen," Mal said. Two drops of blood dripped onto Mal's appointment calendar. He grabbed a tissue.

"But once the issue of mishandling a specimen is brought into question," Les said, "it weakens the overall findings. And remember, they're most likely dealing with degraded DNA fragments. That will make matching speculative and inconclusive."

"You lost me, Les. You're talking legal arguments. I don't want this damn mess to come to that. Maybe we should negotiate with the bitch for an out-of-court settlement. Keep it out of the papers. Especially if there's a kid."

"Slow down, Mal. We have to be careful. If she's already reported this to the police, any such move might be construed as obstruction of justice."

Mal's head throbbed. He placed the ice-bag on the top of his head and reached for his tumbler of scotch. "We can't just sit on our hands waiting for them to haul my son's ass to jail."

"Call Michael. Make sure he doesn't do anything foolish. He must not have any contact with her. And my guess is that she has no intention of going to the police. In that case we sit tight and wait for her to make a move. If blackmail is what she has in mind, we nail her for extortion. That would remove all credibility from her testimony if it were ever to go to a criminal trial."

"There are a hell of a lot of ifs and suppositions in there."

"That's what you're paying me for, Mal."

"Maybe you should check out her background. Dig up some dirt."

"That's SOP. Rana's already working on that angle," Les said.

"Let me know if he comes up with anything."

Michael Greene was on duty that evening and hadn't seen the television interview of Dr. Corbett. When his father phoned and told him about the news report, Michael was incredulous. "How do you know it's her doctor?"

"Les put a private investigator on her tail when she left Philly. Les insists you're not to have any contact with her."

Michael wondered if the private detective had followed her as she left the hospital in his car. If he had taken down the license plate number, he'd have discovered whose it was. Did his dad already know about that?

"I'm not an idiot, dad. Why would I even think of contacting her?"

He wasn't about to tell his father that he had printed one of the photographs of her naked body. He had used a computer software program that allowed him to transpose digitally a picture of her smiling face atop her naked body. The result was near perfect. It would take an expert to detect fraud. He had been on the verge of mailing it to her but had changed his mind at the last minute. The ploy might backfire if she decided not to back away from prosecution or filing a civil complaint.

Between trips to the operating room and the surgical ward, Michael managed to catch a few minutes of the evening news on television. A couple of medical students were in the on-call room as he watched.

"God almighty!" One of the students exclaimed. "That's amazing. After several years his DNA was still recoverable!"

The second student was skeptical. "One doctor, one case, sounds like a hoax to me. Probably never happen again."

"Well, if I were that guy," the first student said, "I'd be changing my underwear about now. What do you think, Dr. Greene?"

"It's irresponsible of the doctor to rush out and have a news conference before submitting her findings to her peers in a refereed medical journal."

"But isn't it sometimes in the public interest not to wait?" the student asked.

Their ensuing discussion of the ethics of going public with preliminary medical findings was interrupted by Michael's beeper. He headed for the general surgery intensive care unit, where he was asked to see several patients. From there he was called to the emergency room.

On the way, Michael had time to ruminate. Why would Laura have subjected herself to major surgery on the remote chance of finding his DNA if she didn't intend to go to the police? Even if Les could somehow get him acquitted, the mere suspicion of him having been a rapist would dog him throughout his life and would certainly impact his medical career.

He was becoming more and more convinced that he had to take matters into his own hands. One look at that picture and Laura would almost certainly decide to let the whole matter drop. He'd have to somehow get it to her so it couldn't be traced to him. He could drive to New York City and mail it from there. No note, just the picture. He would tell no one. But how he'd love to see the expression on her face when she opened that envelope. She might even believe she had gone along willingly with his little game until things got out of hand. In that case she wouldn't dare show it to Bruce or the police.

But what if those photos he had given her, and his implied threat that he might have other compromising photos, had been enough to discourage her from coming after him? How would he know? And how long would he have to sit around biting his nails, not knowing if and when he might be arrested?

In the emergency department he was asked to see a couple whose car had run off the road and rolled over twice before coming to rest on its side. The driver, a twenty-year-old male, had only minor injuries. His companion, an eighteen-year-old girl, was less fortunate. She was thrown against the car door as the boy came crashing down on her. The ER intern was concerned about possible damage to the young girl's spleen. Both she and the driver had alcohol levels above 2.0.

Michael examined the girl's abdomen in silence. She was near the same age as Laura had been the night of the party at Luke's. He wished Laura had gone to the police back then. Teenagers were always doing stupid things. A bunch of teenagers out of control from alcohol and surging hormones. It was Luke's parents who were really to blame. He probably would have gotten off with a slap on the wrist. And what about this girl's parents? Did they have a clue where their daughter was?

"Did you contact her family?" Michael asked the medical student. "We'll need their permission if my attending decides to operate."

"They're on the way."

X-rays and an abdominal CT confirmed the presence of free air, indicating a ruptured bowel. She was immediately taken to the operating room.

Two hours later he took off his scrubs and flopped onto a bed in the on-call room. The repair of her damaged bowel was routine but tedious, as her abdominal cavity had to be scrupulously cleansed of fecal material. Despite Michael's fatigue, sleep did not come easily.

Someone was shaking his shoulder. "Wake up, Michael. It's me, your date. Remember?" He was on his back, his arms tied to the bed rails. He was naked. She was dressed as she had been at the party. She was holding a whip. She snapped it several times in the air, and then began to beat him savagely across the chest and abdomen.

He screamed in pain. "Laura, stop, stop!"

"It's just a game. It doesn't really hurt, does it?"

The room was suddenly full of other girls screeching and clapping with every snap of the whip.

Some of the girls chanted, "We begged you to stop...We begged you to stop...."

Others chanted, "Don't stop. This is fun, don't stop. This is fun."

When he thought he could endure no more, the restraints that bound him to the bed suddenly fell away. He sat up. He screamed when he saw welts crisscrossing his chest and abdomen.

Someone was shaking him by the shoulders. "Dr. Greene, Dr. Greene, it's okay. It's just a bad dream."

He sat on the edge of the bed, clutching his chest, still not sure what was real or imagined.

"Heard you screaming from down the hall," the medical student said. "Must have been a hellofa dream."

"What time is it?" he asked, as he staggered into the bathroom, still not fully awake.

"Rounds start in thirty minutes," the student said. "The resident wants you to discuss the girl with the ruptured gut. I'm presenting the history and physical exam."

In the shower Michael winced as the hot water struck his chest. He looked down and was startled to see that his chest s was covered with purplish welts. No one had actually truck his chest. Had he caused the trauma that brought on the rash? As he watched in disbelief the rash began to fade, but didn't fully disappear. He recalled that as a child he developed itchy welts after being given baby aspirin. Was stress causing a resurgence of aspirin sensitivity?

Peter Rizzolo

Chapter Nineteen

Lester Knowles assigned his private investigator, Rana Akthar, the task of getting hold of the pathology report on the specimens submitted by Dr. Corbett. Rana's parents, originally from India, had immigrated to England when Rana, their only child, was an infant. After retiring from a position in British Intelligence, Rana had found leisure boring. He sought employment as a private investigator.

"We need to know why Laura had her fallopian tubes removed. Her motivation would be important in determining if she would be satisfied with a financial settlement," Lester said.

"I don't believe that will be too difficult," Rana said. "How would you suggest I proceed?"

"I don't want to know how you do it. My assumption is that you will not break any laws."

"I see," Rana said. Straddling the fault between legal and illegal was what his job was all about. "Why is this report important?"

"If finding the DNA had been pursued as an interest of Dr. Corbett's," Lester said, "Laura and her husband might not want to suffer through a court battle."

After speaking with Lester, Rana dialed Dr. Corbett's office.

"Good morning. Dr. Jane Corbett's office. How may I help you?"

"I represent Pro-Path," Rana said. "We're a national contract laboratory interested in offering doctors in your area our extensive diagnostic services." He quickly added, "Our prices are very competitive. Might I set up an appointment with Dr. Corbett?"

He was switched to the office manager. "We already work with a local laboratory, Broach Labs," she said, irritated at being interrupted by yet another solicitor.

"We have a presence in over forty states. We're able to offer significant discounts over local providers," Rana said. "I know we can beat Broach's prices. I'd be more than happy to fax you a copy of our information."

She gave him Dr. Corbett's fax number. So far so good, he thought.

Pathologists always request medical information on specimens submitted to them for analysis. Broache would have on record the reason Laura Hamby's fallopian tubes were removed. Rana had to figure out how to obtain that information. He wondered if Broache also did the DNA testing.

Rana called the Broache Lab's home office. He asked to speak to a staff person in charge of pathology reports. He said that he worked for Dr. Jane Corbett in South Orange, New Jersey. She would like them to fax a duplicate copy of the report on the pathology specimen on Laura Hamby. The original copy had been apparently misfiled, and she needed one for insurance purposes.

"You do have her fax number?" Rana asked.

"We should," the woman said. "Hold on while I check."

"That won't be necessary," Rana said. He gave her the fax number.

"I'd better double check." She put him on hold. "Yes, that's the number we have listed for Dr. Corbett."

Rana explained that Dr. Corbett would not be at her office that day. Would they send the report to her home fax?

"We don't have a home fax number listed."

"I have that right here." He gave her the fax number at a local commercial copy center. "We'd like that as soon as possible," Rana said.

Within minutes Rana had the report in hand. "A twenty-six-year-old white female presented for infertility workup. She was considering *in vitro* fertilization. Her infertility was secondary to pelvic inflammatory disease presumably secondary to untreated gonorrhea she incurred at the time of a sexual assault."

A detailed description of the diseased fallopian tubes ensued. Had the report been written in a foreign language it would have been no more undecipherable. The report indicated that numerous cytology sections were sent to the Broache DNA laboratory for further analysis.

While preparing for rounds at Pennsylvania hospital, Michael Green was paged. The operator informed him that someone named Lester Knowles was calling. Michael agreed to take the call.

"Michael, we need to talk. Your dad is also on the line."

"Make it quick. Rounds are about to start," Michael said.

"My private investigator has learned that Laura had surgery to remove her fallopian tubes. He got hold of a detailed report on the surgical findings."

Rounds can wait. Got to hear this. His luck was improving

"Why in hell would they remove her tubes when she wants to get pregnant?" his dad asked.

"A couple of possibilities," Michael said. "Diseased tubes can cause painful periods. And if she's considering having a test-tube baby, getting rid of the diseased fallopian tubes would increase the chances of the procedure being successful."

"You lost me there," Les said.

Michael went on to explain the complicated procedure of *in vitro* fertilization. "It can take two, three or more tries before a fertilized egg is successfully implanted. At tens of thousands of dollars a pop, IVF can get pretty expensive."

"We know yet what her husband does for a living?" Mal asked.

"He's manager of an auto parts franchise. Doubt if he makes more than $30,000 a year."

"Les," Mal said, "set up a meeting between us and her attorney. We offer them 150 grand to go away and they agree not to press charges."

"I want to be there, dad," Michael insisted. He wasn't exactly impressed by the way Lester had handled the situation so far.

"Okay," Mal said. "But we have to speak with one voice."

"I agree with your father," Les said. "You and Mal sit on either side of me. I do all the talking. Whatever you have to say, whisper in my ear."

"Of course, Less," Michael said. But he had no intention of remaining silent.

Laura contacted several law firms in New Jersey and asked who had the best track record in sexual assault prosecution. One name, Shelly Spinks, showed up on everyone's list: a woman in her mid-fifties, a former prosecutor who had sent many a rapist off to prison. The State at times sought her counsel in the prosecution of high-profile cases. After a brief telephone conversation with the attorney, she and Laura set up a meeting.

Shelly looked nothing like Laura had expected. She had the trim figure of a woman twenty years younger, long dark hair that reached below her shoulders, large, intense dark eyes, blemish-free skin that a teenager would die for, and an open, disarming smile. Laura told her every detail she could recall of the evening the rape had occurred. She told her of Dr. Corbett's findings.

"So you're Ms. Jane Doe," Shelly said. "Those of us in the business of representing rape victims certainly sat up and took notice. But how did you know the DNA was his? Had you saved an item of clothing?"

Laura explained how she had gotten a sample of Michael Greene's blood.

"You understand, my dear, that evidence would most likely not be admissible," Shelly said.

"I just wanted to be certain the DNA was his, before going ahead. Dr. Corbett also found a second specimen."

Shelly opened her eyes wide in disbelief. "But Dr. Corbett's report didn't mention that."

"The doctor told me the second DNA she identified wasn't relevant in terms of the significance of her findings."

"Please don't be offended if I ask," Shelly said, "but was the second specimen your husband's DNA?"

"No. She checked that out," Laura said.

"Good." Shelly thoughtfully chewed on the eraser end of a pencil for a few moments. "You're fortunate to be prosecuting this case in New Jersey. It's the only state in the northeast where adult sexual assault is not restricted by statutes of limitations."

Laura had done her homework and was already aware of the New Jersey law. "But the assault occurred in Pennsylvania. Can the case still be prosecuted here?"

"At times a state will waive jurisdiction, but that's at the discretion of the Attorney General. They'd probably hold onto this one. Statutes of limitations is twelve years in Pennsylvania...so that's not a problem. If you had waited much longer, we would have other options."

'Laura moved to the edge of her seat. "Oh?"

"For one, we could bring suit for bodily injury and not for rape."

"I don't understand."

"You only recently discovered that you had contracted a disease that rendered you infertile and necessitated major surgery. It's called time-of-discovery. That's when the clock starts ticking."

"You mean to say even twenty years after the fact, we could still use time-of-discovery?"

"In Pennsylvania, since you were still legally a minor, you would have nine years after reaching age of majority in which to use the deferred discovery rule."

Laura eased back in her chair. She liked this lady. "Will you be able to represent me in either New Jersey or Pennsylvania?"

"Yes, I'm licensed to practice law in both states. I can represent you in a civil action. But if you decide what you really want is to convict those guys, especially Michael Greene, of criminal assault, the state-appointed prosecutor makes all the decisions. I can join the team if the prosecutor is willing to have me, but I wouldn't be in charge. It's not how I like to work. On the other hand, in a civil action I would have a free hand."

"I've been struggling with civil versus criminal. I thought that with your experience you might help me make the right choice."

"Do you mind if I smoke?" Shelly asked. Laura shook her head. "I'm trying to kick the habit. I'm down to four half-cigarettes a day." She reached into a side drawer of her desk and removed a pack of filter-tip Marlboros.

She paced as she smoked. "The prosecutor will decide what's in the interest of the state, not in yours." Shelly took a deep drag from her cigarette, exhaling through her nose. "If the prosecutors are convinced they can't prove guilt beyond a reasonable doubt, they may go for a plea bargain. Two teenagers, both drunk, and potential witnesses also under the influence of alcohol, and an alleged assault that happened years ago...it would be extremely difficult to prove guilt beyond a reasonable doubt."

Laura thought over what the attorney had said. "I guess my greatest fear is that his lawyers will use that photo of the boy carrying me up the stairs to make it look like I was a willing participant."

"You're right. As unbelievable as that might seem, even with the DNA evidence you have, any defense attorney worth their salt could convince a jury there was reasonable doubt he committed a crime. He could get off with a misdemeanor charge. No jail time."

Laura watched as Shelly exhaled a plume of smoke, and snuffed out the half-smoked cigarette. She recalled how angry she felt when she first saw Michael in the hospital snack bar at U. Penn. Was she looking for revenge or justice? Was there really any difference between the two?

"I don't care if he goes to jail or not," Laura said. "I just want to prove that Michael Greene committed premeditated rape."

"Then my advice to you is to go ahead with civil action. There the burden of proof is more like fifty-one forty-nine."

"I'd like you to represent me, but I'm not sure we can afford you."

"Honey, you pay nothing unless you win. If you do, my fee is forty percent of the award. And considering your years of pain and suffering and the infertility that resulted from the assault, we're going to be asking for one hellofa lot of money."

The sign in front of the small building that Laura had entered listed three attorneys: Shelly Spinks, Rodger Appleby and Ira Simon. Rana called 411 and got their office telephone number.

"Good morning. Spinks, Appleby and Simon."

"Do any of your lawyers handle sexual assault cases?" Rana asked.

"Why, yes. That would be Ms. Spinks. Would you like to make an appointment?"

"No. I'm calling for a friend." Rana smiled. Shelly Spinks. What an interesting name.

Peter Rizzolo

Chapter Twenty

Dr. Jane Corbett became somewhat of a celebrity following her presentation in Orlando and subsequent exposure on national television. She made the rounds of several daytime talk shows, as well as the Larry King Show, where she appeared with a gynecologist, a forensic pathologist, and a woman who had been the victim of sexual assault.

In all of Dr. Corbett's encounters with the press, she steadfastly refused to go beyond identifying her patient as Ms. Jane Doe. A recurring question was how many times had she searched for DNA in specimens removed from women with diseased fallopian tubes? Was the DNA preserved because of the untreated gonorrhea infection? Yes and no, Dr. Corbett asserted. The infection may have created an environment that contributed to the preservation of the rapist's DNA in the case of Jane Doe. But other mechanisms might be involved.

Other fertility experts shared the limelight. Some pooh-poohed her results, while others considered them interesting and provocative. Mal

Greene, Michael Greene and Lester Knowles also thought them provocative, but could not decide on a course of action. They met in Lester's office in downtown Philadelphia.

Mal Greene wanted to do something, but didn't know what. Michael Greene vacillated between doing nothing and taking a leave of absence from his residency training to spend a year at sea. His dad owned a thirty-six foot, sea-worthy sloop that the family seldom used. Michael, as a young boy, had crewed for his father, who was a skilled sailor but an overbearing, demanding skipper. As a teenager Michael refused to sail with his dad, and instead took private sailing lessons. He grew to love the sea. Of course, to circumnavigate the world, Michael would need an experienced crew.

"Might just as well sign a confession as cut and run," Mal said.

"Dad," Michael said, "I've gone from high school through premed, medical school and now residency without a break."

"I agree with your dad, Michael. A hard-working doctor will generate more sympathy than a playboy tooling around the world in a yacht."

A thirty-six foot sloop was hardly a yacht, Michael thought. But he had just thrown out the idea, and wasn't convinced taking off for a year was the right thing to do. And he wasn't worried about resuming his training after a long break. His credentials were outstanding. He'd have his pick of training programs. But he would like to at least complete his internship.

"I don't think we can take the risk of waiting for her to make the first move," Les said. "If she decides to go to the police, we're in for a public scandal regardless of the outcome."

"What are you suggesting?" Mal asked.

"I call her attorney and suggest a meeting."

"Her attorney? She has an attorney?" Michael asked.

Lester looked at Mal. He obviously hadn't told Michael what Rana had discovered. "Got a call from Rana," Les said. "She went to an attorney's office a couple of days ago."

Michael shot an angry glance at his father. He wondered what else they might not have told him. The photos he had given her had obviously not dissuaded her from moving ahead with her plans. Her going to a lawyer changed everything.

"Meant to call you, Michael. I know how busy you are."

"I'm the damn client here...."

"I should have contacted you directly," Les said. "You're absolutely right."

Mal's face reddened. "Yeah, you're the client, son, but as long as I'm the one paying the bills, I'm making the decisions."

"I might just get my own attorney," Michael said.

"On your salary? I can imagine the kind of second-rate hack you could afford."

"Mother will give me whatever I need."

"Over my dead body!"

"Come on, you two," Les said. "We're a team. We have to pull together. Laura Hamby going to a lawyer is the best thing that could have happened."

"No," Michael said. "The best thing would have been for her to drop the entire matter, and neither of you were able to figure out a way to abort the situation." Michael was angry with himself for not having gone ahead with his plan regarding the photographs he had taken of her naked body.

Mal shook his head dismissively. "Like what? Hire a hit man? Okay, so her going to an attorney is the second best possible outcome. Where do we go from here, Les?"

"The fact that she's gone to a lawyer suggests that she's entertaining the possibility of at least a civil action. I contact the attorney. See what her client really wants. Will she settle for money, with a guarantee not to go public, and not pursue further action?"

"Could we hold her to that?" Michael asked.

"We can draw up a contract."

"So she banks the money, and then goes to the police," Mal said.

"I agree with Les, Dad. If we throw enough money her way, why would she want to risk going to trial?"

"Because my gut tells me she won't be satisfied with just money," Mal said. "She has no family to embarrass, other than her husband, and he already knows about it. Besides, the rape happened so long ago she probably doesn't really give a crap about public scrutiny."

"Let's say she signs a contract, takes the money, and then turns around and goes to the police," Les said.

"Exactly," Mal said. "What's to stop her?"

Michael was weary of the endless speculation. He had to bite his lip to keep from telling them about the photos. He stood and walked to a tall window that offered an expansive, twenty-story view of downtown Philadelphia. He asked, still gazing at the bumper-to-bumper traffic below, "Has Rana dug up anything on Dr. Corbett?"

"She's been an expert witness in a couple of rape cases," Les said. "He got a list of her published articles. Half of them are about rape and the use of DNA evidence."

"Makes you wonder if she's ever been a victim," Mal speculated.

"I have a team of paralegals checking that out."

"Anything else?" Mal asked.

"She had one malpractice suit that was settled out of court. Never had her license suspended."

"Any personal stuff?"

"Divorced, two young children and a live-in nanny."

"Legal?" Mal asked.

"Don't know yet."

"I don't care if she ate her grandparents," Michael said. "What the hell difference does it make?"

"If this ever goes to trial, her credibility makes a hellofa difference," Les said. "And if she's ever been raped, her motivation definitely comes into question."

Michael's cell phone rang. "Hi, Jay. Thanks for covering for me....Okay....Okay. I'll be there in fifteen minutes. Sure, I'll go directly to the ER. Thanks, Jay." Michael slipped the phone into his pocket. "Lester, Dad, I've got to run. School bus accident just showed up in the ER."

"Sure, son. Go do your thing. Don't worry, we'll work this out."

I am going to do my thing, Michael thought. Two highly paid attorneys are not getting the job done. It's time to take matters into my own hands.

Chapter Twenty-One

Before leaving Shelly Spinks' office, Laura signed a release of medical information, enabling Shelly to obtain a copy of her medical record from Dr. Corbett. In addition, Shelly asked Laura to prepare an account of when she met Michael Greene, their first date, and a detailed chronological recounting of the night of the party at Luke's house. She was to include any contact she might have had with him in the weeks following the assault.

Laura decided to take the remainder of the day off in order to prepare the information. Jubilee, who usually greeted Laura at her apartment when she arrived home from work, was sleeping peacefully on the sheepskin rug in front of the fireplace. She opened her eyes, stared at Laura for a moment, then glanced at the mantle clock before dropping back off to sleep.

Laura laughed. Could Jubilee actually tell time? Laura kicked off her shoes and sat next to her cat. She stared at the unlit ceramic logs. Both she and Jubilee jumped when the phone rang. It was Shelly.

"I just got a call from an attorney named Lester Knowles. He's representing Michael Greene."

Laura flopped back into a chair next to the phone. "How can that be? No one knew I was going to see you."

"You didn't tell anyone?"

"Bruce knew, of course. We talked last night. But no one else."

"Either your phone's bugged, which I seriously doubt, or someone followed you to my office."

It gave Laura the creeps to realize that someone could still be following her. But at least she knew she had Michael's attention.

"What did his lawyer want?" Laura asked.

"They want to set up a meeting. Me, you, his lawyer, Greene, and Greene's father."

"But we haven't even charged him with anything. What's there to talk about?"

"That's exactly the point. They're looking to settle out of court. They throw a bunch of money at us and Michael walks away without a scratch. They also may be looking to see what kind of case we have. Maybe stall things long enough to dig up some dirt on you, honey."

"Dirt? There's no dirt."

"They don't know that," Shelly said.

"Why should we meet with them?"

"We have nothing to lose. We play our cards close to our chests. See just how much money they're prepared to offer."

"Do they really think they can buy me off?"

"I'd try if I were in their shoes."

"I have no intention of settling out-of-court," Laura said. "When should we meet?"

"The sooner the better. I'll call them back. Will ten in the morning, a week from today, be okay with you?"

"Yes."

"In the meantime," Shelly said, "I'll prepare an official complaint. We'll be ready to file that afternoon."

Laura spent the remainder of the day at the dining room table hand-writing an account of everything she could recall about her one and only date with Michael and the party at Luke's. She used her junior-class yearbook to look up the last names of some of the kids she only recalled on a first-name basis. As she flipped through the pages she saw a picture of Jimmy Caniglia posing with the swim team. She had had a big-time crush on him their junior year. They didn't really date, but he and she were part of a group of kids who palled around together. Someone had once referred to them as the "Brainy Bunch." The name stuck.

One Saturday night in the fall of Laura's junior year at Central High, the Brainy Bunch went to see Clint Eastwood in *The Unforgiven*. Afterwards Ginger suggested they go swimming at the abandoned limestone quarry outside of town. Everyone but Laura was excited. She was spooked about swimming after dark.

The previous summer, a kid had drowned at the quarry. Jimmy, whose dad had been a diver in the Navy, told them that swimming in such deep water was risky, even for strong swimmers. He said that below fifteen to twenty feet you lose your natural buoyancy and begin to sink. And in the dark, that would be especially disorienting…believing you were rising to the surface, but instead you're heading for the bottom. He had told her that if you didn't know which way was up, just let out a little air, and follow your bubbles.

"My mother expects me home by nine. She'll have the National Guard out."

"Cool," Ginger said. "Might be some cute guys."

Ginger had long, flaming red hair and a figure the boys appreciated, the girls envied.

"Call her," another girl said. "Tell her we're going to get something to eat. You'll be home around ten-thirty."

"But we have no bathing suits or towels," Laura said.

One of the girls said, "I'll stop by my house, it's on the way. I'll grab a bunch of towels."

Laura wasn't about to skinny-dip, but she knew some of the other kids might. She was thinking about the condition of her underwear. Jimmy came to her and put his arm around her shoulder.

"Come on, Laura. Going won't be any fun without you." Jimmy had dark curly hair and a smile that did strange things to Laura's knees. "We can build a fire," Jimmy said. "You can explain the ending of that movie. Besides I want to show you a new dive I've been working on."

Suddenly everyone was looking at Laura. She was too embarrassed not to go. "Okay. But I'm not going in the water. It's icy cold this time of year."

The boys led the way in Jimmy's green 1980 Toyota Corona. The girls followed in Ginger's red Mazda coupe.. The quarry had been abandoned years ago, but the property still belonged to the mining company. The quarry was the size of two football fields, with steep banks on three sides and a beach area that trucks had once used to carry away the limestone. Laura said a little prayer of thanksgiving that there was only a sliver of moon and plenty of clouds

As soon as they got there, the four boys threw their towels onto the gravelly beach, stripped down to their jockey shorts and went running into the water, shouting for the girls to join them. The girls stood looking at each other; no one wanted be the first to undress. Finally, Ginger slipped off her jeans and t-shirt. She stood there in her black lace bra and frilly panties.

"Well, come on, you gals! I'm not doing this alone."

Within minutes they were all in the water. The boys were playing water tag. The girls joined in. Laura, not the greatest swimmer, was the pursuer a good deal of the time. No one could catch Jimmy, but Ginger went for him with determination. He dove deeper than any of the others dared to go. As Ginger jack-knifed to dive after him, her panties remained on the surface of the water. Laura wasn't so sure it was an accident. A boy grabbed them and started throwing her panties from boy to boy. Ginger splashed around, pretending she was trying to retrieve them.

"What the hell," Ginger said. She slipped off her bra and threw it to Jimmy. Pretty soon they all started taking off their underwear. They played in the water like a school of dolphins, swimming in ever wider circles until they were some distance from the beach. Laura was growing tired, but she didn't want to admit it. She was relieved when one of the other girls said she was pooped and started heading back.

The boys promised to face the other way as the girls dried off and got dressed. As they ran up the beach Ginger looked back and shouted. "Hey, you guys, you promised."

Laura wondered how many bras and panties had settled to the bottom of the quarry over the years. As the girls were drying off, a police car pulled up, flashing its lights and directing its high-beams on the four of them. They covered themselves as best they could with their towels. Two troopers stepped out of the car. They looked as though they had just won the lottery. One of them drew his gun. "Put your hands over your heads, ladies," he ordered

They hesitated. "Come on now," the second officer said. "Put your hands over your heads."

Their towels dropped to the ground as they raised their arms.

"Didn't you see that no trespassing sign back a ways?"

As he spoke to the girls, the second officer ordered the boys out of the water. While they were scrambling to shore he went to the patrol car and came back with a Polaroid camera. They herded the naked kids together and snapped a few pictures.

"Okay, now. You all get dressed."

Before they left, the policemen searched the girls' purses and made the boys empty their pockets. One boy was carrying a pack of condoms. Another boy had a couple of reefers in his shirt pocket. They found a six-pack of beer in the trunk of Jimmy's car.

"You are all under arrest for trespassing, indecent exposure and possession of illegal and intoxicating substances."

No one said a word as they followed the police car to the station. Finally Ginger spoke up. "Screw them. We didn't do anything wrong. Everybody swims in the quarry. And I'm telling the magistrate he drew his gun on us and made us drop our towels."

Laura was shaking so badly she could hardly speak. All she could think about was those Polaroids. Would they wind up in the papers?

The magistrate was angrier at the officers than at the kids. He said he and his friends swam at the quarry all the time when he went to high school. When Ginger told him about the officer drawing his gun on them, the magistrate reprimanded the officer and demanded he turn over the Polaroids. He studied them for longer than Laura thought was necessary. He looked up. "Now, I'm not charging you with trespassing or indecent exposure, but Tom Watkins, who had the reefers in his possession, is charged with a misdemeanor. Since he's had no previous offense, we will not lock him up. But he will have to do sixty hours of volunteer work at the drug treatment center. For the rest of you, your parents will be notified and asked to come down to the station."

Two days later an article appeared in police blotter of the Allentown Daily:

"Saturday night at the abandoned stone quarry on Satterville Road, Officers Tim Jorden and Claude Langley arrested eight teenagers for trespassing, indecent exposure, and drug and alcohol possession.

One received a misdemeanor charge for possession of marijuana and ordered to 60 hours of community service at the Victoria Jones Treatment Center. The other seven were charged with trespassing and released into the custody of their parents.

A son of one of the arresting officers was a junior at Central High. He had overheard his mother and father talking about what had happened. His dad was showing his mother one of the Polaroids that he hadn't given to the judge. They were looking at the photo and laughing when the boy entered the room.

"What's so funny?" he asked.

His dad folded the photo. "Nothing that would interest you, son."

But the boy was very interested. He returned home on his lunch hour and went into his parents' bedroom. His mom and dad were both at work. The boy found the photo on his dad's dresser.

"Holy crap," he exclaimed. He went to his computer, scanned in the photo and printed himself a copy. That afternoon he showed the photo around at school. Although Laura and her friends, except maybe Ginger, were mortified, they did bask in a kind of celebrity status among the other students.

Laura decided that her skinny-dipping adventure, the newspaper story and notorious Polaroid, should be included in the report she was preparing for Shelly.

Chapter Twenty-Two

Although Lester Knowles arranged for Michael and Michael's father to meet with him to plan their strategy, unknown to them, Michael had decided to move ahead with his own plan. He wanted to arrange a face-to-face with Laura. No Lester. No big daddy. Just the two of them. He called her at work.

"Laura?"

"Yes?"

"It's me, Michael."

She was shocked. They were to get together with the attorney in just a few days. Why was he calling? Had his lawyer put him up to it?

"Laura, are you there?"

She was at her desk. There were a number of people milling about. She cupped the mouthpiece. "What do you want?"

"To meet with you."

"But we..."

"Just the two of us. No lawyers. I have so much I want to say to you."

"Oh? Like what? You were just a kid. You were drunk?"

"Please, Laura. I can't do this over the phone."

This was insane. Was he ready to admit his guilt and beg her to forgive him? How she would love to see him grovel. She would listen unmoved, then tell him some hard jail time was what he needed to appease his new-found remorse. But what exactly did he have in mind? Her curiosity won out over her better judgment.

"Where? When?" Laura asked.

"Morrisville is about midway between South Orange and Philadelphia. There's a great restaurant at the Morrisville Inn. Meet you there at 8:30?"

"No." Laura was familiar with Morrisville. She was not about to meet him at a damn hotel. "There's a coffee shop on Main Street, the Gourmet Beanery."

"I've been there. See you at 8:30 tomorrow night."

As Laura replaced the handset, she considered calling Shelly, but decided not to. Nor would she tell Bruce. He would never agree to let her go. Was Michael really doing this without his lawyer's knowledge? For some reason she believed him. Why? Why should she trust him? Maybe she should wear some sort of recording device. Was that legal without a court order? She couldn't wait to discuss this new wrinkle with Rose and Lilly. They were getting together for lunch the following day.

Laura, Lilly and Rose sat in a booth at a small Greek luncheonette famous for its salads. They had finished eating and were working on their baklava when Laura brought up the meeting with Michael Greene.

"You haven't told Bruce or your lawyer?" Rose asked in disbelief.

"No. I'm sure they would talk me out of it."

"Damn right they would," Lilly said. "Do what your gut tells you. You have nothing to lose."

"I'd be afraid to go," Rose said. "He's desperate. Who knows what he might do?"

"Come on," Laura said. "Do you really think I would be in any danger? It's not as though we're meeting in a back alley somewhere."

They drank their coffee in silence as the waiter cleared the table.

"Maybe this was his lawyer's idea," Rose said. "How will meeting with him look to a jury? A man you accuse of raping you. Maybe he'll wear a wire. Maybe someone will be there to photograph you. I would have told him to go to hell."

Laura laughed. "You're reading too many who-done-its."

"What good can possibly come of this?" Rose asked.

"I don't know. I'm just dying to learn what he's up to."

"I know exactly why you're going. You want him to admit his guilt," Lilly said. "To tell you he is sorry for the pain he's caused you. Even if it's all bullshit, you would love to hear him beg."

"That is pretty close to how I feel," Laura said.

"But where was he all those years?" Rose asked. "It's only when you threaten to expose him for the bastard he is, that he comes to you. Forget the meeting. It's time to make him pay."

Laura felt better having unloaded her concerns on Rose and Lilly. Rose had almost convinced her not to go, but Lilly had been somewhat supportive. The thought of confronting Michael, face-to-face, increased her determination to follow her own instincts.

Would Michael's private admission of guilt and remorse be enough to make her willing to agree to a financial settlement? Her intellect told her that particular resolution of her dilemma made a lot of sense. She and Bruce needed money, lots of money if they went ahead with their plan for a test-tube baby.

After lunch, Laura stopped by the chapel at St. Joe's hospital. It was deserted except for a nun sitting in a pew at the rear, reading from a prayer book. Laura walked to a side alter where there was a bank of votive candles. She lit one and prayed for guidance. She looked at the large cross suspended above the altar, recalling Jesus' words as he hung suspended by the nails that pierced his hands and feet, enduring unimaginable pain: "Forgive them, Father, for they know not what they do." No mere mortal could possibly live up to that standard of compassion and forgiveness. She recalled the newspaper account of Pope John Paul's visit to the imprisoned man who shot and almost fatally wounded him. Although John Paul forgave his would-be assassin, as far as Laura knew, the Pope did not advocate granting him a pardon. Yes, the Pope would be her role model. She would do all she could to see that Michael be found guilty in a court of law.

On the way home to change her clothes, Laura stopped at a local electronics outlet and inquired about a tape recorder that would be small enough to hide. The clerk showed her a miniature digital recorder with a built-in microphone that she could clip to an undergarment. Unlike a tape recorder, it made no noise. There were no moving parts. It could record for up to two hours. He gave her a quick lesson in how to use it.

"Is taping a conversation without the other person's knowledge legal?" Laura asked the clerk. She assumed he might be asked that question a lot.

"It's legal in most states. As long as the person doing the taping is part of the conversation. It's called one-party consent."

"What about New Jersey?" she asked.

"It's perfectly legal here."

At home she clipped the recorder onto the front of her bra and put on a loose-fitting sweater. She checked herself in the mirror in various positions. The recorder was totally undetectable. She taped a few nonsense lines, and then played them back to make sure the unit was working. It functioned perfectly. Before leaving their apartment, she wrote Bruce a note saying she'd be back by around ten. Minutes later, she was speeding toward Morrisville in her Volkswagen Beetle.

Laura was of course unaware of the tracking device Rana Akthar had attached to the underside of her rear fender. He was seated in his parked car a block from her apartment. He wondered where she might be going. Bruce's car was gone from its usual parking place. Was she slipping out for an evening with her two lady friends? Or better yet, maybe a gentleman friend? Before taking off after her, he checked his photographic equipment: an SLR with a telephoto lens and a miniature digital camera. This might prove to be a very productive evening.

Michael Greene smiled as he replaced the handset. He wasn't surprised that Laura had agreed to meet him. Courage, imagination and more than a little recklessness were involved in her decision to go to the University of Pennsylvania Hospital and steal a sample of his blood. His plea had tweaked her curiosity. Too bad she hadn't agreed to meeting at the Morrisville Inn. He was hoping that after convincing her of what really happened that night, she'd agree to drop all charges against him. He, in a seemingly impulsive gesture of benevolence, would agree to pay her medical expenses. Then he'd order a bottle of the hotel's most expensive wine, and vow to help her track down the boys who raped her. He had reserved a room at the Inn just in case a second bottle of wine might put her in the right mood. As Michael prepared to meet Laura, he taped a recording device to his chest.

Chapter Twenty-Three

Laura had stopped at the Gourmet Beanery on her last drive to Philadelphia. She arrived there a few minutes late, and when she prepared to call Rose, as she had promised, Michael pulled into the parking lot. She scrunched down in her seat. Michael stepped from the car. He was wearing chinos, a sports shirt, and carried a ski jacket over one shoulder. He checked his watch as he passed her car and entered the café.

Her heart raced as she dialed Rose's number.

"Laura! I've been staying by the phone waiting for your call."

"He just went inside. He didn't see me sitting here."

"Good. Don't go in. The bastard raped you, for God sakes."

"I'm not afraid of him."

"You sound scared to me," Rose said.

"I'm a little nervous, that's all."

"You tell Bruce?" Rose asked.

"Are you crazy? He'd never let me come."

"Call me before you head back home. I won't be able to sleep not knowing what happened."

"I will," Laura promised.

Laura ordered a cappuccino and looked about the room. Michael, sitting at a corner table, stood and waved to her.

"I thought I was about to be stood up." He smiled. "Can I get you a Danish or a biscotti?"

She ignored his offer. "Let's dispense with the small talk, Michael. Why did you ask me here?" She draped her coat over the back of her chair.

"I don't want to see you blindsided at that conference with my lawyer and my father."

She sipped her coffee. "Blindsided?"

"Have you ever heard of blackouts related to alcohol?"

"I was wide awake and kicking."

"Do you know what time it was when you began to scream, and the girls rushed into the room and found you with your hands tied to the bedpost?"

"You heard me scream?

"No. Martha told me the next day."

She wondered where this might be leading. She had gotten home a little before eleven thirty.

"It was nine thirty when Arnold picked you up after you had fallen. I knew that because I snapped your picture. My camera marks the date and time. You were in that bedroom an hour and a half before those boys raped you."

Laura remembered trying to get Martha's attention, telling her it was nine-thirty and that she had to be home by ten. "I must have been sleeping."

"You weren't sleeping, Laura...For a long time I didn't understand why you didn't call me. I wanted to call you, but the way you looked at me at school I knew you were angry. I was frantic when I learned you had dropped out of school and left home." *And that you might be pregnant, he thought.*

This wasn't what Laura had expected or hoped for. She shook her head in disbelief. "You were frantic I might go to the police. Relieved that I left."

"I went up to the bedroom where Arnold had brought you. You appeared to be asleep. I sat on the edge of the bed. I kissed your cheek. You opened your eyes. I touched your breast. You smiled. You pulled me toward you."

"You're lying."

"We made love."

"That's preposterous," Laura said.

"It was the first time for me," Michael said. "And I could tell you were a virgin. Afterwards you fell off to sleep. I got dressed and went downstairs. Whoever attacked you must have come into the room soon after I left."

Laura stabbed her index finger in his direction. She punctuated each word with a jab. "Sober, drunk or drugged, I would NEVER make love to you."

"I was shocked and angry when Martha told me of hearing your screams, then finding you in the bedroom naked and bleeding."

"And why didn't you come to my rescue?"

"After I left the bedroom I went downstairs. I flopped onto a couch. I must have passed out."

Laura, aware of the recorder nestled between her breasts, chose her words carefully. She wanted to tell him his story was pure bullshit, but said, "I've had vodka since then. What you gave me was definitely mostly water."

"Alcohol can do different things to your brain, Laura. It can make you sick as hell, and if you drink it fast enough you can pass out. A blackout is alcohol-induced amnesia that can last a few minutes, a few hours or even a few days. You can be fully awake in a blackout."

Laura had always assumed that a blackout was the same as passing out. She knew that alcoholics had memory lapses, but had never thought of those as blackouts.

"It's the only possible explanation for you not remembering us making love," Michael said.

"It never happened. That's why I don't remember."

"Those boys raped you. I had nothing to do with that."

"You were one of them. I recognized your voice, remember?"

"You were terrified, disoriented," Michael said. "I can understand why you'd make such a mistake. Not until after I had some medical training that I learned how common alcohol-induced amnesia really is. If you're not used to drinking it doesn't take much."

She knew he was lying. There was no way she could have made love to him and not remembered. But she didn't know enough about alcohol or amnesia to argue. Could what he had told her about alcohol amnesia be true? She had no witnesses placing him in the room with the other boys. "Was this fairytale your lawyer's idea?"

"This meeting was entirely my idea. No one else knows. I'm convinced you can't win this suit. I don't want to humiliate you."

"You have already humiliated me. That's what this fight is all about." Laura stood and grabbed her coat. She realized how naïve she had been, believing he might say something to incriminate himself. He had caught her totally by surprise. "I have nothing more to say to you, Michael."

"There's one other thing, Laura." He reached into his pocket and unfolded a photograph. He held onto it as she looked at it in disbelief. She was lying naked on a rumpled bed. She recognized the bed, the room. In the photo she lay smiling at the camera. Laura's face was crimson as she studied it. In the photo her legs were crossed, her panties were dangling from her foot. She could not bring herself to look up at Michael. Laura was too shocked to speak. She reached for the photo. He pulled it from her grasp and crumpled it in his fist. "This is the only copy I have," Michael said. "No one else will ever see it. I would never use it, even to prove my innocence."

"It's impossible. I . . . I don't remember . . ."

Michael stuffed the photo into his empty coffee cup and ignited it with a cigarette lighter. As flames rose from the cup, a young man from behind the counter rushed over to their table with a pitcher of water. The flames were quickly extinguished. Ashes and water flooded the table.

"How'd that catch fire?" the boy asked.

"We finally got our mortgage paid off. We decided to burn the document," Michael said. "Sorry about the mess." He removed his wallet and handed the boy a ten-dollar bill.

The boy pocketed the money. "Okay. Don't worry about it."

Laura watched in disbelief. The photo was his trump card. Why would he burn it?

"I haven't told my father or my lawyer about this photo or what really happened."

"I don't believe you. I don't believe any of this." Even as she said those words her mind was suffused with the image of her naked body; the birth-mark on her right hip; the dark mole below her left breast; the stupid smile on her face. God in heaven, how could she not remember?

"My attorney intends to offer you cash in return for a written agreement to drop the case. If they knew about that photo they'd offer you nothing." Michael slipped on his ski jacket. "Take the money, Laura."

Rana Akthar had entered the coffee shop, ordered a double espresso and sat two tables from Michael and Laura. He was able to snap several pictures with a miniature camera he held in his palm. He was almost certain Lester Knowles had no knowledge of this meeting. What had Michael shown her? Why did he torch it? *This case is getting very interesting,*

He surmised from the way Laura stomped out of the coffee shop, and from the smug expression on Michael's face, that he had gotten the better of her. Too bad he hadn't sat close enough to have overheard their conversation. The photos Rana had taken might prove useful in Michael's defense. Lester Knowles would be very pleased. Rana anticipated a handsome bonus. A jury, Rana thought, would question the motivation of a woman who would meet with the man she accuses of having brutally raped her. Rana could almost hear Lester Knowles saying: "Her behavior, ladies and gentleman of the jury, has the rotten smell of a scheme to extort money from a man, a physician she knows to be innocent, not the behavior of a woman in the pursuit of justice."

Peter Rizzolo

Chapter Twenty-Four

Laura left the turnpike at a rest area, removed the digital recorder, hit the play button, and slumped back in her seat. Their conversation had taken less than thirty minutes. Michael sounded poised. He chose his words with such precision that she was certain he was wired. No doubt he was hoping she would say something stupid. Something he could use to support his case. His explanation as to how his DNA had gotten into her body seemed unbelievable until he sprang that photo on her. Despite the photo, she refused to believe she had willingly had sex with him. But whether a jury believed him or not, his amnesia theory would establish grounds for greater weight of evidence. She was incredulous that he would have destroyed his only copy. Did he have others, even more outrageous?

She called Rose as she had promised. Laura wanted to sound composed, reassuring, but on hearing her friend's voice, she couldn't control herself. She began to cry. "The son-of-a-bitch ...."

"My God. What happened?"

"You were right. I shouldn't have met with him."

"You want to come by before you go home?"

"I called Bruce. Told him I'm on the way. Can you stop by tomorrow morning before you leave for work?"

"Seven-thirty too early?" Rose asked.

"Okay. Don't eat breakfast. I'll fix something."

When Laura arrived at her apartment, Bruce was on the kitchen phone. He hung up as she entered. "I can't believe you didn't tell me."

"Rose called you?"

"No. I called her. I thought you might be there."

Laura sat at the table. "I wanted to tell you, but I knew you'd talk me out of it."

"You're damn right I would. First you run off to Philly to steal a blood specimen without telling me. Now this. God almighty, this business is screwing up your brain."

Laura's eyes flooded with tears. He was right. In both instances she had prejudged his reaction. She hadn't trusted that he could be supportive. He had every right to be pissed. "I'm sorry. You're right. This thing is making me crazy."

Bruce walked over and stood behind her. He pulled her toward him. "It's okay," he whispered. "If he bullied you, I swear...."

"No. He was disgustingly polite." She reached for a napkin to wipe her eyes. "He tried to convince me I had no case. To take the money and move on." Laura couldn't bring herself to tell him about the photograph. She couldn't believe she would have had consensual sex with Michael Greene. She handed Bruce the digital recorder. "Listen to this."

He listened to the entire recording in silence. "Does he really expect us to believe that crap about you being blacked out, not remembering what happened? What the hell did he show you?"

"A picture of me in that room. Smiling like an idiot at the camera."

"That doesn't prove a damn thing, except that he was there. If he took that picture, that is."

She couldn't look at Bruce. He grasped her head and turned it toward him. "What aren't you telling me?"

"The photo he showed me. I was naked. I swear I don't remember." She pressed her head against his chest.

"Because it didn't happen. That's why."

"But the picture--it was me. Could he be right? Was I really blacked out?"

"Did you get a good look at the photo before he burned it?"

"Yes," Laura said. "I can still see every disgusting detail when I close my eyes."

"Wasn't he the photographer for the school paper?"

Laura searched his face for the answer she wanted to hear. "You think he altered the picture?"

"Why else would he destroy it?"

"I should've been able to tell."

"Not if it's done well."

Laura was puzzled. "How do you know that?"

"I'm on the computer all the time at work. I've been playing around with a graphics program on my lunch hour."

Laura kicked off her shoes. "I'm feeling better already. You hungry?"

"I'm always hungry."

She microwaved some left-over Chinese take-out. They sat at the table eating shrimp, chicken, rice and water chestnuts from the same bowl. Neither spoke for several minutes. Laura desperately wanted Bruce to be right. But what if she made that assumption and the picture wasn't doctored? Michael almost certainly had other photos of her.

"Didn't you tell me he gave you a flask that he had half-filled with vodka?" Bruce asked between bites.

"It tasted pretty watered down. There's no way I could have drunk straight vodka."

"Even if it were straight vodka, half a flask would amount to maybe three drinks at the most. I don't think that would be enough alcohol to make you black out."

"I could hardly stand."

"I'm not saying you weren't drunk. But you remember everything up to the time you fell asleep?"

"There was an hour and a half between the time I fell asleep and the time I remember waking up. He says we made love. I say I was passed out. Who is a jury going to believe? He's going to appear to be noble as hell for having destroyed a piece of evidence that would have showed his innocence."

"There's got to be a way to prove he's lying."

Even if his story was pure fabrication, Laura thought, what had happened was Michael's word against someone whose only defense was that she was in an alcohol-induced stupor. Michael had succeeded in planting a degree of doubt in her mind. For the first time since wanting to see him convicted of rape, Laura felt she had little chance of succeeding. There must also be at least a splinter of doubt in Bruce's mind that the photo Michael showed her was real. If she were to drop charges and take a cash payoff, that splinter could develop into a festering wound.

Laura put her arm around Bruce's waist and leaned into his shoulder. "I love you, sweetheart. I don't want this or anything ever to come between us."

"I'll be damned," Lester Knowles said as he studied the photos Rana had taken at the Gourmet Beanery in Morrisville. "I would love to know what in hell he showed her."

"He held an eight-by-ten photograph. Unfortunately the lighting was poor. I couldn't make it out," Rana said.

Lester removed a rosewood canister from his desk drawer and offered Rana a Generics cigar. Despite the embargo on the importation of cigars from Cuba, Lester was willing to pay the price on the black market to insure a steady supply. They enjoyed their cigars in silence.

"Too bad you weren't able to overhear their conversation," Lester said.

"The deaf, it is said, listen with their eyes. Might I offer a theory?" This was the part of his job that Rana relished. His boss was a genius in the courtroom, but by no means a shrewd analyst.

"Absolutely."

In the past Lester had given Rana sizable bonuses for his input over and above his investigative efforts. "The ritual burning of a photograph after showing it to a woman who has accused you of rape does not require words. The metaphor is double-edged. One interpretation is, 'I am such a nice guy I'm willing to destroy damaging evidence.'"

"And the other?" Lester asked.

"'If you come after me, I will burn you.'"

Lester leaned back in his chair. "If he intends to blackmail her, it makes no sense to destroy the evidence."

"Burning the photo would seem illogical if she assumed he intends to use it to blackmail her," Rana said. "But if he claimed he did it to protect her reputation, despite the fact that she seemed determined to destroy his future career and quite possibly send him off to jail, that would be quite a remarkable thing to do."

"That's not the Michael I know," Lester said.

"He is a complex young man."

"What could he possibly have shown her? All you came up with was that skinny-dipping story. Hardly a smoking gun."

"I saw her shocked expression. Whatever it was, he had reason to believe the photograph was a powerful disincentive for her to want to go to court."

"But why didn't he show us whatever it was he had?"

"If Michael were to come to you and tell you about the damaging evidence he has, then his motive would be for you to drop that on her at the pretrial meeting. You would most likely offer her nothing."

"Interesting, interesting." Lester extinguished his cigar. "And since he hadn't come to me?"

Rana carefully put out his cigar. He would save it to enjoy later. "I see two possibilities. He might have asked her to take the money and not pursue charging him with rape...."

"That makes sense. It's his father's money."

"Or he might have asked her to agree to split the award with him."

Lester laughed. "Scam his own father? Now that's the Michael I know and love."

Lester decided not to inform Mal Greene about Michael's meeting with Laura. Technically, doing so would violate attorney/client confidentiality. Furthermore, he had already planned his strategy for the conference with Laura and her attorney. Lester would maintain that despite the purported DNA evidence suggesting Michael at some point in time may have had sex with Laura Hamby, there was no evidence establishing when that had occurred.

Michael was to maintain that he had not sexually assaulted Laura, but that he did feel some sense of responsibility for what had happened. He had seen a boy carry her upstairs to the bedroom area. In fact he had a photograph that showed her awake and smiling. He could only assume that whatever followed was consensual. He regretted that he had made that assumption. If he hadn't, he may have been able to prevent the assault.

Lester would argue that no one would gain from taking this matter into court. That in defense of his client he would use every means necessary to discredit the accuser. And if the defense were to prevail, what would Laura Hamby have gained? Her presumably happy marriage would be in crisis, her reputation sullied, and she might well be at risk of a countersuit for defamation of character. She had invaded his client's privacy by illegally gaining access to Michael Greene's medical record and subsequently stealing a specimen of his blood.

Lester felt reasonably confident that Shelley Spinks would understand that the likelihood of convincing a jury of Michael's guilt was not good. Mal Greene had authorized Lester to go as high as $250,000. This was more than generous, considering she would most likely end up empty-handed if she went to court. Shelly would advise her client to agree to a pretrial settlement, Lester thought. Michael walks, and Mal is free to become campaign manager for his brother, State Senator Joe Greene, poised to toss his hat into the ring to become governor of Pennsylvania. Lester's fee would be relatively modest, but to have Mal Greene's brother in the governor's mansion would be priceless.

Chapter Twenty-Five

Rose sat at the kitchen table sipping a cup of black coffee while Laura scrambled eggs, popped a couple of slices of bread in the toaster and removed a platter of bacon warming in the oven.

"So much trouble," Rose said. "A cup of espresso works for me."

Rose was wearing Gabriella Rocha leather boots, tailored slacks and a long-sleeve cotton turtle-neck. Laura was still in a knee-length flannel gown that had seen better times.

"That's why you're svelte, and I'm svelte plus," Laura said.

"It is the *plus* some men like," Rose said. She forked another slice of bacon. "You told me nothing on the phone except that he is a son-of-a-bitch. I already knew that."

Laura poured herself a cup of coffee and sat at the table. She recounted her meeting with Michael.

"It is impossible a woman does not remember making love to a man," Rose said. "Alcohol does not turn a seventeen-year-old girl into a *puttana.*"

"I felt like a whore when I saw that photo." She looked at the photos anchored to her refrigerator door by tiny magnets: smiling friends; she and Bruce white-water rafting: and of course a few of Jubilee.

"It's a shame you didn't take it from him."

"I wish I had! I was too shocked to move."

"So what do you do now? Take the money and let him get away with this?" Rose asked.

"I couldn't sleep last night. I was on the internet learning about blackouts. Alcohol can mess up a person's brain. And it takes a lot less to mess up a woman's brain. It's related to body weight and how fast and how much you drink. I'm convinced it wasn't just alcohol that made me pass out. He must have put something in the vodka."

"Like what?"

"There are all sorts of drugs he could have used. Some of them are tasteless. Bruce says that at Penn State they were pretty easy to get."

"So what will happen now?" Rose asked.

"What would you do?" Laura asked.

"I would spit on his filthy money."

Laura wanted to hug Rose. The thought of pocketing his bribe and walking away made her feel cowardly, spineless. "My lawyer's convinced there's very little chance of convicting him in criminal court."

"She does not know of the photo?"

"Not yet. You think it makes him more vulnerable?"

"I don't know. I am not a lawyer. To me it is as though he has attacked you a second time." She glanced at her watch. "I must go or I'll be late for class."

At the door they hugged. Laura whispered. "The idea that he has kept that photo all these years . . . makes me crazy."

Laura dialed Shelly's office number. She told Shelly that it was urgent they get together.

"Oh?" Shelly asked.

"I met with Michael."

"You what? Are you insane? Damnit, Laura, I told you to avoid all contact with him!"

Laura respected Shelly. She was a woman frustrated by the number of men who were getting away with sexual assault. She had given up her career as prosecutor to represent women in civil action against their predators. And Laura had betrayed her confidence. "I'm so sorry," Laura said.

"Sorry doesn't cut it, honey. You may have screwed up everything."

Laura and Bruce met at Shelly's office that afternoon. Laura brought the digital recording. Shelly smoked and paced as she listened. She had Laura play it a second time. She sat at her desk, lit another cigarette and inhaled deeply before speaking. She looked at Bruce.

"Why in God's name did you let her do that?" Shelly asked.

"She didn't tell me. I'd never have let her go."

Shelly waggled her index finger at Laura. "You pull another lame-brain stunt like this and I'm off the case. You understand?"

"I understand. That's the last thing I want to happen," Laura said.

"That blacked out business and you having consensual sex with him....that's going to be tough to refute."

"I don't think she had enough to drink to black out," Bruce said.

"We need some expert medical testimony to refute that," Shelly said. "I agree, I don't think it's plausible, given the amount of alcohol she consumed. I'm more concerned about the photo."

"Bruce believes it was doctored..." Laura's voice trailed off.

"It's been destroyed. We can't prove that." Shelly leaned back in her chair and stared at the ceiling. "You've weakened your position, probably beyond repair."

"I didn't admit to anything. I told him he was lying."

"It's what you said after he showed you the photo," Shelly said. "To that point, you were adamant, certain of your position. Your voice changed dramatically. Listen again." Shelly replayed the recording, fast-forwarding it to the part that concerned her.

"That bothered Bruce too," Laura said. "It was as though someone had smacked me in the gut. I could hardly speak. What the hell was I supposed to say?"

"Your reaction was predictable," Shelly said. "It was exactly what he wanted. I haven't the least doubt he has it all on tape."

"How can a photo that doesn't exist hurt us?" Laura asked.

"It doesn't matter. You saw it. In a deposition or on the stand you'll have to testify as to what you saw.

With what we have now, if we go to court we're coming out losers."

"Honey, I agree with Shelly. Your meeting with him has screwed up everything."

Laura set her jaw. She had tainted the evidence, she knew it. But now she was even more determined not to let Michael off the hook. "You said we can't win with what we have now. What are you thinking?"

"The girls who came into the room," Shelly said. "We need to talk them. You said it was just a minute or two after the three guys left."

"You think they may have seen them leave?"

"If they saw them coming out of the room or even coming down the stairs...."

"Martha and Ginger had been looking for me. Someone probably told them they had seen a boy carry me upstairs. They must have been nearby when they heard me scream."

"We need to contact them. All may not be lost," Shelly said. "First we'd have to gather enough evidence to convince a magistrate that there is probable cause to suspect the young men were guilty of sexual assault. Then he can issue a court order that all three be tested. Maybe there'll be a second DNA match."

"You're sounding like a prosecutor," Laura said.

Shelly nodded. "You're right. I may be talking myself out of a job, but I'd rather turn the case over to a prosecutor than risk losing a civil action."

"Isn't it possible for you to work with a prosecutor?" Bruce asked.

Peter Rizzolo

"It's not unheard of, but it's ultimately up to the discretion of the prosecutor." Shelly said. "The nephew of someone being talked about as the Republican candidate for Governor is accused of rape. Folks in the prosecutor's office will kill for a chance to handle this case."

Laura sat at the edge of her chair. "What should I do?"

"You've done too much already, young lady," Shelly said. "I'll put one of my paralegals on the case. She'll need the names of everyone at the party who you can remember."

"Most of the kids I only knew to say hello."

"You told me Jimmy and Ginger were there," Bruce said.

"Yes, their names were in the report your wife gave me," Shelly said. She removed a legal pad from her desk drawer. "So we'll start with Martha, Jimmy and Ginger. She'll need last names, addresses, and phone numbers, whatever." She turned to Bruce. "You stayed in the area after Laura left. Do you know what happened to these people after they graduated?"

"They all went off to college. Luke Larson went to Stanford. Martha Carver, I think, went to Berkeley," Bruce said.

"That figures," Laura said. "She was Luke's girlfriend."

"Didn't you tell me Jimmy got a swimming scholarship to UNC in Chapel Hill and that Ginger went to Duke?" Laura asked.

Bruce nodded.

"What are Jimmy's and Ginger's last names?"

"Jimmy Caniglia and Ginger Spaulding," Laura said.

"Good." Shelly scribbled a note. "I'll pass this on to Tessie. She may call you if other names come up."

"What about that meeting with Michael and his lawyer?" Laura asked.

"*They* asked to meet. We listen. See just how badly they want to get rid of us. We commit to nothing. The meeting's set for next Friday. We have five days to see if we can build a case, or resign ourselves to settling out of court."

Peter Rizzolo

Chapter Twenty-Six

The more Laura thought about how Michael had tried to shame her, the angrier she became. Shelly was right. Laura had only two options. Either accept a financial settlement or go ahead with criminal prosecution, knowing that, if she chose to prosecute, she might not have strong enough evidence to convict him.

After learning how the sexual assault had affected her ability to get pregnant, Laura had directed all her venom toward Michael. Why hadn't she thought to identify the other two boys? How did they get involved? Had all three of them planned it? Were they looking for any vulnerable girl or had they targeted her? If they had, then Martha Carver, who had invited her to the party, was either knowingly involved or was used by Michael to get her there. That would suggest that Luke was involved. Was it a coincidence that Martha was nearby when Laura began to scream?

Tessie Dearing, Shelly Spinks' junior associate, was a plump, thirtyish brunette, who chewed nicotine gum, not to kick the habit, but to insure a steady supply of her drug of choice in places where smoking was prohibited. She did not possess Shelly's courtroom sparkle, but she had a bulldog's tenacity when it came to building a case. It was she who arranged the meeting with Martha Carver.

Martha extended her hand as Tessie Dearing entered her sparsely furnished office. Tessie thought Martha looked nothing like the photo in Laura's high school yearbook. She had gone from a cute, chubby-cheeked, corn-silk-haired teenager to a tall, disgustingly slim, attractive young brunette in a red Pendleton blazer, silk open-collar shirt and tapered, white flannel pants.

She hadn't been hard to track down. She had returned to Allentown, Pennsylvania, after graduating from Berkeley with a degree in Health Administration. The Allentown phone directory was all Tessie needed. She agreed to meet with Tessie at her workplace. The sign on Martha's office door indicated she was vice president in charge of the claims division of Health USA Inc.

She led Tessie to a leather couch. "I was fond of Laura. She just disappeared. We didn't know if she was dead or alive."

Tessie placed a tape recorder on the seat between them. "Do you mind?"

Martha's eyes widened as she stared at the tiny device. "I---I guess it's okay. Sure. Why not?"

"What did you think really happened?" Tessie asked.

"At the party at Luke's?"

"Yes."

"A lot of us kids felt really bad," Martha said. "We didn't know what to say to her. There were rumors that the guys hadn't forced her."

"But you heard her scream. Weren't her hands tied to the bedpost when you came into the room?"

Martha nodded. "Yes. At first I was almost certain she had been raped. Yet I couldn't understand why she refused to go to the hospital. And after Michael showed me the photograph of Arnold carrying her upstairs, waving and smiling . . . I didn't know what to think."

"When did he show it to you?"

"Early the next day a bunch of us kids went out to Luke's house to help clean up."

"The party broke up pretty late. How did he have time to have the picture developed?"

"He had his own darkroom. Or he might have used a digital camera. In that case he could have downloaded it onto his computer and printed a copy."

"Did they have digital cameras back then?" Tessie asked.

"I'm not sure," Martha said.

"What was your reaction to the photograph?"

"I had heard about Arnold carrying her up to the second floor. But seeing Laura awake and smiling. . . I was shocked. It just didn't seem like something she would do."

"Arnold? Do you know his last name?"

"He was a friend of Luke's. A college freshman. I only met him that one time. Luke would know."

"Did you have any idea who the other guys might have been?" Tessie asked. She decided not to tell Martha about the DNA evidence implicating Michael. She didn't want to prejudice her response.

Martha stood and began to pace. She sat next to Tessie. "I thought I was in love with Luke," she said. "When he went off to Stanford, I decided to go to Berkeley to be near him. He was full of the devil. Fun to be with. The cute 'bad boy.' It was okay in the beginning..."

"It sounds like maybe things changed," Tessie said.

Martha crossed her shapely legs. Tessie studied her face. She appeared to be genuinely stressed. Tessie hadn't expected Martha to be so forthcoming, especially since their conversation was being recorded.

"Luke got into drugs big-time. I tried to get him to quit. Go into rehab. He'd laugh and say he could quit anytime he wanted to."

"So did he?" Tessie asked.

"Not really. One night when he was high on something, uppers I think, he talked about the party. He never brought it up before. He told me that he and Arnold had gone to the bedroom to see how Laura was doing. Michael was in bed with her. She was awake. He and Arnold started to back out of the room, but then Laura said, 'Oh, what the hell. The more the merrier.'"

"I didn't believe him," Martha said. "I guess I always suspected he was involved. The way he pressed me to get Laura to come to the party...I wouldn't let myself believe he could do a thing like that."

"Did you have any other reason to believe he might have been involved?"

"The week after it happened, he kept asking me to talk with Laura. To ask her if she was going to the police. He got really mad at me for refusing."

"Did you have any contact with Arnold after that night?"

"No, but Luke told me Arnold was going to transfer to West Point after his freshman year."

"I see. That night, both you and Ginger had pleaded with her to go to the hospital," Tessie said. "You must have realized the hospital would have notified the police?"

"Laura said she'd been raped. We believed her at the time. She should have gone to the hospital. She should have gotten the police involved."

Martha was silent for a few moments.

"The more I thought about it," Martha said, "the more I suspected that Luke, Arnold and Michael might have planned the whole thing. And I was the one who had talked her into coming."

"So a year later, when Luke told you his version of the story, it confirmed your suspicion?"

"I was furious. Like I was part of it. I didn't ever want to see him again. He called me every day for the next couple of weeks. I didn't respond to his messages. I haven't seen him since."

"Did anyone else hear him tell you that story?"

"We were in his dorm room. Just the two of us," Martha said.

"How long were you and Ginger in the bedroom with Laura?"

"About fifteen minutes. No more. There was so much blood. We cleaned her up the best we could. We helped her get dressed."

"No one else responded to her screaming?"

"The party was going strong, the music was loud. We wouldn't have heard her if we weren't already upstairs."

"Did you see anyone upstairs?" Tessie asked.

"Not that I can remember."

"Did you see Michael, Luke or Arnold when you went back downstairs?"

"I didn't see Luke or Arnold. But as we were getting into Ginger's car, Michael came running out of the house. I had just gotten Laura into the back seat. He asked what the hell happened. Where were we going? When Laura saw him she started screaming for him to get away from her. Ginger gunned the motor and yelled for Michael to get out of the way. Then she damn near ran over him as we tore out of there."

Tessie's heart raced. *She'll make a great witness. I wish I hadn't turned off the damn tape recorder.* "Why was Ginger so angry at Michael?" Tessie asked.

"Laura had told us that she thought Michael was one of the boys who raped her."

"You both believed Laura's account of what had happened?"

"Ginger more so than I. I knew Laura was drunk. I'd seen her stumble and almost fall into the pool. And she told us they covered her eyes with something. She hadn't actually seen any of the boys. Her story just sounded so bizarre."

"Did you see anything they might have used to blindfold her?"

"Not really. There was so much bloody stuff on the floor beside the bed."

"If this goes to court, would you be willing to testify for the prosecution?"

"What good would it do? Luke'll say he doesn't recall telling me that. It's been so many years. Aren't there statutes of limitations?"

"There are ways to get around that. Did you and Ginger go back to the party after you took Laura home?"

"Ginger's date, Jimmy Caniglia, was still there. When we got back almost everyone had cleared out. Luke, Jimmy and Michael were the only ones there, as I remember."

"Why didn't you talk with Laura at school? Laura told us that everyone treated her like a leper." Tessie searched Martha's face carefully. Tessie had shepherded a girl and three boys through their teens. She was pretty good at telling when someone was lying. She was convinced Martha was telling the truth.

"Rumors were flying. Pretty soon kids were saying that half of the senior class had had a go at her." Martha looked at her hands. She took a deep, tremulous breath before speaking. "I was as cowardly as the rest. We all thought she'd eventually go to the police. I had talked her into coming to the party. The police might think I had set the whole thing up. I'm ashamed to say I was relieved when she left town."

"You didn't answer my question about testifying on Laura's behalf."

"Do I have a choice?"

Tessie shook her head. "We could subpoena you. But I'd rather you come forward voluntarily."

"I owe Laura that much. But tell me, why now, after so many years?"

"Laura's married. She wants to have children. She recently learned that she's infertile. Almost certainly it was the result of an infection she got from one of those boys who raped her."

The color drained from Martha's face. "Oh my God. Oh, my God."

"What is it?" Tessie asked.

"When Luke told me his version of what had happened he also said, 'Little miss goody two-shoes was no virgin. She gave me the clap.'"

"You didn't know he had gonorrhea at the time?" Tessie asked.

"No. He never mentioned it."

"You don't have to answer this, but had you been intimate with Luke either before or after the party?"

Martha looked at the tape recorder. Tessie turned it off.

"We had started going steady our last semester in high school and before going off to college."

Martha closed her eyes as though transported back to that summer a long time ago. She didn't speak for several moments. "We were in love---at least I thought so then. He was persistent. I started on the pill. But it was long after the party. And he was perfectly normal, I'll say that much. Not a rapist. No way!"

****

Ginger Spalding was more difficult to track down. The Duke Alumni office supplied her current address after Tessie told them she was Ginger Spalding and hadn't been receiving her alumni newsletter. She wondered if maybe they didn't have her current address.

"I'm sorry about that. Let me check. Hold on please."

Tessie held her breath. She hoped the alumni office wasn't overly cautious about giving out private information over the phone.

"Here we are, 240 Sharon Drive, in Cary. Isn't that right?"

"No. It's 2400 Sharon Drive."

"I'll correct that. Thank you for calling, Miss Spalding."

The Cary phone directory listed two phone numbers for Ginger. A recorded message at Smith Barney led her through a series of options. She eventually reached Ginger and arranged to meet her.

Tessie phoned Shelly about her session with Martha. She listened in silence, except for a few, oh my Gods, as Tessie played the tape of her interview.

"It's not a smoking gun," Shelly said, "but it might be enough to convince a magistrate to issue a court order for DNA samples from Luke and Arnold. In addition we have Michael on tape, saying he and Laura had consensual sex. That directly contradicts what Luke told Martha. We need Arnold's version of what happened. Can you run him down? Meet with him. Ask for his recollection of what happened that night. If we get three different versions, we pretty much destroy Michael's credibility."

"Okay, as soon as I track him down."

"And Ginger?"

"I've arranged to meet with her."

"Good. We need to see if she supports Martha's statement."

"She lives in Cary, North Carolina. I've already booked a flight to Raleigh. Should be there by seven tonight."

"Call me afterwards. Then, if possible, get with Arnold. We meet with Greene's lawyer in just a few days. I want to walk in there with as much ammo as possible."

"You convinced they're counting on a settlement?"

"Pretty much. And I wonder just how far his jaw will drop when I tell him to keep his quarter-of-a-million bucks."

"How'd you know how much?" Tessie asked.

"An educated guess."

From the airport, Tessie took a cab to Ginger's home. Hers was an impressive neighborhood with new super-sized McMansions on one-acre, manicured lots. A white Mercedes convertible was parked in the drive. Looked like the rising stock market was kind to Ginger.

Ginger led Tessie to the kitchen. "I had to work late. Skipped lunch and dinner. I'm starved. Care to join me?"

"Thanks, but I've already eaten."

Ginger was wearing a pin-striped form-fitting business suit. She, unlike Martha, hadn't changed much from the photograph in Laura's yearbook. She still had flaming red hair that reached to her shoulders, intensely blue eyes and a mischievous smile.

Ginger slipped on an oven mitt and removed a foil-covered platter and a basket of bread from the oven and placed them on the granite counter-top. "Maria works for me afternoons. Does a little housework, shops and prepares dinner. She's an angel." She went to the fridge. "At least have a little wine."

"Yes. Thank you."

"I was stunned when you called. The way Laura disappeared. . . I thought maybe she was dead."

The smell of the Mexican food was making Tessie sorry she had declined the invitation to eat. "Do you mind if I tape record our conversation?"

"I'd rather you didn't. I can't really tell you that much. Martha and I were in the pool most of the evening. I remember Laura calling out to Martha that she had to go home. Later Martha asked me to help her look for Laura. Then some kid said they saw a boy taking her upstairs."

"Do you remember who told you that?"

Laura buttered a slice of bread. "No, not really."

"Did you see Michael Greene?"

"No. Martha thought that maybe Laura had asked him to take her home."

"Did you hear Laura scream?"

"We were upstairs when we heard screaming."

"Are you sure you were upstairs?"

Ginger thought for a moment or two. "Yes. I remember because it startled me. It was coming from somewhere down the hall. I ran in that direction. Martha had already entered the room."

"Can you describe what you saw when you entered?"

"Laura was standing beside the bed, shaking, crying. Martha had her arm around her shoulder. Laura's back was to me. I could see blood on her legs, on the bed, on the floor. I ran and got some towels. When I got back she was on her knees, crying."

"What did she tell you?"

"I can't remember her exact words. She said she had gone to sleep, and when she woke up, her hands were tied. There was something covering her eyes and mouth."

"Did you see anything that might have been used to cover her eyes and mouth?"

"No. But I really didn't think to look."

"She said her hands had been tied."

"They might have been. But they weren't by the time I came from the bathroom."

"Are you sure?"

"Yes."

"I see. Did she tell you who had attacked her?"

"She said there were three guys. She heard them talking just before they ran out of the room. She was sure one of them was Michael Greene."

"What made her think that?"

"She kept saying, 'It was him, it was him.' It wasn't until we were driving her home that she said she recognized his voice."

"Anything else you recall her saying before you left the house?"

"She kept insisting we take her home. We cleaned her up and got her dressed. We slipped on her overcoat. We pleaded with her to go to the hospital. I drove. Martha sat in back with Laura. She cried the whole way."

"Did you see Luke, Arnold or Michael as you took Laura to the car?"

"Michael came to the car. I couldn't hear what he was saying. Laura was screaming at him to get away from her. At the time I totally believed he had raped her." Ginger paused. She drained her wine glass and refilled it. "I swear if he hadn't jumped out of the way, I would have run over him. It wasn't until we had driven off that I started shaking pretty bad. I kept thinking that I could have killed him."

"You took Laura home?"

"Her mother met us at the door. She almost fainted when she saw Laura. She grabbed her, pulled her into the house and slammed the door in our faces."

"Did you go back to the party?"

"Yes. The place was practically deserted. I guess no one wanted to be there when the police arrived."

"But the police were never notified, were they?" Tessie asked.

"The kids at the party didn't know that. Besides alcohol, some of them had been smoking pot. Who knows what else?"

"Was Michael Greene still there?"

"He, Luke, Jimmy Caniglia and Arnold were the only guys still there."

"Can you recall anything Luke said or did?"

"He seemed really nervous. He kept asking me if I thought Laura might call the police."

"What about Michael Greene? Did you talk with him?"

"On the drive back to Luke's house, Martha and I talked about what Laura had said about Michael. We were hoping he wouldn't still be there. It's hard to believe someone you know would do something like that."

"How did he seem?"

"He took me aside. He wanted to know what Laura had told me. He said we should have insisted on taking her to the hospital."

"Where were the others? Martha, Jimmy, Luke and Arnold?"

"Luke and Martha and Jimmy went to the bedroom to clean up."

"What did you tell Michael?"

"Just how we found her. That she said she'd been raped. That she insisted we take her home."

"What was his reaction to what you told him?"

"He got really pale. His hands were shaking. He sat next to me. He looked like he was about to cry. He kept saying, "Poor Laura--I can't believe this. God! Who would do such a thing?"

"You didn't say that she had accused him?"

Ginger shook her head. "He was so broken up, I couldn't. To be honest, I was beginning to doubt her story. Why would Michael want her to go to the hospital if he were guilty? When Michael went upstairs, Arnold came over to talk with me. He said he was worried because lots of kids saw him carry her upstairs. He wanted to know if Laura said anything about him. Did I think she intended to go to the hospital? I told him she hadn't mentioned him, that I had no idea what Laura and her mother might decide to do. He told me he and Laura did have sex, but that he didn't force her. He said he had no idea what happened after he left the room."

"Did anyone hear him tell you that?"

"No."

"You never told anyone?"

"On the way home I talked to Jimmy about it."

"What did you think really happened?"

"My opinion so many years after the fact doesn't count for much."

"I'm curious. What did you believe happened?"

Ginger shrugged. She kicked off her shoes and put her feet on the edge of the table. "She was drunk. Arnold brought her upstairs. I believe they had sex. She went off to sleep. When she woke up and saw all that blood, she freaked out."

"Why do you suppose she'd lie?"

"I don't know. Maybe she dreamed the business about being tied up. Maybe it really happened. I don't know."

"I understand you and Laura were close friends."

"We hung out with the same bunch of kids." Ginger smiled. "I sort of moved in on a boy she had a crush on. Laura wasn't too happy about that."

"And who was that?"

"Jimmy. He was my date that night."

"Why didn't you or her other friends call her afterwards?"

"We were all kind of in shock. At school she wouldn't look at or talk with anyone. We didn't know what to do. I thought she just needed some space."

Tessie realized Ginger's testimony would be problematic. She didn't recall seeing anything that might have been used to restrain Laura. And her conversation with Michael afterwards had convinced Ginger that he was innocent.

If Ginger, who had seen Laura bloodied and hysterical, believed that Laura lied, how was Shelley to convince a jury otherwise?

Chapter Twenty-Seven

If Arnold had graduated from West Point, as Laura's husband believed, it would have been the class of 1996. After checking several internet alumni-locator services, Tessie found her man. Although there were three Arnolds in that graduating class, only one had transferred from Pennsylvania State University. After graduation, Captain Arnold J. Sommers joined an Army Airborne Division, based at Fort Bragg, North Carolina. He was married and had two children.

The day following her interview with Ginger, Tessie called Captain Arnold Sommers and explained that her firm was representing Laura Hamby regarding a sexual assault that had occurred in 1994.

"Hamby? Laura Hamby?"

"Her name at the time was Carnahan," Tessie said.

There were several seconds of silence. "This is a bit of a shock."

"I understand how you must feel. Did you know her well?"

"I was a year ahead of her. I saw her around school but never really spent time with her. Why are you interested in talking with me?"

"We're talking with a number of people who were at the party. You were identified as someone who was present at the place where the alleged incident had occurred. We hope you might have information that might be helpful to her."

Tessie and Captain Sommers met at the main entrance to Fort Bragg early that afternoon. He was wearing Army fatigues, boots and a baseball cap with the 82nd insignia above the visor. He told her that he was participating in a Special Operations Anti-terrorism Task Force. That she had thirty minutes tops. His posture was West-Point-erect, his shoulders broad, and his face clean-shaven. His intense blue eyes and rugged good looks made Tessie wish she had met him under different circumstances. He would make a credible witness. She followed his car to the officers' club.

They sat at an elegant wood-paneled bar. Tessie sipped a coke. Arnold ordered a ginger ale.

"You mind if I tape record our conversation?"

"I'd rather you didn't. In fact, should I even be talking with you without first getting an attorney?"

"You were the last person to see Laura. You're not a suspect. I'm hoping you might be of some help," Tessie said.

"I'm not at all sure I should be doing this. But I felt sorry for Laura and would like to help."

"You said on the phone that you hadn't actually met Laura before that night," Tessie said.

"I admired her from a distance, but never got up the nerve to ask her out."

Tessie smiled. "She probably would have jumped at the chance. What do you remember of that night at the party?"

"Luke Marshall invited me. I had been a year ahead of him in high school. We were on the wrestling team together."

"I understand you saw her fall."

"I was watching some of the kids playing water polo. I could see she was unsteady on her feet. I was afraid she might fall into the pool. I went over to her, but she fell before I got there. Hit her head pretty hard. I helped her up. Her scalp was bleeding some. I carried her upstairs to one of the bedrooms. Got some ice. The bleeding had pretty much stopped by then."

"How did she seem?"

"She was laughing. Thought it was funny." He removed his cap. He was silent for a few moments. "Why is this coming up now?"

"Sorry, I can't tell you that."

"Am I a suspect? Should I be talking to a lawyer?"

Tessie could see beads of perspiration gather on his forehead. She spoke in a gentle, reassuring voice. "We're just gathering information. I was hoping you might recall something. At this time we haven't even decided we can make a case for legal action."

Arnold removed a pack of Marlborro cigarettes from his breast pocket. He offered one to Tessie.

"Don't mind if I do," Tessie admitted. They smoked in silence. She decided to give him time to compose himself.

"She must have some kind of evidence. Why else would she be dredging this up?" Arnold speculated.

"Do you recall telling one of the girls that you had had sex with Laura?"

Arnold set his jaw. "I don't remember telling anyone that."

"Did you have sex with Laura that night?"

Arnold snuffed out his cigarette. "Do you intend to call me as a witness?"

"Probably. You were the last person to see her before the alleged assault."

"Shit. I didn't intend to. I didn't want to leave her until I was sure she was going to be okay. We just talked at first. I don't really remember how we got started. It just happened. And later I was afraid that if she went to the hospital and got tested, it would appear that I was one of the guys."

"So you believe she was sexually assaulted?"

"I do. She didn't impress me as the kind of girl who would lie."

"How do you explain that she doesn't recall having sex with you?"

"That's hard to understand. I don't know. She had bumped her head pretty hard. Besides, she must have drunk quite a bit to have passed out."

"Are you saying she wasn't conscious at the time you had sex with her?"

"No, I mean at the pool. She seemed out of it. But after a minute or so, she was awake and responsive."

Tessie decided not to push that line of questioning. "How long were you with her in the bedroom?"

"About an hour."

"You sure?"

"No. That's just a guess. When Ginger came back to the house after taking Laura home, she told me that I had picked up Laura at the poolside around nine-thirty."

"You didn't use a contraceptive?" Tessie asked.

He shook his head. "I'd been drinking. It was stupid, I know." He looked at his watch. "Sorry. I really have to go soon."

"Did anyone see you enter or leave the bedroom?"

"I can't recall seeing anyone."

"You sure?"

"As sure as a person can be after six years."

They talked about his willingness to testify if the matter went to court. He said he didn't think his testimony would help Laura, but he would if called on.

Tessie called Shelly as soon as she exited the base.

"He confirmed Martha's account about having had sex with Laura! He claims it was consensual."

"Of course," Shelly said. "At the time it happened, he was covering himself in case Laura had gone to the police. And he couldn't very well deny it now."

"Do you think Michael might have contacted either Luke or Arnold or both of them?" Tessie asked.

"I doubt it. But if we do file criminal or civil charges against Michael, we can get a court order to check out his phone records."

"So, as it stands now, all three are claiming they had consensual sex with Laura, although Luke's story is different," Tessie said.

"I wish we knew who the second DNA specimen belonged to. If it belongs to Luke, he can't very well deny what he told Martha about his involvement."

"And if it's Arnold's?" Tessie asked.

"Then Luke will claim that he never told Martha he had sex with Laura. It's Martha's word against Luke's."

"Sounds like we're going to court."

Laura invited her friends, Lilly and Rose, to an early morning get-together at her apartment.

"So, tomorrow's the day you meet with his lawyers," Lilly said. She was dressed in a tee-shirt and Capri pants. She sat on the floor, cross-legged, Indian style.

"I have a hunch Michael might also be there," Laura said.

Rose, who was dressed for work, sat on the couch alongside Laura. She smelled as good as she looked. Why is she so made up, Laura wondered? Was the Language Department at Seton Hall spawning a romance?

Laura, in contrast to Rose, did not look her best. Her hair was tangled, her eyes bloodshot, and her face puffy from lack of sleep. Jubilee snuggled contentedly in Laura's lap, unaccustomed to having her mistress available that time of day. As Laura stroked Jubilee's underbelly, she described in detail what Tessie had learned in her interviews with Martha and Ginger.

"If Martha always suspected Luke was one of the guys who raped you, why didn't she break off with him right away?" Rose asked.

Laura shrugged. "I guess she just didn't want to believe that someone she loved could act like that."

"Yeah," Lilly said. "My ex was cheating on me even while I was pregnant with Angela. There were plenty of clues. I was stupid as hell."

"With the DNA evidence and Martha's testimony, wouldn't I be foolish to settle?" Laura asked.

"*Chi troppo vuole nulla stringe,*" Rose said.

"You're a big help," Laura said.

"One who wants too much holds on to nothing," Rose translated.

"They offer you money, take it," Rose continued. "Why put yourself through all that misery?" She downed her espresso in a single gulp. "Even if you win, many will not believe you."

"Don't listen to her," Lilly said. "They should rot in jail."

"You two arm-wrestle," Laura said. "I'll go with the winner."

Lilly held up her arm and flexed her biceps. "No contest. I bench-press Angela three times a day. Forty-five baby pounds and a full diaper."

"One minute I'm prepared to go to court," Laura said. "The next, I think, no way. It's driving me nuts."

"And Bruce?" Rose asked.

246

"We were up half the night. Said he'd stand by me either way. But I'm sure he'd be relieved if we settle and go on with our lives."

Rose stood. "I must leave or I'll be late for class. Bruce is a good man, Laura. He will lose face if you do this."

"Speaking of face," Lilly asked, "Why all the makeup? You having an affair with one of your students?"

Rose blushed. "I'm having lunch with Gino."

Laura had introduced Rose and Gino. She was glad they had hit it off. In a way it took the pressure off Laura. She had felt guilty about being so attracted to Gino. Although there was never anything overt between them, there was an undercurrent, a sexual tension that she felt whenever she was with him. He too felt it. She could see it in his dark eyes.

Lilly had another cup of coffee, but said she couldn't stay long. She had to get Angela to day-care. She hugged Laura at the front door. "You think too much with your head," she whispered. "Do what your heart tells you."

Laura sat at the kitchen table, sipping her third cup of coffee as she leafed absently through the morning papers.

Their kitchen window looked out onto a small cement patio, beyond which was a patch of disorderly crab-grass and beyond that, a copse of bare hardwoods. It was a cold, grey March. She longed for spring. For this time to pass. Maybe Rose was right. Settle and be done with it. But this was no error in judgment, no accident. It was deliberate, premeditated violence. What if everyone took the easy way out? Most women do. Why should she expose her private life to the ridicule and judgment from others?

Laura had been drinking at the party. She couldn't honestly recall how things had started. Many would say that she was somehow responsible. Others would flat-out not believe her story. Her own mother had blamed her, not that she doubted the rape, but she had put herself in an unsafe place.

Laura knew that what she decided to do in the next twenty-four hours would change her life in ways she couldn't begin to imagine. Her lawyer had told her that she could remain anonymous by being identified as Jane Doe, and that her testimony could be read to the court. But Shelly had quickly added that once witnesses began to testify, it wouldn't take much digging to identify her. The media was skillful. A case based on DNA evidence retrieved from the victim's internal organs several years after the assault would be a very important story, even though her identity was being concealed.

The phone rang. It was Shelly. She told Laura what Tessie had learned in her interviews with Martha, Ginger and Arnold. Laura was not surprised to hear that Martha believed that Laura had been raped. But she was stunned that Ginger had thought Laura could have been a willing participant.

"Lord," Laura said. "That's going to hurt us, isn't it?"

"Some. But Arnold's story contradicts what Michael told you. We have that on tape. Remember, Michael said he went to the bedroom soon after he took that picture of Arnold carrying you upstairs."

Laura had felt bad going against Shelly's advice about Michael. Now she was somewhat vindicated. "So his meeting with me at the coffee shop may not have been such a disaster, after all?"

"That kind of mistake does bring into question his overall credibility. But the blackout fairytale he concocted still looms as his best chance to produce a greater weight of evidence in his favor," Shelly said.

"Has Tessie met with Luke?"

"She tried. Luke said he was advised by his attorney not to talk with anyone about the alleged assault. Someone must have gotten to him. Maybe Michael, maybe Michael's attorney."

"Maybe Arnold," Laura said.

"No. She talked with Luke before she called Arnold. If we go to court I can subpoena his phone records. Hopefully they'll show that it was Michael who called him. His attorney has a legitimate reason for calling a potential witness. Michael doesn't."

It was almost too much for Laura to hold onto. Her heart said to forge ahead, but her brain, overwhelmed by theories, facts, contradictions and fear, lurched back-and-forth, like a new driver with a stick shift.

Michael Greene, as he did every morning, was preparing to visit his assigned patients prior to general rounds with the attending and the rest of the surgical team. It was 5:30 AM as he walked the city block from the residents' quarters to U. Penn Hospital. His woolen sweater and scrub suit offered him little protection from the penetrating wind that roared along the concrete and steel canyons of downtown Philadelphia.

He had spent the previous evening discussing strategy with his attorney and his father. They were prepared to offer Laura a quarter of a million dollars to agree not to pursue civil or criminal charges against Michael. If she were to accept their offer, that would be the best possible outcome. Although Lester was convinced there was virtually no chance they would lose in court, it would be an empty victory. In the eyes of many, Michael would be yet another rich guy who got away with rape. He shivered as he pushed through the doors at the hospital's main entrance.

"Good morning, Michael."

He looked over his shoulder. Lin Chen was coming through the door behind him. She was wearing a faux fur hat, knee-length faux fur fringed coat and high-heeled leather boots.

"Hi, Lin. Want to join me for coffee?"

"I'd love to, but I came in early to prepare some slides for the noon conference." She smiled. "I'm free this evening."

"Sorry. Can't do. I'm on call." He hurried off. He thought of their ski trip to the Pocono's. She had lied about her skiing ability. He could barely keep up with her. They had stayed at a nearby Swiss style lodge that night. She had insisted on separate rooms. They drank mulled wine and danced until three in the morning. Lin clung to him, pressed her cheek to his as they danced, kissed and bit his neck, but when he responded by dropping his hand to her buttock she laughed and gently pushed it away. "You mustn't. This is our first date, Michael."

She led him to his room and kissed him goodnight at the door. She had been coming on to him the entire evening. He was certain she wanted to make love as much as he, but didn't want to seem too easy a mark. He had to be careful. He would most likely be asking her to testify as to how Laura had stolen a specimen from her laboratory. A torrid affair would neutralize her credibility as a witness. He kissed her long and hard.

"You owe me, babe," he said.

He gently pushed her in the direction of her room, then staggered into his room and flopped onto the bed. He was accustomed to having his way with women. But after a full day of skiing, and alcohol, eighty-hour work weeks, plus his legal problems with Laura Hamby, a rain check wasn't such a bad idea.

After rounding on his assigned patients and checking out his orders with his supervising resident, Michael had a few minutes before having to report to the operating room. He stepped into an unoccupied patient room and called his lawyer.

"I'm almost certain Laura's not going to settle this without a fight," Michael said.

"There's no way she'd win in court," Lester said.

"But if we go to court, I lose no matter what the verdict. You've got to have a backup plan if she refuses to settle."

"Michael, I already discussed this with your dad. He's willing to up the ante to a half a mil, tops. She refuses that, we have no choice."

"She wants *me* to pay for what I did. Not my father. Can't you understand that?"

"Sorry, but I don't agree, Michael. After all these years, it's not justice, it's greenbacks she's after. The meeting's set for ten tomorrow at my office. See you then."

Michael was beginning to believe that Lester wanted to go to trial. His firm's business would flourish with the inevitable national exposure and rounds of the television talk shows that would result. Lester was his dad's college roommate, an old and trusted friend. His dad would never suspect that Lester would be driven by ambition and self interest, not loyalty.

"Hey, Dr. Greene."

Michael turned. A medical student was standing in the doorway. "The OR's looking for you. An earlier case was cancelled. Said they've been beeping you."

Michael checked his beeper. Damnit! He'd forgotten to turn it on. "Okay. Thanks. Tell them I'm on the way."

That afternoon Michael called Laura's work number. He didn't want to call her at home and risk getting Bruce on the line. He was told that she hadn't reported to work. He had no other choice. He dialed her home number.

"Hello, Laura, it's me, Michael."

Her spine stiffened. Why was he calling? Was he going to plead with her to settle? She sat at the kitchen table. "We're meeting tomorrow..."

"Laura, please hear me out."

"Is this conversation being recorded?"

"My God. Of course not. They're going to offer you a quarter of a million dollars to settle."

"You already told me that," Laura said.

"They're prepared to go higher. You could end up with a lot more. Take it and let's be done with this nightmare."

"I've lived with it for six years."

"I have other pictures like the one I showed you. God knows I don't want to use them."

"Why would you even hesitate to use them if they would indicate your innocence?" Laura asked.

"Because nobody wins if we go to court. I'm working hard to make something of my life. I'm a damn good doctor, Laura. And I'll be in a position some day to help a lot of people."

"Once you get out of prison."

"A cute one-liner, but you're not as smart as you think. You have as much to lose as I. How will you afford IVF if you turn your nose up at hundreds of thousands of dollars and then lose in court?"

"Your concern for me is really quite touching."

"We can prove that you stole a specimen from the lab at University of Pennsylvania Hospital. That's a criminal act, a felony. It will also bring into question the honesty and credibility of your doctor. She accepted the specimen knowing it was stolen. You may end up being the convicted felon in this case."

Laura's hand shook as she pressed the off button on her phone. Shelly had said the illegally obtained blood specimen was problematic but she hadn't made much of it. Was Michael exaggerating its importance? It was an angle she hadn't considered until now.

Chapter Twenty-Eight

The walls of the conference room in the law office of Knowles, Faraday and Pfister displayed a collection of impressionist art. At an exhibition at the Philadelphia Museum, Laura had been bowled over by the dazzling colors and their extraordinary use of light. She stared at *Sunrise* by Claude Monet. It couldn't possibly be the original, it would be worth millions.

"You have good taste, Mrs. Hamby," Lester said. "It's breathtaking, isn't it?"

Laura didn't respond. She wasn't there to make small talk. She studied some of the other paintings. She recognized some...Degas's *Dancers in Pink* and *The Bather* by Renoir.

At the center of the room was a massive granite slab mounted on two steel pedestals. A dozen or so leather armchairs were arranged about the table. Lester sat at one end, Michael to his left, and Mal Greene to his right. Shelly sat at the opposite end, flanked by Tessie and Laura.

Tessie wore a navy blue, double-breasted suit, knee-length skirt and cap with black leather visor. Shelly's first mate, Laura thought.

Shelly wore a St. John's designer powder-blue woolen pants suit and silk turtleneck sweater. Even without makeup or jewelry she looked stunning. Laura felt dowdy in a workaday loose-fitting jumper and long-sleeved button-down shirt.

Sitting next to Lester was a young woman, Maria Faraday, whom he introduced as an associate partner. She looked to be in her mid-thirties, sporting a blond, strait-hair classic bob and sunny smile. After introductions, Lester was first to speak. "The ground rules are: no notes, no tape recorders. This meeting is strictly off the record."

Shelly nodded.

Tessie leaned over and whispered to Laura, "My guess is that Lester warned Mal not to say anything he would not want to have to testify to since he was subject to subpoena by us."

"My client and I called for this meeting to ascertain if we can come to an amicable resolution of this difficult situation. When Michael ran into Laura Hamby at University of Pennsylvania Hospital he was shocked, first of all, to see her after all those years, and second by her vehement outburst accusing him of having sexually assaulted her. Michael, as you might guess, was deeply offended by such a groundless accusation."

"Hardly groundless," Shelly said.

Laura studied Michel's face. He had not made eye contact with her, except for a nod when she first entered the room. Mal Greene leaned over and whispered something in Lester's ear.

"We'll never know exactly what happened that unfortunate night six years ago," Lester said. "What we do know is that a young girl, Laura Hamby, had been drinking, as had most if not all of the teenagers at the party. We have spoken to the two women who heard Laura scream, the first to come to her aid. Laura told the girls that her hands had been tied. That she had been blindfolded, gagged, and raped by three boys. She told the girls that she believed one of the boys was Michael."

Laura stared at Michael. "I was certain one of them was Michael."

"Laura, that's absolutely not true," Michael said.

Laura wanted to call him a rotten liar, but had been advised by Shelly not to engage directly with him.

"Let's not beat about the bush," Lester said. "We know that Dr. Corbett recovered DNA from pathology specimens she removed from Laura's body. And that you have reason to believe this finding incriminates my client in the alleged sexual assault."

"She was familiar with the sound of his voice," Shelly said. "They had been in a class together in their junior year of high school. Her testimony that she believed he was one of the boys is sufficient cause to get a court order for DNA testing of your client."

"It's a moot point. My client admits to having had sex with her prior to the alleged assault," Lester said.

Laura whispered to Shelly, "Michael obviously intends to use his blackout theory to explain why I don't remember having had sex with him."

"I believe we are making progress here," Shelly said. "Your client admits to having had sex with my client that very same night. He says it was consensual, she says it was rape. Perhaps we should let a jury decide?"

"We are not denying that one or more boys sexually assaulted Laura," Maria Faraday said, trying to sound conciliatory. "Michael was not one of them."

Shelly looked at the young attorney with a bemused smile. "Oh, really? I was fully expecting your client would admit his guilt and ask for forgiveness."

"He didn't have to admit to having had sex with her that night in order to explain assumed DNA evidence," Lester said. "They had dated prior to the time of the alleged assault." He turned to Laura, his eyebrows raised. "Did you not?"

If Michael's attorney used the term, "alleged assault" one more time Laura was afraid she would explode.

"You don't have to answer that, Laura," Michael said. "We went to a basketball game. I drove her home afterwards. Nothing happened."

Mal Greene glared at Michael. It apparently was not what he wanted to hear from his son.

"That's not entirely true," Laura said. "You were very aggressive on the drive home. I had to fight my way out of your car. I walked home, remember?"

"I don't recall it happening exactly that way. But I'm sorry if I was overly amorous. I was seventeen. I was fond of you. I just wanted to fool around a little. Believe me, Laura, I'd never force you to do anything you didn't want to do."

Laura bit her lip. Lord! He was such a rotten, unbearably smug liar. She turned to Shelly, who shook her head ever so slightly, signaling for her not to respond.

"You have several major problems if you decide to take this to court," Lester said. "Permit me to discuss them." He paused for a few moments.

It was an obvious rhetorical ploy, Laura thought, to heighten the significance of what was to follow. He was a bit of a dandy, she thought. The way he dressed. The way he moved his hands as he spoke.

"In an alleged rape prosecution, as you know," Lester said, "the statutes of limitations in Pennsylvania is twelve years...I suspect that Ms. Hamby was aware of that. Her time was running out."

"There is a DNA exemption to that statute," Shelly responded.

"There is no way the DNA evidence in this case would be admissible. But please allow me to continue."

Shelly nodded.

"Most important," Lester said, "there are no witnesses to the alleged assault. Without witnesses you must have hard evidence or a credible victim. But the accuser's credibility is very much in doubt, since she claims to having been blindfolded, and was undeniably so drunk that she was unable to stand. The fact that she refused to report the incident to the police or even see a doctor is strong circumstantial evidence to suggest that her story was highly exaggerated. We have in our possession photographs that support this assumption. Furthermore, prior to our meeting today, Laura and our client met, against my advice, and without my prior knowledge. You are going to have a hard time explaining to a jury why a woman would meet in secret with a man she is accusing of having raped her."

Lester nodded to Maria, who picked up a folder and handed it to Shelly. She removed several eight by ten glossy photographs. They were the same set of pictures Michael had given to Laura. She gave them in turn to Laura and Tessie. The photos showed Laura drinking directly from a flask, one of her teetering at the edge of the pool, one of her on the ground, one of Arnold picking her up, and worst of all, one of Arnold carrying her, awake, smiling and waving, up a flight of stairs.

There were also photographs taken of her and Michael at the café in Morrisville. How was that possible, Laura wondered? She didn't recall seeing anyone with a camera. But Shelly showed no sign of surprise at seeing the photos. Had she already known of their existence?

Laura whispered to Shelly, "Should I explain that Michael called me?"

Shelly shook her head.

"Very interesting photos, wouldn't you say?" Lester asked.

"They prove nothing," Shelly said. "The insobriety of the victim does not justify rape."

"Her insobriety does bring into question Laura's reliability as a witness. But let's move on," Lester said. He turned to Laura. "Is it not true that Dr.

Corbett suggested the tissues removed at the time of your surgery be tested for DNA?"

Laura wondered where this was leading. She looked at Shelly before answering. Tessie stepped in.

"Dr. Corbett is a fertility expert," Tessie said. "Our client never dreamed that there was a possibility that someone's DNA could still be in her body after all those years. Of course it was Dr. Corbett's idea. She had looked for DNA in other cases."

"Indeed. Dr. Corbett had a lot to gain by discovering DNA, other than Laura's, in those specimens," Lester said. "She also had a personal axe to grind. Did you know she had been raped as a young girl?"

"Yes, we were aware of that," Shelly said. "I assume that is one reason she has a special interest and commitment toward helping victims of sexual assault."

"Special interest can also be construed as self interest or bias. And how is anyone to know that Dr. Corbett didn't purposely contaminate those specimens with my client's DNA?"

"That's preposterous," Shelly said.

"Not so preposterous," Michael said, staring at Laura. "Your client has shown great ingenuity in obtaining DNA specimens. She got into my personal medical record at the University of Pennsylvania Hospital. Then she stole a specimen from the immunology laboratory. Not just any specimen. It was a sample of my blood."

"We can prove that she did in fact do that," Lester said. "We have very credible witnesses, who have agreed to testify. A grand jury can call Dr.

Corbett to testify how she came into possession of a specimen of my client's blood. Armed with that information, the court would certainly decline to prosecute. It might well be your client who is subject to criminal prosecution."

"No one wants to prosecute this nice young girl for anything," Mal Greene said. "Listen, let's cut all the legal bullshit. A bunch of teenagers many years ago got drunk at a party. Something very unfortunate happened to one of the girls. It was the goddamn parents whose asses should have been hauled off to court for allowing their kids, without adult supervision, to party at their home. Let's face it, we'll never know exactly what happened."

His remarks were met with silence. He continued, "Why rile things up after all this time? If we go to court nobody wins. People will believe my son's guilty no matter what the jury decides, and others will be sure this young woman is lying. It's a lose/lose situation. Let's talk turkey. Settle this thing right here and now. That way everybody comes out ahead."

"Thank you, Mal," Lester said. "That was well put." He turned toward Shelly, Laura and Tessie. "Please don't be offended by his language. I have known Mal Greene from my college days. He speaks from the heart. The masters whose works you see in this room splashed paint on canvas to express their passion. My friend uses his words."

"I'm a bit confused," Shelly said. "I presumed you called us here to talk about Michael Greene, not his father."

"We understand Laura is infertile," Lester said, "and that she believes it was a direct result of rape. We also understand she wants to have a family. Michael has made me aware of how expensive it is to undergo *in vitro* fertilization. My client is prepared to make you a reasonable offer. In return, you would have to sign a contract in which you agree not to press charges against my client in either civil or criminal court, and that the settlement is not an admission of guilt, but an effort to spare both Michael and Laura the pain and suffering that would result from a public airing of this unfortunate situation."

"There has already been considerable pain and suffering on the part of my client," Shelly said.

She waited several moments before continuing. "What are you willing to offer?" Shelly asked.

Lester smiled. He removed a small note-pad from his breast pocket and jotted down something, then slid it across the table toward Shelly. She looked at it and handed it to Tessie.

"I'd like to huddle with my team before proceeding further," Shelly said.

"Of course," Lester said. "Maria will lead you to an empty room."

"Thanks," Shelly said, "There's a coffee shop in the lobby. We'll go there. We won't take long."

"Sure, that's fine," Lester said.

As they exited Laura glanced at Michael. Their eyes met. His blank stare was that of a predator. He had committed premeditated rape. She was certain of his guilt. But could she convince a jury?

"You suppose his offices are bugged?" Laura asked, as she backed into a booth at the far end of the coffee shop, a steaming cup of black coffee in hand.

"Those little games are SOP in this business," Shelly said. "I'm desperate for a smoke."

Tessie opened a pill-box of nicotine gum and offered it to her boss. Shelly grabbed a couple, as did Tessie.

"Well, are you going to show me that paper or what?" Laura asked, pretending to be impatient. But she knew why Shelly hadn't shown it to her in the conference room. She was afraid Laura's expression would reveal too much excitement at the sight of all those zeros.

She handed it to Laura. "It's what I expected. They offer $200,000, we ask for a million. They counter with $300,000. We counter the counter and so on."

"Michael told me they'd be willing to go much higher than their original offer. Why would he co-opt his own father?" Laura asked.

"We checked out Mal Greene," Shelly said. She turned to Tessie.

"He's a kind of corporate raider, à la T. Boone Pickens," Tessie said. "Sees an ailing company and goes for the jugular. He's a major stockholder in Pennsylvania Mining. Got in when they filed for chapter eleven after a series of mine disasters in the 70s. He turned the company around. Made a fortune."

"I believe we can settle this matter today for a million dollars," Shelly said. "It's your call, Laura."

Laura searched Shelly's face. If Shelly was convinced that the final offer would be a million dollars, why wasn't she leaning on Laura to accept a settlement? Shelly's fee would be $400,000! Not a bad return for her limited investment. But if they go to court and lose, Shelly gets nothing. Was Shelly more confident of winning than she had expressed earlier?

Laura recalled what her friend Rose had told her. Follow your heart, not your head. Her head told her to take the six hundred thousand dollars and move on.

"Laura?"

"I can't put a price tag on the things he took from me. I didn't graduate with my high school friends and my mother died alone, thinking her only child hated her." Laura's eyes filled with tears. "I never had a chance to make things right between us. And now I learn that my insides are all screwed up."

Shelly covered Laura's hand with hers. "What are you saying, honey?"

"If you believe a conviction is hopeless, then there's no point in continuing. Is there?"

"I'd say fifty-fifty in civil court," Shelly said. "But like Mal said, Michael will be seen by many as a rapist, regardless of the outcome. In a sense you will have convicted him even if we lose."

"I'd say our chances are better than fifty-fifty," Tessie added.

Laura was fully aware of what this would cost her personally. She was at a crossroads. She knew the path her heart was pleading with her to take. Tears spilled from her eyes. As she accepted a handkerchief from Tessie, the first-mate, she had this

264

sudden image of herself as skipper of a gigantic ocean liner on its maiden voyage. It is the dead of night, and her ship is on track to shatter the cross-Atlantic speed record. Tessie has informed her that massive icebergs lie ahead. The wise course of action is to slow down, to turn away from impending disaster. Her first mate anxiously awaits her orders.

Laura turned to Shelly. "To hell with the icebergs. Let's prosecute the sons-of-bitches."

Shelly looked somewhat confused, and then laughed. "Honey, that's exactly what I wanted to hear." She hugged Laura. "I'll insist on two mil. Tessie, you know what to do."

Tessie was apparently familiar with Shelly's good cop, bad cop routine. She smiled and nodded.

"Let's have a little fun," Shelly said. "See how much money they're willing to shell out to buy us off. How high they're willing to go is a pretty good measure of how scared they are."

"What's our actual target?" Tessie asked.

"A million, not a penny less," Shelly said.

When Shelly, Tessie and Laura re-entered the conference room, Lester, Maria and Mal were already seated. Laura was surprised to see that Michael was not there. Neither Mal nor Lester could have been pleased with Michael's obviously non-scripted remark about what didn't happen on their first date. Or maybe Michael was pushing for a larger settlement than Mal was willing to shell out. Laura was disappointed. She had looked forward to seeing Michael's reaction to her rejection of his cash offer.

Lester smiled. He held up a sheet of paper. "Maria personally typed up the contract so as to keep this matter absolutely confidential. It basically states that for a lump-sum payment of blank, Laura Hamby agrees not to pursue civil or criminal action against Michael Greene for an alleged rape that occurred November 14, 1994 at the home of Luke Marshall. Michael Green denies such charges and asserts that said payment not be construed as an admission of guilt; rather it is his intention to avoid legal proceedings, which would cause pain and suffering for both the accuser and the accused, regardless of the outcome."

Lester stood, walked to Laura and handed her the paper. Laura read the document. It was essentially as Lester had paraphrased it. The space for the amount of the settlement had been left blank. She handed it to Shelly. She and Tessie took a moment or two to read it.

"My client rejects your offer of $200,000. You do not seriously believe we would consider a token amount."

"$200.000 is a fair and generous offer," Lester said, almost convincingly. "We are talking about an alleged act between two minors. The average award in those cases is $15,000."

Shelly whispered in Laura's ear. Laura nodded.

"My client says that if you add one extra zero to your offer we would give it serious consideration," Shelly said.

Mal's fist struck the table. "Girls, don't you dare play games with us. You have no goddamn case and you know it. This is blackmail, pure and simple."

"Does that mean you will make no counter offer?" Tessie asked. "Are we to gather our things and leave?"

Lester held up his hand. "My client's father is absolutely convinced of his son's innocence, and he obviously finds this entire proceeding exceedingly distasteful." He put his hand on Mal's shoulder. "I know how you must feel, Mal. But please, let me handle this negotiation."

Mal gave Shelly a menacing stare, but said nothing.

Over the next hour, Tessie teased counter offers from the Lester team. Lester played Mister Cool for his side, while Mal fumed and sweated, displaying righteous indignation at every escalation. When Mal removed his jacket, his shirt was drenched in perspiration.

Laura was fascinated by the performance of both teams. From time to time Shelly huddled with Tessie and Laura. She asked Laura relevant questions such as, "Who does your hair, honey?" Or to Tessie, "I love your little sailor girl outfit." Tessie remained dead-pan while Laura struggled to appear angry and resolute.

As the figure closed in on a million dollars, Laura began to think of how all that money could change her and Bruce's life. He could go into business on his own. She could go back to school full time. It wasn't too late. She could tell Shelly she'd changed her mind. She was tired of dwelling on the past. She pictured herself walking out of there with a briefcase full of hundred-dollar bills.

Shelly leaned toward her, "Hey, you with us, honey?"

Laura nodded. She couldn't quit now. They can't buy me, damn it. They cannot put a price on what he did.

At a million dollars, Mal angrily thrust his index finger in Shelly's direction. "This is highway robbery. Not one penny more!"

Shelly looked to Laura to deliver their final counter offer.

Laura's voice shook with emotion. "You gentlemen must be scared, really scared to offer me all that money for something you insist never happened. But you know what? I'm not after your money. This never was about money. I want to hear the jury foreman say, 'Your Honor, we find Michael Greene committed assault." She crumpled the document Lester had drawn up, and tossed it to him. The color drained from Mal's face. Lester's jaw went slack, as did Maria's.

Laura, Shelly and Tessie stood and strode from the room, the only sound the clicking of their heels on the hardwood floor. Tessie, last to exit, turned and smiled, raising her right hand to the brim of her cap, in a mock, three-finger, Girl Scout salute. "See you gentlemen in court."

Peter Rizzolo

Chapter Twenty-Nine

Shelly phoned Laura before filing the civil complaint against Michael Greene in the Lehigh County Court of Common Pleas. "Honey, this is it. There's no turning back once I do this," she said, and began reading the main body of the complaint.

Laura had been preparing to leave for work. She listened to the entire litany of legal jargon. It sounded so cold. So matter-of-fact. It was her body, her mental and emotional state it described. Her private life was about to be public record. She carried the phone to the living room where she sank into her favorite chair. "So what'll you charge me if I tell you to tear it up and forget the whole thing?"

"It's scary--I know."

"I'm more than scared. I'm terrified. The people in the courtroom, the jury, the people at work...all judging me. Tell me we're going to win, please."

"Cross my heart and hope to die," Shelly quipped. "Will that do?"

"It helps."

"Seriously, you know, honey, nothing's for sure. Juries are unpredictable."

"What about jury selection? Can we get an all-female jury?"

"That would be lovely. But the other side might not buy that option. We'll probably have to settle for six out of ten."

Laura raised her eyebrows. "Ten? Aren't there usually a dozen?"

"Criminal cases are usually twelve. But even there it can vary. People with driver's licenses are chosen at random to serve. Attorneys for both sides get a crack at them. Each side can strike up to four jurors, who are then replaced by other randomly selected jurors. It's called the *voir dire* process."

"My French is a bit rusty," Laura said.

"It means to speak the truth."

"Does that mean the prospective jurors are under oath?"

"No, but if later they are found to have lied about something that might have disqualified them, they would be dismissed from the jury. It might even result in a mistrial."

Laura, who had never served as a juror, wondered why anyone would lie. But her main concern right now was to get sympathetic, unbiased jurors. She asked, "Wouldn't anyone who appeared to be good for our side be rejected by Lester and company?"

"You're right. It's a poker game. If I like a potential juror I play it cool. Act as though they're the last person I want sitting in that box."

"Sounds like a long process."

"In most civil cases a few hours suffice. But there's a lot at stake here. I'm hoping the judge will give us a couple of days."

"What about the petition to have Michael, Arnold and Luke tested?" Laura asked.

"That's part of the complaint. It shouldn't be a problem. The DNA findings by Dr. Corbett precipitated this action."

During the six months before the trial was scheduled to begin, Bruce and Laura tried to go on with their lives. They were advised by Shelly to speak to no one about the impending trial. Not family, or even their closest friends, and especially not newspaper or TV reporters.

"Jury selection will be hard enough with all that has been reported in the news media," Shelly said. "Nothing, honey. Nada."

"Since I'm no longer employed, I might as well sign up for few more courses at Pace College," Laura said. "I'll be too busy to think about the trial."

"And Bruce?"

"He's used to fending for himself. I run an equal opportunity household. Besides, he's sick of thinking and talking about the suit. Spanish inquisitors couldn't get him to utter a word."

*****

Jury selection was held in a small, windowless courtroom that smelled of floor wax and furniture polish. It was located on the second floor of the Allentown Municipal Building.

272

Shelly and Tessie sat at one of two tables before the bench. Lester Knowles and Maria Faraday sat at the second table. Shelly assumed that Lester had deliberately chosen a female associate, so the proceedings would not resemble a boy/girl confrontation.

The presiding judge, the Honorable Matthew Glasser, a white haired, bushy-browed man, was known by Shelly to have a short fuse, as well as a disdain for attorneys, plaintiffs and especially the sorry masses that paraded through his court. But his demeanor did not intimidate the first potential juror who sat before him.

Barbara Maloney, a married middle-aged woman, appeared relaxed and somewhat bemused by the proceedings. She had the posture and assurance of someone accustomed to being listened to. Lester Knowles held in his hand the questionnaire she had completed as part of the jury screening process.

"Have you, or anyone in your family, or a close friend, ever been the victim of sexual assault?" he asked.

"Not that I'm aware of."

"What possible relevance could something you are unaware of have on your suitability as juror?" the judge asked.

"But if I were to say no, without qualifying my answer..."

"Ma'am, mine was a rhetorical question. Just answer *yes or no* to the questions posed by the attorney."

Before speaking she gave the judge a withering look. "No. I have never been sexually assaulted, and to my knowledge no family member or close friend has ever been sexually assaulted."

"Everyone's a damn lawyer these days," Glasser said. "Proceed, Mr. Knowles."

Shelly whispered to Tessie, "I like this lady. She can think for herself and isn't easily intimidated."

Lester asked the woman several more questions, as did Maria Faraday. He conferred with Mal Greene. Lester indicated the woman would be acceptable.

Shelly asked the woman if she had ever been sued, or had she ever sued anyone. She hadn't. After a few more questions, Shelly agreed to accept her.

The next two jurors were both male blue-collar workers. Lester had asked each of them, "Do you agree with the statement that people with lots of money can get away with just about anything?" One man said yeah, the other said probably. Shelly made a valiant effort to play down those statements by getting the men to affirm that they had no bias against the rich. And although they both denied such bias, the defense team dismissed them.

Maria Faraday questioned Louise Costello, a thirty-eight-year-old restaurant owner. No, she had never been sexually assaulted, nor had any close relative or friend. Yes, she had been involved in a civil suit. A customer had tripped and fallen in her restaurant, and had brought a suit against her, alleging poor lighting and a wet floor had caused her misstep. The case was dismissed when in the course of the proceeding it was learned that she had brought similar suits against several other establishments. Tessie was concerned about this woman. Might she have a bias against persons bringing a civil suit? Shelly disagreed. "I like her. She's tough. She won't be intimidated by the male jurors."

Louise Costello became the second person to be accepted by both sides.

Charles Sargent, a twenty-five-year-old married construction worker, passed muster on the usual questions about sexual assault and civil suits. Lester probed him on what he thought about the astronomical amount of money that some juries were awarding plaintiffs.

"Sometimes it seems ridiculous. Like a case I read about in the papers where a lady fell on her ass and broke her tail bone. Can you believe she got ten million dollars for pain and suffering?"

"That's out of sight," Lester agreed. "No pun intended."

"What if someone with AIDS has sex with someone, and the unsuspecting partner later develops AIDS? Would the victim be justified in bringing suit?"

"That's assault with a deadly weapon. They ought to throw the book at the guy."

After huddling by both teams, Charles Sargent was accepted.

After a full day of interrogation, they had selected only six jurors. Four women and two men. Judge Glasser was livid. "Mr. Knowles, and Ms. Spinks, you have run through more than three quarters of our jury pool. You will complete the jury selection tomorrow or suffer the consequences of having to face a judge who will have zero tolerance for any in-court shenanigans. Cross me, I will make your lives miserable."

After the final juror was selected, they were assembled and instructed by Judge Glasser: "Because of the complexity of some of the testimony you will hear in the course of this trial, the court has decided to permit you to take notes, in order to assist your recollection. However, note taking must not distract you from the proceedings. The court will provide you with note-taking materials. Please place your name on the note pad, which will be collected at the end of each day's session. Your notes will be made available when you retire to consider your verdict. During your deliberations, you may request a read-back of portions of the court's transcript, in order to clarify discrepancies in jurors' recollections of the proceedings."

Tessie compiled a list of the ten jurors who had been selected to serve. She wrote a short paragraph about each person that included his or her name, a brief description, and a listing of both positive and negative attributes. Prior to the trial, Shelly, Tessie and Laura met to discuss the jurors. Laura was given a copy to study and to commit to memory. Tessie considered Barbara Maloney and Louise Costello as potential forewomen. She believed Charles Sargent was a likely, but somewhat unpredictable, vote in their favor.

"If we can convince those three members," Shelly said, "they in turn, have to sway at least an additional three members to form a majority."

One week later when the trial began, Tessie waited anxiously to see which juror entered the courtroom first. She was not surprised when Louise Costello strode into the courtroom at the head of the jurors.

Tessie whispered to Shelly, "Looks like we got our forewoman."

Shelly nodded."

"Hey, what's going on?" Laura asked.

"Tell you later," Tessie said. She sketched the jury box and the positions of the individual jurors. She circled Louise Costello's position and handed the sketch to Laura. "She's exactly who we wanted."

Laura scanned the crowd. The small courtroom was filled almost to capacity Mostly women. One group filled an entire row. They were wearing large buttons.

Laura whispered to Tessie, "What's the PCAR"

"The Pennsylvania Coalition Against Rape. They'll be rooting for you."

Laura was relieved not to see anyone she knew. She had asked Bruce not to come, at least not until the final day of the trial. Who were all those people? Were they just curious? Had some been victims?

Dr. Jane Corbett was the first witness called by the plaintiff. After establishing her medical training, various credentials, and her expertise in the area of reproductive medicine, Shelly asked, "Dr. Corbett, I understand the plaintiff consulted you regarding her inability to become pregnant."

"That is correct."

"How did she happen to choose you?"

"I had recently joined the staff of St. Joseph's Hospital, where she worked as record-room supervisor. One of the staff doctors had recommended she see me."

"And what did you find on examining her?"

"Physical examination, ultrasound studies and an MRI of the pelvis all indicated pelvic inflammatory disease as the cause of her infertility."

"Dr. Corbett, would you explain to the jury what is meant by pelvic inflammatory disease?" Shelly asked.

"Pelvic inflammatory disease is infection of a woman's reproductive organs. It may include the cervix, uterus, fallopian tubes, ovaries, and surrounding structures."

"And how would a woman acquire such an infection?" Shelly asked.

"Through sexual intercourse with an infected partner."

"Were all of the plaintiff's sexual organs found to be diseased?' Shelly asked.

"Her cervix, uterus and ovaries were normal. Her fallopian tubes, however, were severely damaged."

"Why did you advise her to have her fallopian tubes removed?" Shelly asked.

"She was considering *in vitro* fertilization. We know from well-documented studies that removing diseased fallopian tubes will enhance the chances of the success," Dr. Corbett explained.

"I see. Why did you search for DNA in the pathology specimens?"

"I had several reasons. Since as early as my residency training, I had suspected that in cases of sexual assault the perpetrator's DNA might survive long after the time of the event."

"Had you searched for DNA in pathology specimens from other patients?" Shelly asked.

"Yes, and never found any. But recent techniques for extraction of DNA from formalin-fixed, paraffin-embedded tissue sections gave me reason to continue to search."

Shelly walked back to her table where Tessie and Laura sat. She gave Laura a reassuring smile. "And your second reason, Dr. Corbett?"

"I theorized that the inflammatory process in her pelvis may have trapped DNA material and prevented its destruction by her body's normal immune processes."

"Perhaps you might explain to the jury what led you to that theory?"

Dr. Corbett turned toward the jury and addressed them directly. "There are numerous examples of live organisms surviving in the human body for years. Tuberculosis is a prime example. Tuberculosis organisms in a person's lungs can be rendered harmless, even if not killed by the body's immune system. But if for some reason the immune system is suppressed, the body's defenses break down, and live organisms are released. This happens in the elderly and in persons with AIDS or other immune deficiency diseases."

Laura could tell Shelly was pleased with Dr. Corbett's cool and authoritative manner. But, while Dr. Corbett spoke, Laura noticed several jury members taking notes. Were they able to grasp. all that she was saying, Laura wondered?

"You said you had several reasons," Shelly said. "Are there others?"

"Researchers at Imperial College, London, published a study in the *Journal of Biological Chemistry* in which they discuss a sperm's apparent ability to dodge the woman's immune response. They suggest there may be many mechanisms in play. Glycoproteins on the surface of sperm may prevent them from being attacked by the female immune system."

Shelly held up a sheaf of papers. She handed it to Dr. Corbett. "You are referring to this study?"

"Yes."

"Your Honor, a copy of this article has been given to the defense team." Shelly turned to the witness. "Dr. Corbett, did you personally check the pathology specimens for DNA?"

"No. The specimens were sent to the hospital pathologist. He made numerous cytology sections, preparing them in such a way that foreign DNA, if present, could be extracted. He then sent those slides to specialty laboratories to carry out tests."

Shelly handed Dr. Corbett some papers. "Do you recognize this, Dr. Corbett?"

Dr. Corbett scanned the three pages. "Yes. These are the reports sent to me by the DNA laboratories."

"Can you tell the jury what they reported?"

"Three genotypes were identified that were not those of Mrs. Hamby. One was consistent with gonorrhea and the other two were human genotypes."

"Dr. Corbett, did you share these findings with your medical peers?"

"I presented a detailed report at a conference of fertility specialists in Orlando, Florida, and subsequently submitted my findings to *The Journal of Assisted Reproduction and DNA Research.*"

"Has the study been accepted for publication?" Shelly asked.

"Yes, it has."

"Thank you, Dr. Corbett."

Lester looked as though he had just stepped out of the pages of Playboy. His Italian tailored suit, flamboyant tie, pastel dress shirt, gold cufflinks, and alligator shoes, all exquisitely coordinated, announced to the jury that he was not a person accustomed to losing. His left hand supported an immodestly sized diamond.

He acknowledged Dr. Corbett's qualifications and expertise as a fertility specialist. "Dr. Corbett, finding someone's DNA other than her spouse's in the pathology specimens removed at the time of surgery in no way established when the DNA might have contaminated her tissues, did it?"

"Based on her history..."

"Please answer yes or no. Could you say when the DNA in question entered the plaintiff's body?"

"No. I could not."

"But you obviously believed she had been sexually assaulted. The entire premise of your published article purported finding DNA many years following a sexual assault. Is that not true?"

"It was based on my belief that her account of what had happened to her was accurate."

Lester looked from juror to juror. "Hardly the scientific skepticism one requires of a research protocol."

"Sir, in all due respect, you obviously have not read my published article."

"Again, not a conclusion consistent with scrupulous scientific analysis. I have in fact read your article several times."

Laura believed Lester was treating Dr. Corbett with condescension and disdain. She was impressed how her doctor was not allowing him to fluster her.

"Then you should recall, Sir, that I concluded that if in fact the woman had not had intercourse with any man, other than her husband, since the night of the reported assault, then I must conclude that the DNA of the rapist had survived many years in the woman's body."

"Looking at your other published articles, it is apparent you have a special interest in sexual assault."

"As a fertility expert, that is not unusual," Dr. Corbett said.

"Might I suggest another motive? Had you ever claimed to have been sexually assaulted?"

Shelly stood. "I object, Your Honor!"

"Objection sustained," Glasser said. "Mr. Knowles, this line of questioning is highly improper. Dr. Corbett, you may decline to answer if you so choose."

Laura exchanged glances with Shelly and Tessie. Shelly had mentioned once in passing that Dr. Corbett may have had a personal reason for her interest in rape, but she had not pursued the question.

Dr. Corbett was silent for a few moments. "Yes. I was twelve years old. The boy was the older brother of one of my friends."

"Did you press charges?"

"Yes."

"And the outcome?"

"He was acquitted."

"The boy's sister testified that you were lying, didn't she?"

"She was trying to protect her brother."

"His sister's testimony was obviously believable. The charges against her brother were dropped. I have no further questions..."

"I object, Your Honor," Shelly said."Study after study has shown that teenage boys accused of statutory rape are rarely convicted."

"Objection overruled," Judge Glasser said. "The jury is not to base their decision on statistical analysis. They must weigh the facts and circumstances and evidence specific to this case."

Tessie whispered to Laura, "It's okay. The jury's not likely to know the stats on rape cases brought to trial. Shelly made her point."

Laura's heart ached for Dr. Corbett. To have that thrown in her face after all that time! Laura had the urge to stand and scream profanities at Lester Knowles.

Shelly, seemingly sensing Laura's anger, whispered, "It's best not to pursue that. If we drag it out, it makes a bigger impression on jurors."

Lester walked to the table where Michael was seated. He picked up some papers. "Dr. Corbett, this is the report of the study that appeared in the *Journal of Biological Chemistry*. They said that glycoproteins on the surface of sperm may protect them from destruction by the woman's immune system. Is that correct?"

"Yes."

"It was supposition, not a scientifically established fact. Isn't that correct?"

"I have shown that DNA did survive in Mrs. Hamby's body," Dr. Corbett said. She looked toward the jury box. "That is an established fact." She turned to face Lester. "I referred to the study as a possible explanation for why the DNA was not destroyed by my patient's immune system."

"You did not answer my question. I asked if the study you referred to scientifically proved that foreign DNA can withstand destruction by the human immune system."

"It did not," Dr. Corbett answered.

"Thank you, Dr. Corbett, that will be all for now."

Martha Carver was the next witness for the plaintiff. She was on the stand for more than an hour. Laura hardly believed she was the same girl with whom she had gone to school. Gone was her flaxen hair and boyish good looks. Now Martha was a striking brunette with cover-girl looks and sensual lips. *The magic of augmentation!*

"Ms. Carver," Shelly asked, "did you invite Laura Hamby to the party at Luke Marshall's home on the evening of Friday, November 14, 1994.

"Yes, I did."

Shelly's long, jet-black hair encircled her face, accenting her penetrating dark eyes and fair complexion. She wore a gray tailored pantsuit. She was in constant motion as she spoke.

"Would you say you were close friends?" she asked.

"No. I knew her, of course. We were in a class together our third year of high school. Luke Marshall told me that his friend Michael Greene was coming and didn't have a date."

"But why wouldn't Michael call her himself?"

"Your Honor," Lester said, "this tedious line of questioning is utterly pointless."

"I agree," Judge Glasser said. "The court is not interested in teenage intrigues regarding party invitations."

"Your Honor, will you not allow the witness to answer my question?"

"Answer the question, Ms. Carver," the judge said.

"He told me she wouldn't go if Michael Greene had asked her directly. He said to tell her that her friends Ginger Spalding and Jimmy Caniglia would be there."

"Why is that?" Shelly asked.

"I don't know. I didn't ask."

"I see," Shelly said. "Did you hang out with her during the party?"

"No. I was in the pool most of the evening. Laura came out on the patio and watched us play polo. I asked her to join in, but she said she couldn't. The way she said it, I assumed she was having her period."

Laura blushed. God! Why did she have to say that? The things people remember! She noticed a Madonna-like smile on the face of juror Maloney.

"Your Honor, I object to this line of questioning," Lester said.

Judge Glasser agreed and addressed Shelly directly. "Ms. Spinks, the court is interested in what the witness knows about the alleged assault," the judge said, "not a detailed description of the party."

"Ms. Carver, did you see Laura Hamby fall?" Shelly asked.

"No. I heard the commotion. I saw Arnold helping her stand. She collapsed in his arms. He carried her somewhere."

"When did you next see her?" Shelly asked.

"A friend of Laura's, Ginger Spalding, reminded me that I was supposed to drive Laura home. We changed out of our bathing suits into party clothes and went looking for her."

"Why didn't Michael Greene drive her to the party? Wasn't she his date?"

"Laura agreed to come only if I agreed to pick her up and drive her home."

"Did she tell you why?"

"She said there was no way she would ever get into a car with Michael Greene."

"Did she explain why?"

"No."

"You didn't ask?"

"No. He had a reputation for being aggressive..."

"I object, Your Honor. That is hearsay and should be stricken from the record," Lester demanded.

"Objection sustained. That remark is indeed hearsay. The witness must testify to what she has personally seen or experienced. The jury is to disregard the witness's last answer."

"Had you ever personally experienced aggressive sexual behavior on the part of Michael Greene?" Shelly asked.

"No."

"I see. Let's move on. How long after Arnold had carried the plaintiff away did you and Ginger go looking for her?" Shelly asked.

"An hour, maybe a bit longer."

Martha went on to describe how she and Ginger couldn't find Laura anywhere. Then someone told them they had seen Arnold carry her up to the second floor.

"We ran upstairs. While we were looking through the rooms, we heard her scream. I was first to get there. Laura was standing with her back to me. As I approached her, I saw that her hands were bound by a pair of panty hose. The other end of the hose was tied to the bedpost. She was naked. There was blood on her legs, the floor, the bed. Ginger came in. When she saw all that blood she ran for some towels."

"I helped her free her hands. She kept repeating that it was three of them. She said her eyes had been covered and mouth taped shut."

"Did you see anything that might have been used to blindfold and gag her?" Shelly asked.

"I really didn't look. She had vomited. The floor was a mess. Her clothes were spread everywhere. We concentrated on calming her down, cleaning her up, and getting her dressed."

"Had she recognized any of their voices?"

"She told me that Michael Greene was one of them. She said she was sure of that. Laura told me that she had freed one of her legs and had kicked one of the boys, knocking him to the floor. He yelled at her. She said it was his voice... Michael Greene's."

Laura scanned the jury. Their heads turned almost in unison toward Dr. Michael Greene. She followed their gaze. He was whispering in the ear of his attorney.

Shelly said nothing for several moments, staring at the jury the entire time. She turned to the witness.

"Ms. Carver, what was your relationship with Luke Marshall?"

"In our last semester in high school Luke and I became close friends."

"Were you boyfriend and girlfriend?" Shelly asked.

"Yes."

"Can you tell the court of a conversation you had with Luke Marshall while he was a student at Stanford?" Shelly asked.

Lester objected. "Your Honor, whatever she says Luke Marshall told her is hearsay."

"Objection sustained. Can you recast your question, Ms. Spinks?"

"Your Honor," Shelly said, "Luke Marshall is my next witness and is present in the court. Since he can speak on his own behalf, I request an exception to the hearsay rule."

"You should have advised the court of that fact before initiating your line of questioning," Judge Glasser said.

"In all due respect, Your Honor, he was on my witness list."

"I have never met or seen Mr. Marshall, so I had no way of knowing he was present in the court at this time. Do not patronize me."

"I object to the plaintiff's attorney's request for hearsay exemption, Your Honor," Lester demanded.

"Objection overruled, Mr. Knowles. Exception granted."

"Martha, did anything he said shock you?"

"I was convinced that he had been lying to me all along about his involvement in the assault."

"Where did this occur?" Shelly asked

"It was after a fraternity function he had invited me to. He had drunk too much and was high on something. I drove him back to his dorm room. For some reason he began talking about the party at his home," Martha said.

"He was referring to the party at which the plaintiff was sexually assaulted?" Shelly asked.

"Ms. Carver, would you tell the court what Luke Marshall told you about the party in question?" Shelly asked.

Martha explained that Luke had described how he and Arnold Sommers had walked in on Michael, who was in bed with the plaintiff.

"He told me that he and Arnold watched for awhile, then started to back out of the room. But then

Laura waved to them and invited them to join her and Michael."

Laura glanced toward the jury box. She looked from juror to juror She doubted any of them understood the intricacies of the rules governing hearsay. Some looked confused. Barbara Maloney looked directly at Laura. It was a penetrating, non-committal look. Shelly had asked Laura not to smile at individual jury members. She must project by her facial expression an attitude of quiet confidence and interest. She engaged Barbara Maloney's stare for a few moments then directed her attention to the witness.

"Ms. Carver, Luke Marshall didn't mention that Laura Hamby's hands were tied to the bedpost?" Shelly asked Martha.

"No."

"Did you believe what he told you?" Shelly asked.

"Ms. Spinks," the judge interrupted, "this is not the Inquisition. The court is not interested in what the witness believes."

"You must have been quite surprised by what he said," Shelly continued.

"I was shocked. My relationship with Luke was already foundering for a variety of reasons."

"For instance?" Shelly asked.

"His drinking, his drug use. I didn't like his friends."

"Did Luke Marshall tell you anything else?"

"Yes. I recall his exact words. He said, 'That bitch gave me the clap.'"

There was a communal gasp from the jury box. They stared at Laura. A woman in the rear of the court stood and shouted "Liar, liar, liar."

Tessie whispered to Laura, "She comes to all the rape trials."

Judge Glasser banged his gavel. "Order in the court. Anyone who disturbs the orderly conduct of this court will be ejected and prevented from reentering." He turned to Shelly, "You may proceed, Ms. Spinks."

"You were not aware at the time that Luke Marshall had been treated for gonorrhea?"

"No. I was furious. I never saw him again."

Lester could do little to shake Martha's testimony. "Did it ever occur to you that the plaintiff had been playing along with the boys? That she might have voluntarily had them tie her hands to the bedpost?"

"When I first discovered her in that condition I had no reason not to believe her story. But when I got back to Luke's house after taking Laura home I talked with Michael. When I described what I had seen in the bedroom he got really pale. His hands were shaking. He sat next to me. Tears filled his eyes. He kept repeating: 'Poor Laura...I can't believe this. God, who would do such a thing?'"

"It was a long time ago. Are you certain that is what he said?"

"Yes, because Ginger Spalding and I talked about it afterwards."

"So Michael's behavior and what he said were causing you to question her story?"

"It wasn't only that. The following day when Michael showed me the photograph of Arnold carrying her up the stairs, smiling, I was even more confused."

"Ms. Carver, if I might paraphrase your testimony," Lester said, "you have told the court that Michael Greene's behavior seemed inconsistent with what the plaintiff would have us believe?"

"That is an unanswerable question, Mr. Knowles. We have not as yet heard from the plaintiff," Judge Glasser said.

"Yes, but Your Honor, Ms. Carver has already told the court that the plaintiff had accused Michael Greene..."

"Rephrase your question or sit down."

Lester sported a rather unconvincing smile. He walked to the witness box.

"Ms. Carver, the plaintiff told you in the presence of a second party, namely Ginger Spaulding, that she had been sexually assaulted by three young men. That she was certain one of them was Michael Greene. Is that true?"

"Yes. She didn't actually see him. She recognized his voice."

"I see," Lester said. "Did you tell Michael Greene that she had accused him of sexual assault?"

"No. I was confused. She repeatedly said that he was one of them. But the way he insisted that we should have taken her to the hospital. And the fact that she hadn't actually seen him...."

"Yes, Ms. Carver... she was blindfolded and emotionally devastated....you were quite right to doubt her version of what happened."

"From observing Michael's behavior and the next day after seeing the photographs, I had reason to believe she might have been mistaken."

"I have no further questions," Lester said.

"May I re-examine, Your Honor?" Shelly asked.

"If the defense has no objection," Glasser said.

Lester shrugged. Shelly approached Martha.

"Ms. Carver, you stated that Michael Greene was upset with you for not taking Laura to the hospital or to a doctor. Is that correct?"

"Yes."

"How did he learn that you hadn't taken her to a doctor?"

"When we returned to Luke's house after taking Laura home, Michael was still there. He asked where we had taken her. I told him that Ginger and I had pleaded with her to get medical help. That she refused and insisted we take her home."

"Did it also occur to you that once he learned that you hadn't brought her to a doctor, that he had nothing to lose by pretending to be upset with you?"

"At the time no," Martha said.

"And later?" Shelly asked.

"The following day when we went out to Luke's place to clean up, I asked Michael if maybe he should call Laura to see how she was doing."

"How did he respond?"

"He said we should respect her decision. That it was better for everyone if we just let her be."

"Did that cause you to consider that he was being insincere when he admonished you for not taking Laura for medical care?"

"I object, Your Honor," Lester shouted. "She is asking the witness to assess my client's motivation."

"Objection sustained. It is apparent what you are getting at, but I must not allow you to continue this line of questioning."

"Thank you, Your Honor," Shelly said. "Since my intention is apparent, I believe I have made my point."

Peter Rizzolo

Chapter Thirty

Ginger Spaulding was next to take the stand. Her flaming red hair had softened to a lustrous reddish-brown. She looked at Laura and smiled as she sat in the witness box.

"Ms. Spalding, did you doubt the accuracy of Laura's version of what happened to her at the party at Luke's home?" Shelly asked.

"We were friends. I often teased Laura about her Catholic upbringing and her determination to wait for that one special guy."

Ginger looked directly at Laura. "I was convinced, at that point in her life, she would not voluntarily have had sex with Michael Greene or anyone else."

"Ms. Spalding," Shelly asked, "did you return to the home of Luke Marshall the day following the party to help clean up?"

"Yes, I did."

"Did you speak with Michael Greene?"

"Yes."

"Can you describe your interaction with him at that time?" Shelly asked.

"He showed me a photo of Laura drinking from a flask. He said it was his father's. That his dad would kill him if he lost it. Michael wondered if, when we dressed Laura, we might have seen his flask anywhere. I told him I hadn't. He and Luke searched the whole house. Luke even checked out the swimming pool, thinking maybe she dropped it when she fell."

Maria Faraday, Lester's associate, cross-examined. "We have witnesses asserting that the plaintiff was so drunk she couldn't stand or focus her eyes. Wouldn't her virtuous resolve have been considerably weakened under those circumstances?"

"I object, Your Honor," Shelly said.

"Sustained. You are asking the witness to speculate about someone else's behavior."

"Had you ever seen the plaintiff under the influence of alcohol before the evening in question?" Maria asked.

"No."

"Not even a little drunk?" she asked.

"No. When we partied she had soft drinks. She didn't like the taste of beer."

"So you cannot say, based on previous observations, how she might react when falling-down drunk?"

Ginger looked at the judge. "Am I again being asked to speculate, Your Honor?"

Judge Glasser leaned toward the witness. "Ms. Spaulding, you appear to have a better grasp of the law than some of the attorneys who stand here before me."

A few laughs rippled through the courtroom.

"I withdraw the question. The witness is excused."

Laura was shocked as Luke Marshall took the stand. He had gone from a scrawny high school kid to middle-aged in a mere six years. His hairline had receded, and he sported a half-dollar bald spot. He was wearing a leather jacket, sport shirt and khaki chinos. His right hand shook as he was sworn in. Was he just nervous, Laura wondered, or was he an alcoholic in need of a drink?

"Martha Carver has testified as to what you told her happened the night of the party at your home. Would you tell the court what really happened?" Shelly asked.

"I heard that Laura had fallen and that Arnold had taken her to an upstairs bedroom. I went to check on her. She seemed to be asleep. I shook her shoulder to make sure she was okay. She opened her eyes. She was covered by a sheet. I could see that she had no clothes on. I told her she could stay overnight. That my parents wouldn't be back for a couple of days."

"She said she wasn't up to going home just yet, but that she couldn't stay overnight. I got her another pillow. I got a towel from the bathroom and used it to dry her hair. I asked if I should get her more ice. She said no, but would I sit with her for awhile. I didn't need much encouragement."

"You had sex with her?"

"Yes."

"Did you force her?"Shelly asked.

"Absolutely not."

"Did you use a condom?"

"No."

"So what you told Martha Carver a year later was not true?"

"I made that up. I had met someone else. I wanted to end my relationship with Martha. And because I knew she had a lingering suspicion that I might have had something to do with what happened to Laura that night. I told her that story, hoping she'd walk out on me."

"Did you also lie about getting a venereal disease from Laura Hamby?"

"No. That part was true. I saw a doctor a week after the party. He treated me for gonorrhea."

Laura nudged Tessie. Tessie had called two or three pharmacies in the general area where Luke had lived at the time. She told them she was a doctor at a local emergency room and had a patient named Luke Marshall who was in anaphylactic shock. She needed to know if he had ever been given a prescription for penicillin. Two pharmacies found no such record. A third pharmacy consulted their prescription archive and confirmed that he had been prescribed penicillin on three occasions. One was issued November 21, 1994.

Shelly asked, "You admit that you lied to Martha Carver, Mr. Marshall. How is the court to know what part of your testimony to believe?"

"I know it sounds somewhat illogical, but we had been drinking and I was more than a little under the influence. It was the anniversary of the party at my house."

"Mr. Marshall, previous witnesses have testified to the fact that when they entered the room, there was blood all over the place."

"There were blood stains on the sheet. I did notice that. I remember seeing that. But nowhere else that I can recall. Whatever happened to cause her to bleed must have taken place after we made love," Luke insisted. He looked directly at Laura.

Laura could barely control herself when he described what he had done as making love. Her face burned with indignation. Tessie squeezed her hand. All three men were claiming they had had consensual sex with her. It was outrageous, but it did make sense as a defense. Neither Luke nor Arnold knew to whom the second DNA specimen belonged. The full DNA report hadn't as yet been presented.

"Mr. Marshall, do you recognize the military officer seated in the third row of this courtroom?" Shelly pointed to Captain Arnold Sommers.

"I do."

"Would you identify him for the court?"

"That is my friend, Arnold Sommers."

"Martha Carver has testified that Arnold Sommers had told her that he had had consensual sex with the plaintiff after bringing her upstairs," Shelly said.

Laura realized that Shelly had gotten around the hearsay rule.

Shelly continued. "We have a signed deposition from the defendant, Michael Greene, asserting that he went up to the bedroom after he saw Arnold leave. And that he had had consensual sex with the defendant. So you were either third in line or the defendant is lying or Arnold Sommers is lying or all three of you are lying."

"I object," Lester shouted. "Ms. Spinks is accusing the witnesses of perjury without any evidential foundation."

"Objection sustained. The witness is not on trial and need only testify as to what he knows and not to hypothetical questions."

"I have no further questions, Your Honor," Shelly said.

Despite being overruled, Laura realized that Shelly had made an important point. If Luke had indeed been third in line, and Laura hadn't bled according to his testimony, where had all that blood come from?

The following morning, Captain Arnold Sommers in dress uniform, his left chest covered with an array of ribbons and medals, took the stand. Laura had only a vague recollection of him as the young man who had carried her to the bedroom.

"You were a freshman at Pennsylvania State at the time. How did you happen to go to Luke Marshall's party, the night in question?" Shelly asked.

"Luke and I were friends. He was a year behind me. But we were on the wrestling team together. I happened to be in town that day. I just called to say hi. That's when he invited me."

"Had you met Laura Hamby before that night?"

"No, ma'am. I did notice her around school during my senior year at Central High, but she was friends with a different bunch of kids."

"Tell us what happened at the party," Shelly asked.

"I noticed her sitting beside the pool by herself. She was drinking from one of those pocket flasks. When I saw her stand and stagger I was afraid she might fall into the pool. I was clear on the other side. I ran as fast as I could, but didn't get there in time."

"She fell as you were running toward her?"

"Yes, sir. She hit the edge of a chaise lounge. She got herself quite a goose egg on the back of her head. She was lucky not to have hit the pavement."

"Was there a lot of bleeding?"

"No."

"Was she conscious when you got to her?"

"She was making jokes about it. I don't recall exactly what she said. I think she might have asked me if I wanted to dance. She was obviously drunk."

"Obviously?" Lester asked.

"Her speech was slurred. She couldn't focus her eyes. When I helped her to stand, her knees buckled and she fell into my arms."

"Why did you carry her upstairs to a bedroom?"

"There was so much noise and so many kids downstairs that I figured it would be better to take her where she could sleep it off."

"How long did you stay with her?" Shelly asked.

"First off, I ran and got some ice to put on the back of her head. Then I sat on the edge of the bed to make sure she was going to be okay."

"What happened then?"

"I really hate talking about this. It was something between her and me."

"I'm afraid you must, Captain Sommers. Did you and Laura Hamby have sexual relations?"

Arnold looked at Laura. He whispered loud enough to be heard, "I'm sorry. I'm really sorry."

"Would you answer the question, please?"

"Yes, ma'am. Neither of us expected it to happen. She called me her knight in shining armor. I kissed her hand as a kind of joke. Then I kissed her arm, her neck. I was lost in the moment, overcome. I kept telling her I was sorry."

"You did not force or coerce her in any way?"

"No."

"How long were you with her?" Shelly asked.

"I don't know. Maybe a half hour. Not more than an hour. She fell asleep in my arms. I got dressed and went downstairs."

"Did you use a condom?"

"No. ma'am. I hadn't expected to have sex. It was foolish. I know."

"You knew Laura Hamby was drunk. You testified to the fact that she couldn't stand or even focus her eyes."

"Yes, ma'am. I believed that at the time."

"Were you morally justified in having sex with someone in that condition?"

"At the time I did not believe I was taking advantage of her," Arnold said.

"And now, how would you assess your behavior?"

"Even the day after it happened I realized I had used poor judgment. I wanted to call her."

"Why didn't you?" Shelly asked.

"She was claiming to have been raped. I was concerned that she would think I was one of those guys."

"The defendant, Michael Greene, stated in his deposition that he went up to the bedroom ten or fifteen minutes after he had seen you carry her upstairs. Yet you claim that you were there almost an hour. How do you explain that?"

"I object, Your Honor. The witness is not compelled to reconcile his testimony with that of my client," Lester said.

"Objection sustained. Would you rephrase your question, Ms. Spinks?"

"How confident are you, sir, that you were with my client about an hour?"

"Forty-five minutes. Maybe longer."

"Captain Sommers, have you ever been treated for a venereal disease?" Shelly asked.

Arnold looked at the judge, then the jury before responding. Laura sat at the edge of her seat. Tessie had tried to get Arnold's medical records released by the Student Health Service at Penn State University. They refused to do so without his permission or a court order. The Magistrate in that jurisdiction had refused.

"My medical history is a private matter that has no bearing on this case," Arnold said.

"On the contrary. We know that the plaintiff developed gonorrhea after that night. . ."

Lester jumped to his feet. "I object, Your Honor. She could have contracted gonorrhea at anytime in the past six years."

"Objection sustained. We have not been presented proof as to when she developed gonorrhea."

Laura's jaw tightened a she sensed the entire jury turn toward her.

Tessie reached over, resting her hand on Laura.

"So you made no effort to contact Laura Hamby after the night of the party?" Shelly asked.

"No, ma'am. I didn't."

"And why is that?"

"I felt embarrassed and guilty. I realized that she might not even remember what had happened between us."

"At least not the way you described it," Shelly said.

Laura instinctively looked at Lester Knowles, fully expecting him to object. He started to open his mouth but must have thought better of it. It wouldn't hurt his client, if the jury had reason to suspect that Arnold was the one who had sexually assaulted Laura.

"I have no further questions," Shelly said.

Lester approached the witness. "Captain Sommers, while a student at Penn State and later at West Point, and in your present military assignment, have you ever been subject to disciplinary action?

"No, sir."

"And in fact, aren't several of those ribbons, and that bronze pendent, awards for outstanding leadership and exceptional moral character?"

"Yes, sir."

"I have no further questions of the witness, Your Honor."

At the close of that day's session Shelly, Laura and Tessie went to Shelly's hotel suite. They kicked off their shoes and raided the liquor cabinet. Laura avoided the vodka. She popped a can of light beer.

"Hey! I thought you didn't like the taste of beer."

"Not when I was seventeen," Laura said. She sat cross-legged on the rug.

"So our entire case boils down to who the jury believes. Martha's account or Luke's testimony?"

"How could Arnold tell that cock-and-bull story with a straight face?" Laura asked.

"That was such a touching scene after the rape; Michael in tears, scolding Ginger for not taking you to the hospital."

Shelly was unusually quiet, as she sipped a tumbler of Johnny Walker scotch.

"Hey, boss lady, you okay?" Tessie asked.

"I'm thinking about your testimony tomorrow, Laura. We may sink or swim, depending how well you do." She reached into her purse and pulled out some papers. "Let's rehearse. I'm going to play Lester, Tessie will be the judge. This will take some time. You ready for it?"

Laura checked her watch. "Bruce is coming by in an hour."

"If we're not finished, he can cool his heels in the bar," Shelly said.

After picking up Laura at Shelly's hotel room, Bruce drove her to their motel. Bruce tried his best to encourage Laura, but was unable to assuage her fears. Although cameras were not allowed in the court, reporters were present in large numbers. Television reporters each evening regurgitated the day's happenings. As much as she wanted not to, Laura scoured the papers and watched the televised reports. Most of the pundits predicted a verdict of not guilty. They maintained that the evidence was circumstantial and fell far short of a greater weight of evidence required in a civil action. Others asked why she claimed to have been raped and then did nothing about it? Ex-prosecutors appeared like raindrops in a summer storm. Most were not convinced, by the evidence presented, that the young doctor was guilty.

Laura told Bruce that she was due to take the stand the following day. She must project an aura of confidence, not be intimidated by Lester's swagger.

Following the mock cross-examination by Shelly and Tessie, Laura was beginning to feel better about testifying. But she was afraid that Lester might come up with something they hadn't anticipated.

Laura stepped into the witness box. She had dreaded this moment from the onset of the trial. But to her astonishment, once she sat before the court she felt calm and eager to tell her story. Shelly had coached her on every conceivable question Lester might ask. Or so she thought.

"Mrs. Hamby, it is your contention and conviction, is it not, that on the night of November 14, 1994, you were brutally sexually assaulted by three young men at the home of Luke Marshall?" Shelly asked.

Laura looked directly at the jury. "Yes, that is my contention and conviction."

"Can you tell me your state of mind in the days, weeks, months following that incident?"

"I couldn't concentrate on school work. My friends shunned me."

"That must have been extremely hurtful," Shelly said. "Can you tell the jury more?"

Laura took a deep breath before answering. Bruce could probably describe her state of mind better than she. "I slept fitfully. I had a recurring dream of being tied down and attacked by wild dogs that tore at my body. I would awaken, drenched in perspiration and shaking uncontrollably."

"What emotions were you feeling, Laura?"

"Intense, unrelenting anger. I wanted to hurt those young men. I wanted them to suffer."

"Why didn't you go to the police?" Shelly whispered.

"I was ashamed to talk about it. Even to think about it made me physically sick. My mother said no one would believe me." Laura paused to compose herself. She didn't want to cry. Not in front of Michael. She must be strong.

"You have told me how it affected you physically. Would you describe that to the court?"

"At times my heart would race, I'd become light-headed and overtaken by overwhelming fear. I thought I was going crazy."

"Was there no one to comfort you?" Shelly asked. "Certainly your mother," Shelly said softly, just loud enough for the jury to hear.

"My mother was in a state of shock. I was her only child. She raised me to be a strong, responsible person. She wasn't ready to forgive me for lying to her. For being weak and vulnerable, for shattering our lives."

"For lying to her?"

"I told her I was going to a movie with my girlfriends that night. She would never allow me to go to a party where there wasn't adult supervision."

"I see," Shelly said. "And was your father supportive of you at that time?" she asked.

"My parents divorced when I was an infant. I know him only from photographs."

"You were an honor student at Central High. Why did you drop out only six months before graduation?"

"Life was intolerable at home and at school. I wanted to go away where no one knew me."

"You got some medical help after you left home?"

"Two or three months after I was on my own I went to a community mental health center. I was losing weight. I couldn't sleep. I saw a psychiatric social worker who said I was suffering from depression and panic attacks. She got her supervising medical doctor to write me a prescription."

"Did the medication help?"

"I took it for a few weeks. It didn't help all that much."

"Did the doctor change your medication?"

"I never saw the doctor."

"Why is that, Laura?" Shelly asked.

"I couldn't bring myself to talk with a man about what had happened. I threw myself into my new job."

"That was several years ago. Do you still have panic attacks?"

"For a long time I rarely had any. But with all that's happened in the last few months, they've started up again."

"Would you tell the jury why after all these years you are choosing to come forward and seek compensation in a court of law?"

"My husband and I want children. We went to a fertility expert. She discovered that as the result of a sexually transmitted disease, my internal organs were so damaged that it would be impossible to conceive. I was shocked. I had never had consensual sex with anyone other than my husband. And he has never had a venereal disease."

"In all due respect to the witness," Lester said, "her husband was not likely to tell her that he had ever had a venereal disease."

"You are out-of-order and you darn well know it, Mr. Knowles," Judge Glasser said. "The court reporter will strike his remark from the record. Proceed, Ms. Spinks."

"I understand you and your husband are considering what is called *in vitro* fertilization."

"Yes. We very much want to have children."

"I understand that is a very complicated and expensive procedure that your insurance would not cover."

"It often has to be tried multiple times to achieve success, and that can be extremely expensive."

"I have no further questions, Your Honor."

Lester approached the witness box. "You have implied that you had reason not to like or trust Michael Green, and yet you agreed to go to the party in question?"

"A couple of my friends were going. I planned on hanging out with them."

"But you did spend some time with Michael Green?"

"I was never alone with him."

"You danced?"

"Once. He cut in on me."

"When did he give you alcohol?"

"I had just opened a can of Coke. He said he had something better to drink. He pulled a flask from his pocket. He said it was mostly water and a little vodka. He took a sip, then offered to give me a taste."

"And you accepted?

"I didn't like it. I added some of my coke to the flask."

"I'm confused. You accepted something to drink from someone who by your own assessment, you didn't trust...is that what you're telling me?"

Laura nodded. She knew he had talked her into a corner.

"Please answer yes or no so the jury can be certain of you response," Lester said.

"Yes."

"You are prone to risky behavior, Mrs. Hamby, are you not?"

Shelly stood. "I object, Your Honor. The attorney for the defense is making a summary judgment and asking the plaintiff to agree with him."

"Objection sustained. Mr. Knowles, you have not demonstrated a pattern of risky behavior."

"If you bear with me I will, Your Honor." Lester stood facing the jury. "Mrs. Hamby, were you ever arrested?"

"Mr. Knowles, as you well know," Judge Glasser said, "you cannot question the witness about arrests, only convictions."

"Your Honor, I am not concerned about criminality but rather about the plaintiff's behavior that placed her in that position."

"You are skating on very thin ice, Mr. Knowles." The judge turned toward Laura. "You may answer the question, Mrs. Hamby."

Laura had discussed the incident with Shelly. They had hoped it wouldn't come up, but Shelly wasn't concerned.

"A bunch of my friends and I went to swim at an abandoned quarry..."

"Please answer my question, Mrs. Hamby. Wasn't the group you were with arrested for trespassing, possession of drugs, alcohol, and indecent exposure?"

"Yes." Laura turned to Judge Glasser. "May I be permitted to explain?"

"Yes, you may."

Laura looked toward the jury, who almost in unison to moved to the edge of their seats. They seemed more amused than concerned...perhaps recalling similar incidents in their youth.

"It was not unusual for local high school students to swim at the quarry. As we were getting out of the water and drying off, a police car pulled up.

They held us at gunpoint. They ordered us to drop our towels and put our hands over our heads. They took Polaroid pictures of us."

"Really, Your Honor, I would like to move on," Lester said.

"The witness is entitled to explain the circumstances of the arrest. You may continue, Mrs. Hamby."

"...The police watched as we dressed, then took us to the police station..."

Lester said to the jury, "Apparently the officers aborted what was about to be quite an orgy."

"You are out of order, Mr. Knowles," Glasser said. "The court clerk is ordered to strike that remark from the record."

"Your Honor, I am in the process of establishing a pattern of risky behavior." He approached the witness box. "Mrs. Hamby, after Dr. Corbett told you that she found someone's DNA in pathology specimens she had removed from your body, did you travel to the hospital where Michael Greene is employed as a surgical intern, for the express purpose of stealing a sample of his DNA?"

"I went there to attend a workshop."

"Yes, and at that workshop did you use one of the record room computers to pull up Michael Greene's medical record?"

"Yes."

"You are supervisor of a hospital medical records department. Isn't one of your prime responsibilities to insure the confidentiality of the medical record?"

"Yes."

"What you did is against the law. I would characterize that as not only risky, but criminal behavior."

"I object, Your Honor. My client is not on trial here," Shelly said.

"Objection overruled. Your client's credibility is a legitimate area of exploration."

"Good," Lester said, "let's move on. After you learned from my client's medical record that he recently had a finger-stick in the operating room, and that a sample of his blood was stored in the hospital immunology laboratory, you stole that blood specimen, did you not?"

"I did not steal the blood specimen. I removed a small amount of serum to prove to myself that the DNA specimen Dr. Corbett found in my body did in fact belong to Michael Greene."

"If you had gotten caught, you would have been in a heap of trouble. I would call that risky and, in fact, irresponsible behavior." Lester turned from the jury and walked toward Laura. "And after you proved to yourself that the specimen you stole did match the specimen Dr. Corbett removed from your body, you arranged to meet with Dr. Greene, didn't you?"

"He called me and asked if we could meet."

"Did you tell your husband or your attorney Dr. Greene called you and asked you to meet with him?"

"No."

"I suspect the reason you didn't tell them was because neither of them would have approved of such a meeting."

"I agreed to meet with him because I thought there was a remote chance he might admit his guilt and ask me to forgive him."

"Do you really expect the jury to believe that was your motive?"

"I object, Your Honor," Shelly said. "He is asking my client to speculate as to what the jury may or may not believe."

"Objection sustained."

"Did you realize that DNA obtained illegally would not be admissible as evidence?"

"My intention was to prove to myself that Michael Greene had sexually assaulted me."

"So you admit that you were not certain?" Lester asked.

"I knew he was guilty. I wanted proof of his guilt," Laura said.

"Might I pose another motive? A clandestine meeting with the man you accuse of sexual assault smacks of blackmail, not intent to prosecute in a court of law."

Shelly objected. "Your Honor, that is an egregious accusation. I move it be stricken from the record."

"Objection sustained. The jury clerk is so ordered and the jury advised to disregard that assertion by Dr. Greene's attorney."

"Excuse me, Your Honor," Lester said. "I got carried away by the power of logic. I have no further questions."

The following morning, the defense began presenting its witnesses, beginning with the supervisors of the two laboratories that had tested the pathology specimens Dr. Corbett had surgically removed from Laura. They described the test procedures in excruciating detail. Each laboratory used somewhat different techniques for extracting and analyzing the specimens for DNA. They both identified two human DNA specimens that were not the plaintiff's or her husband's.

One of the laboratory supervisors said, "I was asked to compare those specimens with a DNA specimen from Michael Greene, Luke Marshall and Arnold Sommers. We confirmed a match with Michael Greene and Arnold Sommers." The supervisor from the second laboratory concurred.

Lester brought to the stand a DNA forensics expert, who was highly critical of Dr. Corbett's technique and procedures in the collection, storing and transport of the pathology specimens she had sent to the independent laboratories.

"There were numerous points along the way where the specimens could have been contaminated," the witness insisted.

"Isn't it relatively easy to secure a person's DNA without his or her knowledge?" Lester asked.

"Absolutely. That is why the procedure for the collection and handling of evidence must be scrupulously followed."

"Thank you, sir. I have no further questions of the witness, Your Honor."

On cross-examination Shelly was unable to budge the witness from his position and certitude.

The defense next brought in an expert witness, Melvin Casper MD, who went into great detail about alcohol-induced amnesic blackout. Melvin Casper had written the definitive text on the subject. He mesmerized the jury. Shelly could not shake his assertion that in susceptible persons, amnesic blackout could be induced by the consumption of a relatively small amount of alcohol, and that individuals in such a state would appear to be quite normal and in control of their behavior. That a person in that state might have a distorted memory, or no recollection, as to what had happened.

Following the morning session, Shelly, Laura and Tessie went for lunch at a nearby café.

"Hell, he had me ready to quit drinking," Tessie said. She nibbled at her food without interest.

"And the forensic expert didn't help any," Shelly said. "She slammed Dr. Corbett's handling of the pathology specimens."

"But Michael admitted to having sex with me." Laura cringed. She had just admitted to having had sex with him. She continued after a long pause..."Why did they spend so much time debunking the DNA findings?"

"That's SOP," Tessie said. "Since there are no witnesses, the DNA is our trump card."

"That's true," Shelly said. "But we also have circumstantial evidence and a ton of conflicting testimony. Martha's testimony that she helped you untie your hands was crucial in confirming your assertion that you were restrained."

"Do you believe that Lester will suggest I already had gonorrhea prior to that night?" Laura said.

"There's a venereal disease expert on their witness list. I wouldn't be surprised," Tessie said.

One more nail in the coffin, Laura thought. "And why haven't they come after me about stealing Michael's blood specimen?"

"My guess is that they're saving that as a basis of appeal if things don't go their way," Shelly said.

"Do you think Michael will take the stand?" Laura asked.

"We have the right to call him. We may well do that, depending how things go. But the defense seldom puts their client on the stand. If he were my client, I wouldn't. Just let him sit there. The young, handsome doctor falsely accused. That plays better than his getting up there and calling you a liar."

"Captain Arnold Sommers looked like an oversized Eagle Scout. Who would not trust him? He almost convinced *me* he was telling the truth," Laura said.

"You know what hurt us most?" Tessie asked. She didn't wait for an answer. "Martha's and Ginger's testimony that Michael was so concerned about your condition, he insisted they should have taken you to the hospital. And Martha's reaction to the photograph of Arnold carrying you up to the bedroom."

"I looked at the jury when she said that. It appeared they made up their minds right then and there," Laura said.

"Shake the gloom, you two," Shelly said. "We still have Martha's testimony that Luke told her all three...he, Arnold and Michael...had sex with Laura at the same time. It contradicts Arnold's and Michael's stories."

"He admitted he said that but insisted he was lying," Laura said.

"But it does raise significant doubt," Shelly said. "If the jury believes the version he told Martha, then Michael and Arnold are lying."

The afternoon session was even more embarrassing for Laura. Lester set up several easels on which he displayed poster-sized blow-ups of the photographs Michael had taken of Laura at the party. There were ten in all. Most were of her at the poolside. They were copies of the photos Michael had given Laura. There were also photos Akthar had taken at the coffee house. Particularly shocking was one of Laura standing beside Michael as they watched flames rising from a coffee mug. If Lester asked her what Michael had burned, she'd be compelled to describe the photo.

The defense then brought in several of Michael's friends, who knew him through college and medical school. They described him as an outstanding student, steadfast friend, devoted physician and a man with an unblemished reputation. The chief of surgery at the University of Pennsylvania Hospital described Michael as a promising young surgeon with knowledge and skill well beyond his peers.

The following morning Rana Akthar took the stand. Laura immediately recognized him as the man she had seen in a car parked by her apartment. She hadn't been paranoid after all. He had been following her.

"Sir, you are a licensed private investigator?" Lester asked.

"Yes, sir."

"You took these photographs at the café in Morrisville, New Jersey, where the plaintiff and Michael Greene met?" Lester pointed to the displayed photos.

"Yes, I did."

"How did you happen to be there?" Lester asked.

"Sir, you informed me of the meeting. You suspected Mrs. Laura Hamby might attempt to shake down your client."

Shelly objected. "That statement is highly prejudicial and should not be permitted."

Glasser agreed. He ordered the jury to disregard the statement.

Lester shrugged. "Mr. Akthar, can you tell the court what you saw and heard between the plaintiff and the defendant at that meeting?"

"The coffee shop was crowded. I was unable to sit close enough to hear their conversation."

"Did you see what it was he burned in the coffee mug?"

"It was an eight-by-ten photograph. At the angle at which I observed them I couldn't tell. But I could see that Mrs. Hamby seemed genuinely shocked at the sight. You might want to ask her to describe the photograph."

Lester smiled. He looked toward the jury. "I may well indeed...I have no further questions of the witness.

"Your Honor," Shelly said. "It has already been established that my client met the defendant at the coffee shop in Morrisville, New Jersey. What we have learned from the burning of this photo is the duplicity of the defendant. I have no questions of the witness."

That evening Bruce tried his best to encourage Laura. She felt that Lester had pretty much taken her apart in his cross-examination.

"Come on, honey," Bruce said, as they sat together on their living room couch. "I think you did great, and Shelly agreed."

She rested her head on his lap. "That amnesia crap...If the jury buys that..."

When the phone rang, Laura was inclined not to answer. They were getting dozens of calls from well-wishers and publications.

"Let it go," Bruce said. "Who would call this late?"

Laura sat up. She walked to the phone.

Chapter Thirty-One

Laura picked up her phone messages. "It's your Aunt Lena. Call me, dearie."

Laura dialed her immediately. "Aunt Lena, hi. How are you? How's Uncle Walter?"

"We're doing just fine, honey. You and Bruce doing okay?"

Tears filled Laura's eyes. Aunt Lena and Walter were the only family she had left. Her voice sounded so much like her mother's. "We knew it was going to be hard," Laura said, "but with stuff in the papers..."

"You just pay them no mind, Laura. You're doing the right thing. Just hold your chin up high. There are lots of folks on your side, praying for you."

"Thanks, Aunt Lena."

"Do you remember that footlocker I filled with some of your things?" Lena asked.

"Yes, of course, Aunt Lena."

"When we read in the papers what that doctor said about alcohol and some of those drugs that can make a person black out, Walter got wondering if maybe that young man put something in the whiskey he gave you."

"We wondered about that too, but there's no way to prove that he did," Laura said.

Aunt Lena told Laura she had found the flask in the coat she had stored in the footlocker. She said it was in a leather case that had the letters "M G" engraved on the side.

"I thought I left the flask beside the pool. I'd seen the coat at the bottom of the footlocker. But it reminded me of that horrible night. I didn't even touch it."

"I can understand that, dearie."

"It wasn't like mother to put it away without checking the pockets."

Aunt Lena explained that her mother never handled anything in Laura's room after she left. That she prayed every day that Laura would return.

Those words, those images...her mother grieving, praying for Laura's return, would haunt Laura forever. She was unable to speak.

"I'm sorry to have to tell you that. I know how terrible it must have been for you. We can talk about this some other time."

Laura's voice shook with emotion. "It's okay. We need to talk."

"I was wondering...should your lawyer know about finding the flask?"

"But there was nothing left in the bottle. And Michael Greene already admits giving it to me."

"Walter says there's always a few drops that don't come out. Maybe one of those CSI guys like we see on television could test it. You never know. Walter told me not to open the bottle. I put it in a zip-lock bag."

"Aunt Lena, you are a genius!"

Laura immediately called Shelly.

"You said your mother threw away everything you wore that night."

"That's what she told me," Laura said. "But later I noticed the coat hanging in my bedroom closet. When I left home I decided not to take it. It reminded me too much of that night."

"Was it soiled? You know, blood or anything else?"

"I don't think so. Martha and Ginger cleaned me up before dressing me."

"But weren't you still bleeding?"

"Yes, but Ginger gave me a hand towel to put between my legs."

"Call your aunt back and tell her that I'll arrange for someone from Allentown social services to pick up the flask and the coat."

"Why not the police?"

"They're not usually interested in getting involved in civil cases," Shelly said. "I've dealt with a very reputable private forensics lab in Allentown. I'll ask social services to deliver the flask there. And tell your aunt to give them the coat, too. It might have been soiled. It only takes a spot or two for analysis."

"And if the flask tests negative?"

"A negative test wouldn't help, but it wouldn't hurt us either," Shelly said. "Just seeing that flask might raise in the minds of the jurors the possibility that he may have spiked your drink."

"How long will it take to get an answer?" Laura asked.

"I'm not sure how long definitive testing will take. But there's a spot test that'll give a preliminary answer in just a few minutes."

"Aren't there dozens of different drugs he might have used?" Laura asked.

"That test is designed to screen for up to a hundred different substances," Shelly said.

The following Monday, the defense called Dr. Gertrude Youngblut, head of the infectious disease department at Johns Hopkins.

"Dr. Youngblut, the plaintiff in this case claims to have contracted gonorrhea as the result of an alleged sexual assault," Lester said. "Are you familiar with the paper Dr. Corbett presented at a recent conference of fertility specialists in Orlando, Florida?"

"Yes, I am."

"Could you describe for the court what she found when she operated on the plaintiff?"

"She described the patient's fallopian tubes as severely scarred and cystic and concluded that the changes were consistent with gonorrhea."

"Would untreated gonorrhea in your opinion have caused such changes and could they account for the plaintiff's infertility?"

"The changes were consistent with, and quite typical of untreated venereal disease of the pelvis, including that caused by gonorrhea," Dr. Youngblut said.

Lester raised his arms in a gesture of revelation and directly addressed the jury. "So, one or more diseases other than gonorrhea could have caused similar changes?"

"That's true."

"I see," Lester said. "We cannot say for sure that gonorrhea caused her infertility."

"That is also true," the witness asserted.

"Is there any way to ascertain exactly when a woman has first contracted gonorrhea or other venereal disease?"

"If she had been examined soon after the alleged sexual assault, tests could have been done to determine if she had contracted a venereal disease."

"Unfortunately the plaintiff for some reason did not choose to seek medical care," Lester said. "So is it fair to say that the assertion that she contracted gonorrhea on a particular night, at a particular place, is pure speculation?"

"Yes. It would be speculative."

Lester grasped his forehead as though in deep thought. "I see. I see. So you are saying that we can't say for sure the organism that caused her disease resulting in her infertility was gonorrhea? Furthermore we cannot ascertain when the plaintiff contracted gonorrhea or some other venereal disease?"

"That is correct," the doctor said.

"Thank you, Dr. Youngblut. I have no further questions."

Shelly approached the witness. "Dr. Youngblut, are you familiar with the testimony of Martha Carver and Luke Marshall?"

"I have read accounts of their testimony."

"Martha Carver testified under oath that Luke Marshall told her that he had contracted the clap after he and two other boys had sex with my client."

"Yes," Dr. Youngblut said. "Clap is a common name for the disease *gonorrhea*,"

"I see," Shelly said. "In your expert opinion, if three men have sexual relations with a woman, and one man develops gonorrhea, he could possibly have gotten the disease from the woman, or either of the other two men?"

"If the man who was first to have had sex with the woman had developed gonorrhea, he obviously would have contracted the disease from her. But if the man second in line were to develop gonorrhea he could have contracted it from the woman or the man who preceded him."

"So, the man third in line could have contracted the disease from either of the two men who preceded him or from the woman?"

"That is true," the doctor responded.

Laura watched the jury as Shelly made these points. Some were taking notes.

"Thank you, Doctor. You said that you read Dr. Corbett's paper, in which she stated that non-human genetic material was found in the plaintiff's cystic fallopian tubes, as well as human DNA that was not her own or her husband's."

"Yes."

"The fact that the non-human DNA and the human DNA were trapped in the plaintiff's scarred and cystic fallopian tubes suggests, does it not, that their presence was temporally related?"

"It's an intriguing speculation, but there is no scientific basis for making that conclusion."

"Dr. Youngblut, the DNA in question belongs to a man who admits to having had sex with my client. And another man admitted to Martha Carver that he also had sex with her that same evening, and that he later developed gonorrhea. That sounds like a temporal relationship to me."

"We have no way of knowing whether the plaintiff already had gonorrhea or might have developed it at a later date," Dr. Youngblut said.

Following Dr. Youngblut's testimony, Shelly Spinks and Lester Knowles approached the bench. Shelly said, "Your Honor, new evidence has come to light. The flask the defendant gave my client has surfaced."

"That's preposterous, Your Honor," Lester protested.

"And where has this mystery flask resided all these years?" the judge asked.

"It was in the pocket of a coat my client wore the evening she was sexually assaulted."

"Did you know about this, Mr. Knowles?" Judge Glasser asked.

"The plaintiff's attorney called me. I was astonished that they would withhold such evidence until so late in these proceedings. Besides, we have no way of knowing it is the same flask my client gave to the plaintiff."

"I believe Mr. Knowles' point is well taken," Glasser said.

"After my client's mother died, her sister, my client's aunt, stored away some of her personal things. She recalled having found a flask in the pocket of the coat my client had worn the evening of the party in question. She called my client, who in turn called me. I had someone from the Allentown Social Services Department pick it up and bring it to a forensics laboratory for testing."

"Had you been made aware of this, Mr. Knowles?"

"Yes. But I could see no way it would be admissible as evidence, so I refused to be part of such testing."

"Your Honor," Shelly said, "preliminary testing confirms the presence in the flask of traces of what is referred to as a date rape drug. As soon as definitive testing is available, I'd like to call Lena Holthauser to the stand."

"But Your Honor, there's no way to prove the authenticity of this supposed piece of evidence," Lester protested.

"The leather case," Shelly said, "that encloses the flask has Michael Greene's initials embossed on the side."

"Mr. Knowles, you displayed photographs of the plaintiff drinking from a flask," Glasser said. "As I recall, it was a silver flask in what appeared to be a brown leather case."

"Your Honor, my team needs time to evaluate the authenticity of this so-called evidence. It raises countless new questions. I maintain that accepting this flask as evidence constitutes a procedural error and grounds for a mistrial."

"I do not agree," Glasser said. "I rule the flask may be entered as evidence if properly authenticated. You can bring in extra expert witnesses if you so choose."

Lester Knowles had no choice but to acquiesce. He conferred with his client and Maria Faraday, his assistant.

The following week Lena Holthauser, a white-haired women in her mid-seventies, walked toward the witness box. Laura's aunt had the tiny features and the plump, rosy cheeks of a child. She wore wire-framed glasses, a blue cardigan sweater, a knee-length, floral print dress and running shoes.

Shelly approached her. "Mrs. Holthauser, would you tell the court how you came in possession of the flask the defendant gave your niece at the party, where she had been sexually assaulted?"

"I object, Your Honor. It has not been established that she had been sexually assaulted."

"Objection sustained. The jury hopefully at this point understands that the plaintiff is claiming to have been sexually assaulted."

"Mrs. Holthauser, how did you come into possession of the flask given by the defendant to Laura Hamby at the party in question?"

"Six months after my niece, Laura, left home, her mother died from breast cancer. She had noticed a lump for over a year but never went to the doctor. When they discovered it, the cancer had already spread."

"Was she your only sibling?"

"Yes, she was my baby sister. There was just the two of us."

"I assume you tried to contact her daughter?"

"Oh, yes. But we didn't know how to get in touch with Laura. We tried. It seemed like she just disappeared off the face of the earth."

"And after your sister died?"

"I handled her estate. She had asked that I sell the house and furniture and put the money in a trust fund for Laura. She asked me to keep some of Laura's personal things, you know, class pictures, yearbooks, things from her grade-school years, some of the clothes Laura didn't take. After Laura left home, her mother never stepped foot in her room. Wanted things left just like they were. She was sure her little girl would come back home any day."

Shelly asked softly, "I asked about the flask?"

"I was getting to that, dear. There was a winter coat hung up in the closet in Laura's bedroom. It was a little worn here and there, but too good to throw out. I decided to pack it away with the rest of her things. As I folded the coat I felt something in an inside pocket. It was a silver flask in a fancy leather case. At the time I paid it no mind. But the other day when my husband, Walter, said maybe someone put one of them tranquilizer pills in Laura's drink, that's when I remembered that flask. I went to the attic and fetched it. I shook it. There didn't seem to be anything inside, but my Walter, who likes to watch those CSI police shows, said maybe there was some way they could tell if there was ever anything in there besides whiskey. I put it in a zip-lock bag. I called my niece and told her about it."

"How did she react to that information?"

"She said she thought she had dropped it besides the pool. She said she was going to talk to her lawyer. You know what happened next, Ms. Spinks."

Shelly smiled. "Would you tell the court?"

"Two women from social services came by the house to pick it up."

"Thank you, Mrs. Holthauser."

Laura noticed that Lester Knowles huddled with Michael before approaching the witness. Probably asked him if there was any reason he should be concerned about the contents of flask he had given her. Michael shrugged.

"Mrs. Holthauser," Lester said. "Didn't Laura Hamby contact you a year after she had left home?"

"She did. I was thrilled to hear from her, but sad to tell her about her mother."

"Did you tell her about the things of hers you had saved?"

"I did. She said all that was past. She said that I should just keep them. That maybe someday she'd come by and see what she wanted to take."

"Did you tell anyone that your niece had called you?"

"Her old high school boyfriend, Bruce, called me every now and then to see if I heard from her. I called him and gave him her address."

"Did Laura ever come by to get her things?"

"The first time she came was after her and Bruce got married. Laura went up to the attic by herself and looked through the footlocker. Took a few things, picture albums, souvenirs from class trips, things like that."

"Did she take the coat?"

"No. I already told you I still had that."

"How long was she alone in the attic?"

"It was some little while. When she came down I could see she'd been crying."

"So she could have removed the flask and poured into it whatever she pleased, or even replaced it with another flask."

"I object, Your Honor. He is asking the witness to speculate."

"Objection sustained."

"She didn't switch no bottle, Your Honor. It was in a leather case that had his initials on the side." She pointed to Michael Greene. "*M.G.* in gold letters plain as life."

"Do you love your niece, Mrs. Holthauser?"

"Of course I do. What kind of question is that?"

The judge smiled. "Mrs. Holthauser, just answer the questions."

"Is it reasonable to assume you'd do anything to help her?"

"That is a leading question. I object," Shelly said.

"Everything I said is the God's honest truth. And I don't like the way you asked."

Laura wanted to run up and hug her aunt. Even Lester Knowles realized he had met his match.

He shrugged "I have no further questions of the witness."

The judge excused her. "Ms. Spinks, you have another witness?"

"Yes. But he is not as yet prepared to testify. He assures me he will be ready in forty-eight hours."

"Ms. Spinks, you are to inform the court and the defendant's attorney of the identity of your remaining witness. For now, the court is recessed until the day after tomorrow. The jurors are reminded of my earlier admonitions not to discuss the case with each other or anyone else. You must not read news articles or view television that alludes to this trial. Or listen to anyone who attempts to discuss this trial with you or if you become aware of any breach of these admonitions, you are to advise the court immediately."

Peter Rizzolo

Chapter Thirty-Two

Two days later, an officer from the Allentown Forensic Division of the Police Department took the stand.

Shelly asked him how he had come into possession of the evidence.

He turned toward the jury. "I received a call from Mrs. Shelly Spinks. She informed me that Mrs. Lena Holthauser had important evidence in her possession. She said that she'd asked the Social Services Department to send two social workers to pick up the evidence, and would I want to accompany them. I agreed. We took the specimen to the forensics laboratory."

"Did you pick up the evidence by yourself?"

"No. I was accompanied by another officer. That's standard procedure."

"What analyses did your laboratory perform?" Shelly asked.

"We checked for fingerprints, genetic material, and illicit chemicals."

"Are you prepared to share those results with the court?"

"I am."

"Do you recognize this report, sir?" Shelly asked. She handed a paper to the forensic officer.

He examined it. "Yes. This is the report my laboratory sent to you."

"Can you tell the court what they found?"

"The report describes the physical characteristics of the evidence. Its size, color, shape and weight. The flask is stainless steel. Its outer surface is sterling silver. It was tarnished. The case is brown leather. On its side the initials, 'M.G.' are embossed in gold lettering."

"I take it's the size and shape of a typical pocket flask used to hold whiskey and other libations?" Shelly asked.

"Yes, ma'am."

She handed him a plastic bag containing the flask. "Do you recognize this, sir?"

He looked at it carefully. "Yes. That's the flask I examined."

"I assume you checked it for fingerprints."

"Mrs. Holthauser's were the only identifiable prints on the leather case and the neck of the flask," the officer said.

"So the plaintiff's prints or Michael Greene's were not on the flask or outer case?"

"No."

"And your chemical analysis?"

Laura carefully watched Michael during the officer's testimony. She was hoping he'd make eye contact with her. She was certain he had never expected this evidence to come back to haunt him. She wanted to see the terror in his eyes. But he stared straight ahead. His hand shook ever so slightly as he reached for a glass of water.

"There was a residue on the inside of the flask. Among other chemicals we identified a drug commonly referred to on the street as a 'roofie.'"

There was chaos in the courtroom. The PWAR women were first to stand and shout their approval. Others joined in. The judge banged his gavel. "Order in the court." As the room quieted, he said, "Continue, Ms. Spinks."

"Isn't a roofie often referred to as a date-rape drug?" Shelly asked.

"Yes. It is one of many."

"Would you explain to the jury what a roofie is?" Shelly asked.

"Your Honor, I object. These last-minute theatrics give the defense no time to bring in our own experts. I move you declare a mistrial!"

"Objection overruled". He turned to the witness. "Answer the question, sir."

"The brand name is Rohypnol. Its chemical name is flunitrazepam."

"If imbibed by an unsuspecting woman, how might she react?" Shelly asked.

"It is a very potent tranquilizer, similar in nature to valium, but more than fifty times stronger. The drug produces heavy sedation, muscle relaxation, slowing of psychomotor responses and amnesia."

Lester again jumped to his feet. "I object, Your Honor. This man is a forensic officer, not a medical or pharmaceutical expert. I move you instruct the jury to disregard his testimony."

"I will do no such thing. Be seated, sir."

"I have no more questions, Your Honor," Shelly said.

Lester Knowles stood and approached the witness.

"Sir, do you have any way of knowing that the bottle you examined was in fact the same one the plaintiff drank from the night of the alleged sexual assault?"

"No."

"You said there were no other prints identifiable on the flask other than Mrs. Holthauser's?"

"It would be highly unlikely..."

"Please, yes or no. Were Michael Greene's or the plaintiff's fingerprints on the bottle?"

"No."

"Now isn't that strange? According to the plaintiff's own testimony she held that flask for an entire evening. Yet there were no prints?"

"Prints are fragile. I seriously doubt they could survive on the surface of the leather after being in a coat pocket for several years."

"Your answer implies they might?"

"It's possible under certain circumstances."

"Such as?" Lester asked.

"The oil in a finger print will retard oxidation on a surface such as sterling silver. We expected to find prints etched on the surface of the flask. We used a number of techniques to bring out latent print images. We couldn't identify any."

"You did not answer my question. Might the plaintiff's or my client's prints have survived?"

"Yes. It is conceivable they might have."

"Sir," Lester said, "Isn't it possible that the reason Dr. Greene's or the plaintiff's fingerprints are not on the flask is because it is not the same flask he gave to Laura Hamby the night of the party?"

"That would be one explanation."

Lester went to the table where Shelly had placed the plastic bag containing the flask. He handed it to the witness. "Can you tell the jury what kind of lid is on the bottle?" Lester asked.

"It is screw-top lid."

"A screw-top lid? Would you agree that anyone over the past six years could have unscrewed the cap and placed in the bottle whatever they pleased?"

"I can't disagree with that," the officer responded, "but..."

"I have no further questions of this witness. What they did or didn't find in that bottle is irrelevant, since it lay about for several years easily accessible to almost anyone."

Shelly stood. "May I conduct a re-direct examination of the witness, Your Honor, since he was dismissed in mid-sentence?"

"Yes, you may."

"You started to say when Mr. Knowles interrupted you?"

"The lid was all but fused shut."

"I see," Shelly said. "And how did you get it open?"

"It was not possible for me to manually open the bottle. If you observe the cap closely, you will see the marks of the instrument we had to use to open the flask."

"Were you able to determine why it had fused shut?"

"After we pried it open we did a chemical analysis. The threads of the cap were filled with crystallized sugar."

"I see," Shelly said. "If the flask had contained a soft drink such as Coca Cola, would that explain the presence of sugar?"

"Yes. In fact we found on analysis compounds used in cola-type soft drinks."

"What compounds were those?" Shelly asked.

"Glucose, phenylketonurics and caffeine."

"In your opinion, could Mrs. Holthauser or her husband have opened the flask prior to its coming into your possession without leaving marks on the cap?"

"My guess is that it hadn't been opened in years."

"I object, Your Honor," Lester said. "The witness is speculating. The bottle could have been opened at some time in the past, then resealed."

"Objection sustained." the judge said.

"Allow me to restate my question. If the flask had been opened recently, would it have remained as tightly sealed as you found it to be when you first attempted to open it?"

"No."

"I object, Your Honor. How recent is recently? A day, a week, a month, a year?"

"Objection sustained."

"Let's move on," Shelly said. "Could you explain to the court how you removed the residue from inside the bottle?"

"We added a solvent to dissolve the residue. We divided the residue into three portions. We tested one sample, and sent samples to two independent laboratories."

"And who was present while you did this?"

"We notified the defense team as you requested. They refused to witness the procedure."

"Did anyone witness the procedure?"

"Yes. The police officer who accompanied me when I picked up the evidence also observed the testing."

"And what did the independent laboratories report?" Shelly asked.

"They confirmed our findings. The drug Rohypnol was identified in all three samples."

"I have no further questions of the witness," Shelly said.

Michael and his attorney huddled. They appeared to be arguing. Michael grabbed Lester by the lapel and brought him to his feet. Lester threw up his hands before turning toward the judge. "Your Honor, my client, Michael Greene, wishes to take the stand."

"I warned you, Mr. Knowles, that I will not tolerate any last-minute machinations. You have previously told the court that your client would not take the stand."

"In light of this most recent evidence he has chosen to do so."

"Are you certain you wish to do this, Dr. Greene?"

"Yes, Your Honor." He walked to the witness box.

"What would you like to tell the court, Dr. Greene?"

"I have a piece of evidence that I have withheld to this point because I did not wish to humiliate the plaintiff." He looked directly at Laura as he spoke. He reached into his jacket pocket and handed Lester Knowles a recording device. "Mr. Knowles, in my briefcase is a jack and speakers. Would you hook up the recording to the speakers and turn it on when I ask you?"

"Would you please tell me what in God's name is going on here?" Glasser asked.

"When I met with Laura Hamby at the Coffee Shoppe in Morrisville, New Jersey, I recorded our conversation. I would like to play it for the court."

"This is highly irregular," Glasser said. "Ms. Spinks, you have the right to preview this evidence before it is presented to the court."

"That won't be necessary, Your Honor. My client has nothing to hide."

"In that case, you may continue, Dr. Greene."

"The first voice you will hear is mine," Michael said. "I can bring forward an expert witness who will attest to the fact that it is indeed my voice and that the recording has not been tampered with in any way." Michael asked Lester to start the recording.

"I thought I was about to be stood-up. Can I get you a Danish or a biscotti?"

"Let's dispense with the small talk, Michael."

"Laura, I don't want to see you blindsided when you meet with my lawyer and my father."

"Blindsided?"

"Have you ever heard of blackouts related to alcohol?"

"I was wide awake and kicking."

"Do you know what time it was when the girls rushed into the room?"

"Around eleven, because it was almost eleven-thirty by the time I got home."

"It was around nine-thirty when that boy picked you up after you had fallen at the poolside. You were in the bedroom at least an hour and a half, before those guys raped you."

"I was sleeping."

"For a long time I didn't understand why you didn't call me. I wanted to call you, but the way you looked at me at school I knew you were angry with me. I was frantic when I learned you had dropped out of school and left home."

"You were frantic I might go to the police. Relieved that I left."

"I went up to the bedroom where that guy had brought you. You appeared to be asleep. I sat on the edge of the bed. I kissed your cheek. You opened your eyes. I touched your breast. You smiled. You pulled me toward you."

"You're lying."

"We made love."

"That's preposterous."

"I could tell you were a virgin. Afterwards you dropped off to sleep. I got dressed and went downstairs. Whoever attacked you must have come into the room soon after I left."

"Sober, drunk or drugged, I would never make love to you."

"I was shocked and angry when Martha told me of hearing your screams, then finding you in the bedroom naked and bleeding..."

"And why didn't you come to my rescue?"

"When I went downstairs I flopped onto a couch. I fell asleep."

"I've had vodka since then. What you gave me was definitely mostly water."

"Alcohol can do different things to your brain, Laura. It can make you sick as hell, and if you drink it fast enough you can pass out. A blackout is alcohol-induced amnesia. It can last a few minutes, a few hours or even a few days. You can be fully awake in a blackout. It's the only explanation for you not remembering us making love."

"It never happened. That's why I don't remember."

"Those guys raped you. I had nothing to do with that."

"You were one of them. I recognized your voice, remember?"

"You were terrified, disoriented. I can understand why you'd make such a mistake. It was not until after I had some medical training that I learned how common alcohol-induced amnesia really is. If you're not used to drinking it doesn't take much."

"Was this fairy tale your lawyer's idea?"

"He knows nothing of this meeting. I'm convinced you can't win this suit. I don't want to humiliate you."

"You have humiliated me. That's what this fight is all about. I have nothing more to say to you, Michael."

"There's one other thing, Laura."

Michael asked Lester to pause the recording. "I had just shown Laura a photograph I had taken of her after we made love. She is naked and smiling at the camera." Michael continued the tape.

"This is the only copy I have, Laura. No one else will ever see it. I would never use it, even to prove my innocence."

"It's impossible. I don't remember..."

Michael signaled Lester to turn off the recorder. He turned to the jury box. "I crumpled the photograph, stuffed it in a coffee mug, and set it on fire. The court will recall the photograph taken by Rana Akthar showing the flaming coffee mug."

"Dr. Greene, did you retain any other copy or a negative of the photograph you burned?" Lester asked.

"I had used a digital camera. I purged the photograph from the camera and the hard-drive on my computer years ago. The photograph I burned was the only copy in my possession."

"You did not make any back-up copies?"

"No. I did not."

Lester took the digital recorder to Judge Glasser. "I would like to enter this in evidence, Your Honor."

Shelly stood. "I have no questions of the witness, Your Honor."

She whispered to Laura, "We have more to lose than gain by a cross exam."

Laura, who after Aunt Lena's testimony had felt almost euphoric, was now concerned about the accusatory expressions of several jury members. But her team was not unprepared for Michael's last-minute gambit.

"Your Honor, might I recall the plaintiff to the stand?" Lester asked.

The judge agreed. Laura whispered to Shelly, "Do I have any choice?"

Shelly shook her head. She whispered, "Say as little as possible. Relax." She patted her briefcase. "We have our little insurance policy in here."

"Ms. Hamby," Lester asked, "Would you attest to the authenticity of the taped conversation you just heard."

"Yes."

"Would you describe the photograph Dr. Greene showed you before he destroyed it?" Lester asked.

"It was a photograph of me."

"Were your hands tied or were you restrained in any way?

"Not in that photograph."

"Dr. Greene described you as naked and smiling. Is that accurate?" Lester asked.

"Yes."

"Do you recall having that photograph taken?"

"No. I do not."

Lester smiled. "Thank you, Mrs. Hamby. I have no further questions, Your Honor."

"Mrs. Hamby," Shelly asked, "were you able to closely examine the photograph Michael Greene had taken of you in the bedroom?"

"He never let go of it. After a few seconds, he snatched it from me."

"He had taken several pictures that evening, hadn't he?"

"Yes."

"Were you smiling in some of them?"

"Yes."

"Were you naked in any?"

"Not while I was conscious," Laura said.

The jury members were on the edge of their seats. Laura forced herself to look at them with a confidence she did not feel.

"We heard Dr. Greene's explanation as to why he destroyed the photograph. Why do you think he destroyed the photograph?"

Lester was quick to respond. "I strenuously object. How is the court to judge the relevance of the plaintiff's opinion as to my client's motivation?"

"Sustained. Ms. Spinks, your client is not exactly an unbiased observer," Glasser said.

Shelly continued, "In your position as supervisor of a medical records department at a major medical center, I expect you work with computers on a daily basis."

"Yes. I have for several years," Laura said.

"Are you familiar with software programs into which one can scan photographs and then edit the photos in a variety of ways?"

"Yes. At our hospital when photographs are submitted as part of a malpractice suit, our IT staff checks them carefully for evidence of tampering."

"Objection! I cannot see the relevance of this line of questioning," Lester said.

"Overruled. The relevance is obvious. Continue, Mrs. Hamby."

"I had no prior experience with this; however I went online and downloaded a photograph of

President George Bush and his wife. I opened a graphics program and proceeded to perform an amazing head transplant."

Tessie removed something from a briefcase and brought it to Shelly.

"Is this the photograph you digitally altered? Shelly asked.

Laura glanced at the photo. "Yes, it is."

Shelly handed the photograph to Judge Glasser. "May I enter this as an exhibit, Your Honor?"

Glasser studied the photograph. "Would the attorney for the defense approach the bench?" He handed Lester the photograph.

"Your Honor, this is totally irrelevant. Of course digitized photographs can be altered."

"We have not assembled a jury of computer experts," Glasser said. "This testimony is indeed relevant."

"But it's utter fantasy to conclude it has any relevance to the photograph my client showed to the plaintiff," Lester insisted.

"That is for the jury to decide," Glasser said. "I will accept it as an exhibit."

Judge Glasser nodded. "Continue with your questioning, Ms. Spinks."

"I have no more questions, Your Honor."

"Will there be any further evidence from the defense?"

"No, Your Honor."

"The court will adjourn for lunch," the judge announced. "The attorneys for the plaintiff and the defense will meet in my chambers for a charge conference. Court will reconvene in two hours to hear closing arguments."

Laura's stomach churned, not for lack of food, but from the fear that Michael Green would be vindicated, and she would be judged a bitter, vengeful woman, seeking, for financial gain, to ruin a young man's reputation and career.

Peter Rizzolo

Chapter Thirty-Three

Laura looked about the crowded courtroom. There was standing room only. The atmosphere was electric. Michael sat between Maria Faraday and Lester Knowles. At a nearby table, Laura was flanked by Shelly Spinks and Tessie Dearing.

"Ladies and gentlemen of the jury," Shelly said, "first of all I wish to congratulate you on your obvious close attention to highly technical and complicated testimony. You have had to digest information from experts in the procurement and testing of DNA evidence. You have had to listen to experts on both sides argue the plausibility that DNA evidence could or could not be recovered from the body of a woman years after a sexual assault. You have had to assess differing opinions of forensic experts, pathologists and a host of medical specialists."

Shelly walked in broad circles as she spoke. Her gaze moved smoothly from jurors, judge, persons in the courtroom, and her client. Laura was astonished at how fresh Shelly looked after weeks of stressful hearings and late night preparations. She wore a white pants suit, classic black, high-heeled pumps and a satin cream-colored blouse. Her long black hair, parted in the middle, hung to her shoulders. She wore no makeup or jewelry.

"You have heard my client's description of the horrific, shattering experience she endured on the night of November 14, 1994. She has been called a liar by the defendant's attorney." Shelly paused and directed the jury's gaze toward Laura. "Laura Hamby is an intelligent young woman, who had a responsible position as supervisor of the medical records department of a prestigious hospital. She knew how difficult it would be to prove her case."

The entire jury was staring at Laura. Shelly had instructed her to engage the jury members, but not to linger more than a brief moment on any one person. Laura felt most comfortable making eye contact with the women. But she was careful not to ignore anyone. Those ten persons would determine her fate. Shelly's entire case rested on Laura's credibility. Every nuance in her behavior would be observed and evaluated by the men and women of the jury.

"Her intellect told her to settle out-of-court," Shelly said, "as the accused had suggested when they met at the Gourmet Beanery Café in Morrisville, New Jersey. She could have accepted an out-of-court settlement and not endure the pain she knew would be associated with a civil or criminal action. But no, this suit is not about money. This," Shelly said as she swept her hand in an arc that included the judge, jury and courtroom, "is about justice. This is about the thousands of women who are assaulted every year, minors and adults, who are intimidated by the legal process and negative consequences of a public airing of their painful, life-altering experiences. In my opening statement I entered into the court record the National Crime Victimization Survey by the Bureau of Justice that researched sexual assault of both minors and adults in the United States in the year 2000. They reported an incidence of 191,000 sexual assaults. These are not isolated outbreaks. This is a crime of epidemic proportions."

Lester objected. "The plaintiff's attorney knows full well that statistics referring to a crime in general are not allowed in a closing statement."

"Objection sustained. The jury is instructed to disregard those statistics. You are charged with determining merits of this trial and this trial alone. You may continue with your summation, Ms. Spinks."

Laura was pleased that Shelly was painting a broad picture of what this trial was really about. The jury wasn't likely to forget those numbers.

"Evidence presented here by Dr. Corbett," Shelly continued, "indicates that women who previously believed that if they had waited weeks, months or even years, they would not be able to prove they had been raped based on DNA evidence. Now justice has an expanded window.

"I would like to remind you that, according to one of our expert witnesses, fewer than two percent of reported sexual assaults are believed to be false accusations. In fact, sexual assault remains the most underreported of all violent crimes.

"The vast majority of women, victims of this brutal crime that results in physical and emotional trauma that can last a lifetime, never experience justice. The predators go unpunished, emboldened to repeat their heinous crimes."

Shelly stood with her head bowed for several moments. There was absolute silence in the courtroom.

"Martha Carver has testified that Laura Hamby's hands were tied to a bedpost when she responded to the plaintiff's screams." Shelly looked at Laura. She spoke quietly, her voice tense with emotion. "How utterly terrifying that must have been." She did not speak for several moments.

Laura closed her eyes. Sounds, odors, images, flooded her mind. She must hold on. She mustn't have one of her panic attacks. *Dear God, make it pass.*

Shelly looked from juror to juror. "No one has reconciled that testimony with their claims of consensual sex. Did the victim tie her own hands to the bedpost?

"Three men each claim to have had consensual sex with the plaintiff. But what choice did they have? They knew that there was DNA evidence that proved two of them had had sex with my client. They could not afford to play Russian roulette with a gun partially loaded with DNA bullets. They had no option but to claim they had consensual sex with the plaintiff. But their stories contradict each other's. Luke Marshall told Martha Carver that he and Arnold Sommers walked in on Michael Greene, who was in bed with the plaintiff. That she had invited them to join her and Michael Greene. This account contradicts the testimony of Michael Greene and Arnold Sommers.

"The defense attempted to explain the fact that the victim denies having had consensual sex with Michael Greene because she was in a state of alcohol-induced blackout. They would have you believe that an ounce or two of watered-down vodka induced amnesia and turned Laura Hamby, a young woman with an unblemished reputation, into a nymphomaniac. Dismiss that bit of fantasy." Shelly repeated, as she looked from juror to juror, "Dismiss that bit of fantasy."

Shelly walked to her table and poured a glass of water. Laura was surprised to see Shelly's hand shake ever so slightly as she raised the glass to her lips. Was the nicotine patch she put on that morning wearing off, or was she nervous? Her voice didn't carry the slightest hint of tension.

"I would like to briefly discuss the whole DNA question. The defense has attempted to discredit the DNA Dr. Corbett recovered from the plaintiff's fallopian tubes, because the specimens were not handled in conformance with police protocols and because she did not process the surgical specimens as a police investigator would had done. Dr. Corbett is a reputable physician. She sent the tissues she removed from Laura Hamby's body to the hospital pathologist. She requested the cytology sections be processed, using techniques suitable for the extraction of DNA. The hospital pathologist in turn sent samples to specialty DNA testing laboratories. Exhibit number twenty-seven. Exhibits twenty-eight and twenty-nine are reports from those laboratories. They are all dated weeks prior to the time my client decided to obtain a DNA sample belonging to the defendant. The DNA she obtained could not have been used to contaminate the surgical specimens Dr. Corbett had sent to the laboratories for testing. She was not looking for evidence to be used in a court of law. She wanted proof for what she believed to be true...that it was Michael Greene who had sexually assaulted her.

"My client made a mistake. Neither I nor her doctor was aware of her decision to procure a sample of the defendant's DNA. But you must not let that fact cloud the true issue here."

Shelly paused. She and Tessie, the night before, had disagreed on whether to bring up the issue of the DNA. Tessie had maintained it was a moot point because the finding of the rape drug in the flask was evidence enough to convince the jury of Michael's guilt. But Shelly had insisted it had to be addressed, since the DNA evidence had been their original reason for pursuing legal action.

"When this suit was filed we procured a court order to obtain a DNA sample from the defendant, based on Dr. Corbett's findings. The sample that the Allentown police subsequently took from Michael Greene matched the DNA found in the tissues removed from the body of the plaintiff at the time of surgery by Dr. Corbett.

"Yes, DNA evidence got our attention, but the flask that Michael Greene gave to the plaintiff contained all the proof my client needed."

Shelly looked a Lena Holthauser, who was sitting in the first row, flanked by her husband, Walter, and Bruce Hamby. "Aunt Lena has put all that to rest. The rape drug Rohypnol was found in the flask Michael Greene had given Laura Hamby. Three independent laboratories came up with this indisputable fact. To what extent Arnold Sommers and Luke Marshall were involved in that criminal act is yet to be established. But we know for certain that Michael Greene gave the flask to Laura Hamby. She insists that the flask never left her possession, at least until the time she collapsed at the side of the swimming pool at the home of Luke Marshall. We also know that Michael Greene searched frantically to recover the flask. He said it was his father's. But we know now why he was so desperate to find it."

Of course he was desperate to find it. He had slipped a roofie in there, Laura thought. If I were a juror what would I believe? Look at Michael..... confident, poised, a young surgeon with impeccable credentials.

Shelly continued, "The mystery as to why she appeared to be severely intoxicated after consuming a small amount of alcohol over the course of an evening is now solved. It wasn't the vodka. It was the potent drug, Rohypnol, that three independent laboratories found to be present in Michael Greene's flask. It was used for one purpose and one purpose only. To render the plaintiff helpless, as he and two other young men brutally raped her.

"Laura Hamby's life was forever changed. She must be compensated for the severe physical and emotional consequences of premeditated sexual assault. We rest our case."

Laura whispered to Shelly as she sat beside her, "That was magnificent."

Lester stood. He was sporting an exquisitely tailored Brioni two-button blue suit and color coordinated accessories. Laura glanced at the jury. They had no doubt grown accustomed to his flamboyant attire, but many wore bemused expressions.

He addressed the jury. "I too want to congratulate you on your patience and attention to what at times was rather tedious testimony. My esteemed adversary has just asked you to ignore a mountain of testimony from credible witnesses that exonerates my client. He admits to having had sex with the plaintiff. So it is no surprise that his DNA could possibly be recovered from her body."

Lester paused for a few moments. "Two noted forensic DNA experts were highly critical of the sloppy manner in which Dr. Corbett collected and transported pathology specimens to the testing laboratories. And at a later date, Dr. Corbett accepted an illegally obtained sample of my client's DNA with a wink, and no questions asked."

He walked to where Maria Faraday was sitting. She handed him a copy of the paper Dr. Corbett had presented at the conference of fertility specialists. He held it up for the jury to see. "How Dr. Corbett's report of her findings was accepted for publication in a prestigious medical journal is completely beyond my comprehension."

He walked back to the table and dropped the report as one might drop a dead mouse a cat had dragged in.

"But why belabor this point when the DNA evidence, even if valid, which it is not, does not prove sexual assault, but would merely establish that they had intercourse at some point in time.

"I bring it up because it demonstrates the duplicity of the plaintiff, who proffered a stolen serum specimen, and the duplicity of her physician, who accepted it.

"Why didn't the plaintiff go to the police to obtain a court order to have my client tested after Dr. Corbett informed her that she had discovered human DNA in a surgical specimen? We have heard repeatedly and even in the plaintiff's own voice, that she does not seek money. What she is after is justice. Those are her words. But what of her actions? She did not choose to pursue her case in criminal court where issues of guilt or innocence are decided. No. she chose to file a civil action in which she seeks financial compensation for her grievances. What are you to believe?" Lester paced before the jury box. "Her actions, ladies and gentlemen of the jury, shout, they scream for your attention." Lester took a deep breath before continuing.

Laura watched the jury as Lester spoke. They appeared to be entranced by his every word, his every gesture. Her confidence, which had soared after Shelly's summation, was now being dismembered piece by excruciating piece. Tessie apparently felt the same way. She leaned over and whispered, "The little prick is good."

"And as to the other side's claim that the plaintiff drank too little to produce alcohol-induced amnesia," Lester said, "how can we possibly know exactly how much she may have drunk over the course of the evening? From whom else had she accepted something to drink? Or how many times might she have refilled the flask? You, of course, have no way of answering those questions. But you have seen photographs showing her repeatedly drinking from the flask."

Lester extended his hand toward Michael. "My client is a young man with no previous or subsequent criminal record. We have heard from a stream of people who have known him over the years, and who attest to his integrity and dedication as a friend, student and physician. On the night of the alleged assault, he showed concern for her wellbeing. Two women have testified that he admonished them for not taking her to the hospital or a doctor's office. Does that sound like a man who is guilty of sexual assault?

"We do not dispute the fact that after Michael left the bedroom the plaintiff may have been assaulted. But that is not the issue you must decide.

"I accept the evidence as determined by three separate laboratories that a valium-like drug was present in the flask," Lester said. "But my client denies having placed anything in the flask other than vodka. That flask has been on the loose for years. Who knows when, or by whom the drug might have been placed in it?" He paused for several moments. "I ask you...who had access to the flask?" Lester stood before the jury box, engaging each juror before continuing. "And who had most to gain?" He held his hand palm up and extended in the direction of Laura and her attorney.

"Is it a coincidence or an act of desperation that this so-called evidence surfaced when it was becoming obvious that the plaintiff has little or no chance of success? The drug in question is readily available. It wouldn't be difficult for someone to place a bit of a crushed tablet in a drop of water and plant it in the flask. After a day or two the water would evaporate and leave a residue. The flask could then be tightly resealed. Is that what really happened? I don't know. What I do know is that the reason that police confiscate evidence is so that it cannot be tampered with. I objected to the court accepting this evidence. Unfortunately the court did not agree with me. It may well be that a higher court will have to decide.

"What I am certain of is that Michael Greene put nothing in that flask other than a little watered-down vodka.

"My client denies, and the plaintiff has not established, that he had venereal disease either before or after the night of November 14, 1994. So there is no way you can decide that he is responsible for the plaintiff's subsequent medical problems. I implore you to let this young man, who has such a promising future, go on with his life and not to ruin his reputation with false accusations and unsubstantiated claims. The defense rests its case."

Judge Glasser instructed the jury. "Sexual assault occurs when physical force is used to sexually abuse a person or when he or she engages in sexual intercourse or other sex acts with a person whose power to resist is substantially impaired by drugs or intoxicants. That is true whether the victim has become impaired because of his or her own actions or by substances employed by the perpetrator without the knowledge of the victim.

"Although you are not here to make a pronouncement as to the defendant's guilt or innocence of having committed a felonious action, you can make the defendant liable for the consequences of such action.

"There are generally two levels of proof required. The lower level, which is applied in civil suits, requires the plaintiff to present evidence that provides a probability of guilt greater than fifty percent. Your verdict therefore does not have to be unanimous. A simple majority is all that is necessary.

"Because of the complexity of some of the testimony, you are reminded that you may request portions of the recorded proceedings to clarify disputes. I would also remind you that a recorded note by a juror carries no more weight than another juror's recollection."

On the first day of the jury deliberations the jury forewomen, Louise Costello, requested that Judge Glasser clarify his instructions. Two jurors interpreted what he had said to indicate that it was considered sexual assault if a person has sex with someone who is substantially impaired by intoxicants, whether or not he or she had voluntarily consumed the intoxicants.

"That is true. But do not be sidetracked by that definition of sexual assault. In the case before you, you must evaluate suppositions as to what happened. The defense claims the plaintiff became intoxicated and suffered an alcohol-induced blackout. That during that time she voluntarily had sexual intercourse with the defendant. The plaintiff on the other hand claims the defendant deliberately drugged her and subsequently sexually assaulted her. Both sides have presented evidence to establish their positions. You must decide wherein the truth lies. Is that clear?"

"Yes, Your Honor," Ms. Costello said. "I have another question. We would like to know what constitutes substantial impairment. And also answer the question, how is someone to know when the person they choose to have sex with is substantially impaired?"

"The impairment is considered substantial when the victim is unable to resist someone who wants to have sex with him or her."

"You are speaking of physical resistance?"

"Yes. But it can also refer to emotional or psychological resistance. The so-called rape drugs lower inhibitions. They can render a person docile and indifferent. The intent in using such drugs is for the sole purpose of incapacitating the intended victim."

"But if sex between two individuals is not witnessed by anyone, how is it possible to answer the question of consent versus resistance?" Ms. Costello asked.

"Each of you must weigh the evidence and the credibility of the adversaries. Your job as forewoman is to facilitate that process. But remember, juries in civil actions are not expected to strictly apply the facts to the law in all circumstances. Instead, juries are expected to base their verdicts on extralegal values and their sense of justice."

"For example, Your Honor?" the forewoman asked.

"I was thinking specifically of the flask that surfaced after so many years. In applying the law strictly, I might well have determined it inadmissible. But instead I admitted it as evidence in order to allow the jury to exercise its sense of justice in evaluating the significance of the flask and its contents."

Bruce came to Allentown and stayed with Laura at a downtown hotel while they awaited the verdict. Every time the phone rang, Laura thought it was a call from the court saying the jury was prepared to render a verdict. Why was it taking so damn long? Was it a good or bad sign for their side? Shelly, who checked in on her often, had said it was a good sign. That there was no clear majority either way. She assumed Louise Costello and Barbara Maloney were on their side and would eventually influence the holdouts.

The jury deliberated for two days. As they filed into the jury box, Judge Glasser asked, "Have you reached a verdict regarding the questions the court has asked you to adjudicate?"

"We have, Your Honor."

"Bailiff, please retrieve the answer sheet and bring it to me."

After reading the verdict to himself Judge Glasser handed it to the courtroom clerk.

"The defendant will face the jury," Glasser asked.

Michael, as he had throughout most of the proceedings, looked confident, almost defiant. Laura's heart pounded violently. Had he resigned himself to a guilty verdict and was already planning an appeal? Or was he certain he would be exonerated?

And if the jury decided that the greater weight of evidence was in Michael's favor, a cloud would hang over Laura's life forever. Strangers would be convinced that she had been a promiscuous teenager and was now prepared to ruin a fine young man's life by falsely accusing him of rape. Would her friends and even her own husband begin to doubt her version of what had actually happened? Laura looked where Aunt Lena, Uncle Walter and Bruce were sitting. Aunt Lena gave Laura a reassuring smile. Bruce forced a smile that could not conceal his anxiety and fear.

"Madam Clerk, please read the verdict."

"In the case of Laura Hamby versus Michael Greene, the Lehigh Circuit Court, case number 2000 CV 1234, we the jury find as follows:

"Question one: Did the defendant engage in premeditated conduct that resulted in grave physical and emotional harm to the plaintiff?

The jury foreman responded, "The jury answers yes to question one."

"Since you answered yes to question one," Glasser asked, "do you find by the greater weight of evidence that plaintiff was injured as a result of the assault in question?"

"The jury answers yes to question two."

"Since you answered yes to questions one and two, did you find by the greater weight of evidence that the plaintiff suffer injury as a result of the assault by the defendant?"

"The jury answers yes to question three."

"Since the plaintiff suffered injury as a result of the assault by the defendant, what damages is the plaintiff entitled to recover from the defendant?

The jury foreman responded, "The plaintiff is entitled to recover $5,000,000 as compensation for acts by the defendant that caused grave physical and emotional harm to the plaintiff."

Bruce, Rose, Lilly, Aunt Lena and Uncle Walter stood and worked their way toward Laura. Laura hugged Bruce, each of her friends, Uncle Walter and Aunt Lena. She looked toward Michael and his legal team. They stood in stunned silence. Their eyes met. She was expecting bitterness, anger, that repulsive snarl of his...instead he nodded. *What the hell did that mean? Was that subtle motion of his head an admission of guilt and a plea for forgiveness? She thought of the beating Michael had endured at Bruce's hands, barely resisting, almost inviting the physical punishment he must have felt he deserved.*

"You okay?" Shelly asked.

"I should be feeling vindicated...elated, but for some reason I'm feeling sad. I've been angry so long. Did I ruin a man's life for something he did as a teenager?"

She embraced Laura. "You did the right thing, honey. Now's the time for forgiveness. That's something a jury can't provide."

Chapter Thirty-Four

Lester appealed the amount of the judgment, citing several sexual assault cases where teenagers were involved. Glasser reduced the judgment to $2,500.000. Shelly Spinks' compensation amounted to forty-percent of the judgment, leaving $1,500,000 for the Hambys. That left the Hambys $1,000.000 after the IRS took their share...enough to make some babies and to move from their small apartment into a home of their own.

In the weeks and months following the trial, Laura's and Bruce's lives slowly returned to some semblance of normalcy. Dr. Corbett's first attempt at *in vitro* fertilization was not successful. She advised them to wait a month or two before repeating the procedure. Laura doubled her course load at Pace Junior College, hoping to complete her paralegal degree within the year.

As they awaited the results of their second attempt, they planned a getaway. Bruce took his two-week annual vacation from Carmart. They decided on a flight to Provo, the smallest of the Turks and Caicos

Islands. Scuba diving lessons were part of the package.

"It's something I've always wanted to do," Bruce said. They were sitting at the kitchen table, tri-fold color brochures spread before them.

"Really?" Laura asked. "That's news to me." She stood, grabbed his hand and pulled him to his feet. "Let's go for a walk. It's such a gorgeous day."

They walked along a bike trail separated from their apartment complex by a meandering privet hedge and honeysuckle vines. Laura breathed in the scent of honeysuckle blossoms. Hummingbirds flitted from flower to flower, filling their tiny bellies with nectar.

"When I was a kid I was addicted to reruns of *Sea Hunt*. I dreamed of growing up and exploring the ocean. Maybe working for *National Geographic*."

"Retrieving treasures from the sea?" Laura asked, making waves with her hands.

"I got over it."

Laura studied his face. Why hadn't he ever told her? She wondered what other dreams he had kept to himself. Had she done the same? Were there things she held close to her heart that she hadn't shared? She had told him she wanted someday to work in a law firm as a paralegal, but what she really wanted was to study law at Princeton University. That dream would have to wait. She had other more urgent priorities. She hadn't as yet told him of the conversation she had with Dr. Corbett that morning.

She stopped walking. She put her arms around his chest. She pressed her cheek to his. "The actor who played the lead role in Sea Hunt..."

"Lloyd Bridges," Bruce said.

"As I remember, he had quite a bod."

"Careful, that kind of talk'll get you into trouble," Bruce said.

"I'm already in trouble."

"The kind of trouble I'm thinking of?"

"Looks like you'll be a daddy sometime in the fall."

He gathered her in his arms. "Oh my God! That's great."

"It's even greater than you think. It's buy one, get one free!"

They clung to each other, turning in circles, lost in the moment...caught up in life's unending cycle of new beginnings.

Peter Rizzolo

Epilogue

Turks and Caicos Islands

August 2004

Laura, crouched on an isolated beach on Provo Island, added a bag of charcoal to a pit she had dug in the sand. She lighted the coals, placed a grill over the pit, and lifted a lobster pot filled with sea water onto the grill. She slipped on a pair of goggles and ran into the surf where Bruce was snorkeling in search of crabs.

"Over here," she shouted. "There's a big one!" She was a little squeamish about grabbing it herself.

Bruce scooted over and had to chase after the crab as it scurried away. A few minutes later he stood, triumphantly holding a large crab over his head.

Laura's cell phone sounded. She rummaged through her beach bag to retrieve it. She couldn't imagine who would be calling.

"Laura honey, it's Shelly. Sorry to bother you in paradise, but I know you'll want to hear this."

"Hi. Okay. Sure, what's up?" Laura placed her cell on speaker phone so Bruce could listen in.

"The Lehigh County DA reviewed the civil case and decided there's enough evidence to charge Michael with premeditated sexual assault."

"My God! He's in jail?"

"That's where he belongs," Bruce said as he placed the large and two smaller crabs in boiling water.

"He's out on bail," Shelly said, "and get this...he's pleaded guilty and entered a plea bargain."

"I haven't seen anything in the papers..."

"I have a friend in the DA's office. She called me. He's offered to implicate Luke and Arnold in the planning and execution of the assault."

"And what does he get in return?" Laura asked.

"I understand they're offering him five-years probation and two years of community service."

"There's no honor among the wicked," Laura said. "He doesn't mind incriminating his good buddies."

Bruce stirred the pot of boiling crabs. "Wouldn't expect much more."

"What'll happen to them?" Laura asked her lawyer.

"I'm pretty sure Luke will get jail time. Turns out it was all his idea. He got the drug on one of his college interviews. Not sure what will happen to Arnold. Since the alleged crime occurred prior to his military service, I believe he would be tried in a civilian court. But I'm not sure."

"Shelly, I'm so glad it's all over with. I don't want to waste another minute of my time thinking about them."

"Amen," Bruce whispered as he embraced Laura.

Peter Rizzolo

About the author

After earning an MD degree at Creighton University School of Medicine, and completing a medical internship, my wife, Alyce, and our first-born child, Geri, joined the Navy. I served as a Submarine Medical Officer. After a two-year stint in the Navy, I added a second year of post-graduate training at the Hunterdon Medical Center in Flemington, NJ. As a solo practitioner in general medicine in Flemington, I cared for pregnant women, their babies, young children, adults, their parents and grandparents. It was a dream come true. The practice grew rapidly and within four years the Flemington Medical Group consisted of four family physicians. The Hunterdon Medical Center became one of the earliest sites for training young doctors in the newly created specialty of Family Medicine. It was an exciting time for general practitioners. I was offered the position of director of the program. It gave me the opportunity to combine my love of patient care with my commitment to teaching young doctors both the science and art of medicine. After several years as Director of Medical Education at Hunterdon, Alyce and I and our by then six children headed south and joined the faculty at the University of North Carolina in Chapel Hill. I participated in the training of medical students and Family Practice residents. For several years I directed the residency training program in the Department of Family Medicine.

I took a one-year fellowship in Geriatrics at UCLA Medical Center in their Hartford Scholars program. I'm currently Emeritus Professor of Family

Medicine at the University of North Carolina School of Medicine. My professional areas of interest and publications include the following: thyroid disease, tick-borne diseases, cognitive impairment and geriatric assessment.

Besides writing fiction, I enjoy building furniture, love reading, movies and live theater. I follow national politics closely, play tennis reasonably well, golf poorly, and in my spare time do a little baking.

I've published two novels, *This Thing Called Love*, a coming-of-age story of a teenager navigating his first love as he struggles with an alcoholic father and a family that is on the verge of collapse. *Forbidden Harvest* is a medical drama about a twelve-year-old boy who desperately needs a heart transplant and the extremes to which his family and physicians are willing to go to get him a new heart. Both novels are available at Amazon.com, Goodreads, Barnes and Noble, and independent book stores.